Read These Suspenseful Stories
Of Babies

DELIVERED INTO DANGER

On Newsstands Now:

TRUE STORY
and
TRUE CONFESSIONS
Magazines

True Story and *True Confessions* are the world's largest and best-selling women's romance magazines. They offer true-to-life stories to which women can relate.

Since 1919, the iconic *True Story* has been an extraordinary publication. The magazine gets its inspiration from the hearts and minds of women, and touches on those things in life that a woman holds close to her heart, like love, loss, family and friendship.

True Confessions, a cherished classic first published in 1922, looks into women's souls and reveals their deepest secrets.

To subscribe, please visit our website:
www.TrueRenditionsLLC.com or call **(212) 922-9244**

To find the TRUES at your local store, please visit:
www.WheresMyMagazine.com

Read These Suspenseful
Stories Of Babies

DELIVERED INTO DANGER

From the Editors
Of *True Story* And
True Confessions

Published by True Renditions, LLC

True Renditions, LLC
105 E. 34th Street, Suite 141
New York, NY 10016

Copyright @ 2013 by True Renditions, LLC

All rights reserved. No part of this book may be reproduced or transmitted in any form or by any electronic means, without the written permission of the publisher, except where permitted by law.

ISBN: 978-1-938877-54-4

Visit us on the web at www.truerenditionsllc.com.

Contents

Stolen From Her Bedroom..1

Hushed Cries..30

Help Me! My Son Is Missing..73

Empty Cradle...98

The Baby Was Ripped From Her Body.........................121

My baby girl was
STOLEN FROM HER BEDROOM

I inhaled deeply before I spoke. "Is it another woman?" I held my breath as I waited for my husband to answer. He lay next to me in bed with his back to me. I had made the initiative, just as I had the last three times in as many weeks.

And just like the last three times, I'd been rejected again.

"No, Simone." He'd sounded tired and disgusted. "I'm not seeing another woman. I'm just tired. Your old man runs me ragged. If you want to blame someone, blame him."

I'd stared at the ceiling, fighting tears of frustration. "You used to want to make love nearly every night," I whispered, trying to hold back the tears. "Maybe you should see a doctor."

Well, that had been the wrong thing to say. Mitchell had thrown back the covers and gotten out of bed. He'd turned on the bedside lamp and stood there, glaring down at me.

"You're just like your father," he snarled. "Always wanting, wanting, wanting, but never giving anything in return!"

My mouth had fallen open in shock. "What are you talking about?" I asked. I had given him everything! A home, a beautiful daughter, and sex whenever he'd wanted it. I had even taken a cooking class so that I could prepare gourmet meals for him.

Mitchell slapped a fist into his palm, and his face was red with anger. "I'm talking about understanding, sympathy—hell, a little support would help!"

"Support?" I'd sat up in bed, my adrenaline pumping. "I don't understand, Mitchell. Explain to me exactly what you mean."

"For starters, you could talk to your old man about letting go of that trust fund instead of waiting until you're thirty! Maybe we could get out of this dump, and I could start my own business."

Dump? What was he talking about? We lived in a four-bedroom home, in a nice neighborhood. We had a pool, a privacy fence, and a three-car garage. Dump? I was hurt that he'd considered our first home a "dump."

"I can't ask Daddy to do that, Mitchell," I protested. "He's following my mother's wishes. And, for reasons of her own, she didn't want me to have that money until I turned thirty."

"It's a stupid wish," Mitchell shocked me by saying. "You've been married since you were twenty. You're a grown woman, with a family to help support."

"If you want me to get a job—" I began.

"This isn't about you getting a job!" he shouted. "It's about you getting what's rightfully yours! It's about me, being sick of working for your father, and supervising a bunch of computer nerds, day in and day out."

"He promised that he'd promote you when he thought you were ready." I'd tried to speak calmly, hoping that Mitchell would calm down, too. Our daughter, Missy, was asleep down the hall. I didn't want her to hear us fighting. I knew that Mitchell adored her, and that he wouldn't want her to be upset, any more than I did. I'd figured that maybe a reminder was in order.

"Honey, will you lower your voice? Missy might hear you," I said softly.

My reminder had worked a miracle. His expression had contorted for a brief moment, then cleared. He'd sighed and sat down on the bed. His hand had reached for mine. That was the Mitchell that I knew and loved.

"I'm sorry, babe. It's just that I get so frustrated. I want you and Missy to have nice things," he murmured.

"We do have nice things, Mitchell. Missy is spoiled rotten," I told him.

A hint of his earlier anger had returned. "That's because your daddy buys her the moon. Anything she wants, she gets."

"At least, she's getting it. Isn't that what really matters?" I asked. It might have been manipulation—I wouldn't deny it—but Mitchell always had been a dreamer, a restless soul, and it always had been up to me to keep him anchored in reality. "Come back to bed, honey. Let me rub your back."

Mitchell had reluctantly complied, just as I'd figured that he would. He had never been able to resist a massage. I'd rubbed and kneaded. I'd tried hard to ignore my own sexual needs as I'd touched my husband's smooth, firm skin. Finally, when I'd heard his soft snores, I'd turned over onto my side and tried to go to sleep.

It was no use, though. No matter how hard I'd tried, I couldn't sleep. Mitchell's outburst had just kept playing and replaying in my mind, making me doubt myself. Had I been wrong to keep silent about my pending trust fund?

Mitchell didn't know it, but I had approached Daddy less than a year after Mitchell and I had gotten married. I had just found out I was pregnant, and we'd wanted to buy a house. Daddy had listened without interruption. Then, he'd calmly and firmly reminded me that my mother had had her own reasons for waiting. He'd asked if I'd really wanted to go against my mother's dying wishes. Daddy didn't bring Mitchell into the conversation, but I had known that he was thinking about him.

Mitchell hadn't exactly impressed Daddy with his fledgling computer consulting company. It brought in income, but not enough for us to be able to save for a down payment on a house. I'd been working for Daddy, as his receptionist, just as I'd done since I had graduated high school.

A few weeks after my conversation with Daddy, he'd called me back into his office with a proposition. He'd wanted to hire Mitchell as a supervisor, but he'd also wanted me to stay home with the baby when it came.

"Just for a few years, Simone," he'd told me. "Let Mitchell carry the load for a while. Let him learn what it's like to have a real job—with real responsibility."

Daddy's plan had sounded good to me. And, when I'd approached Mitchell about the offer, he'd seemed excited about it, too. He decided to keep his own company open as a second job that he could work at on weekends and weeknights.

Mitchell had worked hard for Daddy, and I'd settled into the blissful state of motherhood. I'd tried hard to be the perfect wife for Mitchell. I'd wanted for us what my mother and dad had shared for twenty-five years—a wonderful marriage that was built on trust and love.

Missy was three years old and, somewhere along the way, Mitchell had become restless again. He hadn't been happy with his job, and had long since sold his own business to someone else. Why was he unhappy? I'd thought and thought about it, but I hadn't been able to come up with anything that had happened between us that might have prompted the sudden change in Mitchell. We went on family vacations together and had a great time. We spent the weekends with Missy, then together, alone, after she'd gone to bed. We were not only husband and wife—we were best friends. Or, so I'd thought.

When had the rift occurred, and what was causing it? Was Mitchell going through some early midlife crisis? Was he just fed up with working for Daddy, or was he tired of me, as well?

I'd jumped as Mitchell had slipped his arm around me and snuggled close. A thrill shot through me as I'd felt his arousal. Mitchell was an excellent lover, and my body responded to him eagerly.

"Want to fool around?" he whispered as if he hadn't rejected the offer thirty minutes earlier. His hand tunneled beneath my shirt and fondled my breast.

I'd moaned and arched my body, then turned around to face him. I'd looked lovingly into his eyes. "I want you to be happy, Mitchell," I murmured.

He'd kissed me tenderly, gently. "I am happy, Simone," he said gently. "Very happy. You and Missy are my life. Without you two, I would be nothing."

"That's not true," I protested, feeling the need to stroke his ego. I'd wanted assure him that he was a good man in his own right. "You're a strong, loving person, with or without us."

He'd pulled my leg over his hip and moved closer. His eyes had grown more intense, scattering my doubts like ashes in the wind. Had I really thought that he might be having an affair? The possibility had suddenly seemed highly unlikely.

"I would die without you," he vowed. "And I would die without Missy. You two are the lights of my life." He cupped my face in his hands. He'd kissed me deeply. "Let's make another baby," he'd whispered.

Ever since Missy had turned three, I'd been daydreaming about giving her a little sister or brother. I was overjoyed that Mitchell wanted the same thing.

"Okay," I agreed. Once again, everything was right in my world. Little did I know that my world was about to crumble around me.

The next morning, I'd ripped off my birth control patch and tossed it into the trash, along with the box of patches that was supposed to last for the rest of the month. I was elated and very excited. I'd felt almost as I had when Mitchell and I had been on our honeymoon. Even Missy had laughed and giggled more than usual, obviously picking up on my mood.

I couldn't wait to tell Daddy that we were trying to get pregnant again. Mitchell hadn't been exaggerating when he'd said that Daddy worshipped Missy. He did, and I knew he would be as happy as I was at the thought of having another child to spoil.

After breakfast, I'd put a movie in the VCR for Missy and called Daddy. Just as I'd expected, he was overjoyed at the news.

"That's wonderful!" he exclaimed. "It's about time that you gave me a grandson. I'm going to need someone to take over the business when I die, since Garrett doesn't seem to be shaping up."

"Daddy, don't talk about dying!" I was shocked that he would say something like that, with my mother's death four years before still sharp in our minds. Losing her had been very hard on both of us. At first, I'd thought that it had been hard on my older brother, Garrett, too, but considering the path that he'd taken in life, I wasn't so certain anymore.

"You're going to live to be a hundred. Besides," I added, sounding stern, "Missy is just as capable of taking over the business as a grandson would be."

He laughed. "I know. I just wanted to see if I could still get you riled up. Remember how I used to tease you about that boy down the street?"

I'd remembered. "You mean, when I was six and hated boys? He kissed me at my birthday party, and I made my lips raw, washing them." I hesitated. "Daddy, I thought you were training Mitchell with the idea that he would take your place when you retired."

Mitchell certainly thinks so, I mused, thinking about our argument last night. "He's worked really hard, hasn't he?"

My dad was silent for a long moment. "Sure, honey. He's a hard worker, and he's a good supervisor. Mitchell's turned out to be a better man that I expected."

My fingers tightened around the phone. Daddy had said good things, but there was something in his voice that hadn't quite agreed with his words. "Daddy, you aren't thinking about backing out of giving Mitchell that promotion, are you? Because if you are, Mitchell would be very disappointed." I would have been disappointed, too, and I should have told him that. But, I loved my father, and I didn't want to pressure him.

"No, I haven't changed my mind, honey. Say, do you want to have dinner with me tonight?" he asked.

"Sure." My heart leaped with excitement. Maybe Daddy was planning on surprising Mitchell with that promotion! "Where and when?"

"At the steakhouse, around seven. I'll meet you two there. Can you get a sitter?"

It was a weeknight, but if we weren't out too late, I knew that Jade, a teenager who lived on our street, would probably baby-sit for me. "Yes, I can get a sitter. We'll see you there, okay?"

"Okay. Oh, honey? Your brother's in town for a while. Would you care if he joined us?"

I'd grimaced, thinking about Garrett. He'd just gotten out of rehab for cocaine abuse for the third time. I loved him, but I'd given up hoping that he was going to change.

My mother, God rest her soul, hadn't known about his addiction, or his character weaknesses. If she had, I doubted that she would have stipulated in her will that Garrett get his money at age twenty-five, instead of thirty. As a result, Garrett had gone through his inheritance within a year. He'd blown it on gambling, women, and drugs. Daddy had washed his hands of him several times, but, like most parents, he couldn't completely disown him—no matter what he'd done.

I, on the other hand, had found myself having a harder time forgiving him for nearly killing Daddy with his reckless lifestyle. My mother would have turned over in her grave if she had known how her son had turned out, or how he had very likely brought on Daddy's mild heart attack last year. Garrett had blamed everything on losing our mother. He'd claimed that depression had caused him to turn to drugs. But no one had been closer to our mother than I had been, and I hadn't turned to drugs after her death. As far as I was concerned, using my mother's death was a pitiful excuse for Garrett's weak character.

"Simone? You're not backing out of dinner, are you? Because you know that Garrett misses you, and that he wants to see you. He even bought Missy a doll."

"Missy has more dolls than she knows what to do with," I snapped irritably. "Daddy, are you giving him money? You know that he'll just buy—"

"No, I'm not giving him a penny. I've already told him that, and I'm not giving him his old job back, either. I told him that he was going to have to make his own way. And, I told him that he is going to have to prove to me that he's changed."

"And, if he has?" I'd held my breath, ready to do battle. If I could stop my father from getting his heart broken again, I would have done just about anything.

After a short silence, my dad answered. "It was just a figure of speech, honey. Nothing more. I told you after the last time that I wasn't going to let Garrett make a fool out of me again."

I'd heard the hesitation behind his words, though, and my heart sank. Daddy was too softhearted sometimes. Except when it came to Mitchell. Then, he wasn't softhearted enough—at least, in my opinion. Mitchell was ten times the man my brother was. That might have sounded awful, but it was the way that I'd felt. In my heart, I truly believed that Garrett was a weak, manipulating user who had no qualms about taking advantage of Daddy's love.

I'd hung up the phone, resisting the urge to call Mitchell and share my suspicions about that longed-for promotion, and to warn him that Garrett was back in town. There was no love lost between the two. I believed that Mitchell felt threatened by Garrett, and with good reason. Mitchell had worked hard and long for Daddy, and yet, it was Garrett who was given chance after chance.

The reason why I hadn't told Mitchell my happy suspicions about being pregnant was because I didn't want to get his hopes up, just in case I was wrong. I hoped and prayed that I wasn't.

Dinner was every bit as awkward as I'd expected that it would be. Garrett had dominated the conversation, going on and on about how much he'd changed, and what he intended to do with his life. The rest of us were forced to listen to his lies. We knew that none of it was true, but out of an ingrained politeness, we couldn't say anything.

Finally, over dessert, someone else other than Garrett had managed to get a word in edgewise. I was so relieved that I was sure it showed in my expression.

"I had to fire one of my best men today," Daddy commented during a brief lull. He pointed his fork at Mitchell. "Did Mitchell tell you, honey?"

I shook my head. Mitchell had worked late, so he'd had time for a shower and nothing more. I'd been feeding Missy her dinner and giving the baby-sitter instructions.

"We haven't had time to talk. Surely, you're not speaking of Gavin?" When my dad nodded, I'd felt a pang of sympathy. Gavin had worked for my dad for more years than I could count. He'd been not only Dad's assistant and business consultant, but his right-hand man, as well.

Almost immediately, a shameful elation had smothered my sympathy.

Was that why Daddy had asked us to dinner—to ask Mitchell to be his new assistant?

"I'm afraid so," Daddy admitted, muffling a curse. "I can't believe that, after all these years, he would steal from me."

"Are you sure, Daddy?" I just couldn't imagine Gavin Monahan stealing from a man that he'd worked for and admired. Gavin hadn't seemed like the type of person to do such a thing.

"I'm sure." Daddy frowned. "He said that he'd gotten into some financial difficulties. He should have come to me, though, instead of just taking what he needed. I would have helped him."

"Are you going to press charges?" Mitchell asked. He wasn't as good at hiding his excitement over Gavin's leaving as I had been. He'd looked downright hopeful as he'd asked the question.

Trying to be subtle about it, I'd kicked him beneath the table. He'd shot me a narrow-eyed look, but I'd noticed that his expression had changed.

"No, I couldn't do it," Dad said in a gloomy voice. "He's worked for me a lot of years. I suppose I owe him that much."

"You don't owe him anything—not if he was stealing from you," Garrett declared, throwing his arm around Daddy and patting him on the back.

I'd almost gagged. I'd had to bite my tongue to keep from reminding Garrett that the way he'd manipulated Daddy into giving him money over the years had been paramount to stealing. But I'd kept silent, not wanting to upset Daddy further.

Was I the only person on earth that Daddy could really trust? Since my marriage, I had refused to turn to Daddy whenever we'd gotten into a financial bind, no matter how difficult things had gotten at times. My one small concession had been the time when I'd asked him to release my trust fund early, so that we could buy a house. But I had been asking for my own money—not his.

By the time dinner was over, I couldn't wait to get away from Garrett. After Daddy had told us the news about Gavin, he hadn't said much and had just picked at his dessert. I could tell that he was having a difficult time with Gavin's betrayal. Garrett had launched into another long, boring, totally unbelievable story about an idea that he'd had to make an instant fortune.

"I want to get home in time to put Missy to bed," I'd interrupted him. "Mitchell hasn't had a chance to spend any time with her today." Then, I'd stood up and grabbed Mitchell's elbow, hauling him to his feet. "Come on, Mitchell. Good night, Daddy. Good night, Garrett."

"Good night, Simone. Good night, Mitchell," Garrett said in a pitiful voice designed to induce guilt. It didn't work, though. It hadn't worked in a long, long time.

When we got into the car, Mitchell had remembered some papers that he'd left at his office. We'd driven by the building my dad owned so that he could pick them up. I'd waited in the car, realizing that I wouldn't get home in time to kiss Missy good night. It was nearly ten—way past her bedtime. I'd highly doubted that she had managed to stay awake so late. Like most three-year-old children, Missy slept as hard as she played. Once, I'd found her fast asleep on the floor of her room, nearly buried beneath a mountain of dolls, dress-up clothes, and stuffed animals.

With tears in my eyes, I'd rushed to get my video camera, eager to record the scene. I could easily imagining teasing her in her later years by showing the videos to her husband and children. I was lost in my own little daydream about graduation, weddings, and grandbabies when Mitchell had startled me out of my reverie by hopping into the car.

"Sorry that took so long. I couldn't find the new file on the guy I just hired," he told me.

I'd smiled to show that I wasn't upset. "I hope Jade didn't have any trouble getting Missy to bed."

He'd laughed the proud laugh of a father who couldn't believe that his child could do any wrong. "Jade loves her, honey. You know that."

When we'd arrived, Missy wasn't asleep. Jade lay sprawled on the couch, the television just loud enough to muffle her adolescent snores.

Like a typical teenager, she'd popped upright the moment I'd clicked off the television. She'd blinked and looked around, confused. Finally, the fog of sleep had seemed to clear. She'd focused on Mitchell and me, looking sheepish.

"Sorry. I must have fallen asleep," she mumbled.

I'd tried to look stern, but it was nearly impossible in the face of her obvious embarrassment. "Hey, it's okay. I take it that Missy's been in bed for a while?"

Jade sat up and gathered up the schoolbooks that she had spread out on the coffee table. She nodded. "Just after her bath. She soaked the bathroom, though."

She'd gingerly grabbed her still-damp T-shirt and held it away from her chest. "And me. That kid's unbelievable." But she'd said it with affection, so I hadn't taken offense. Missy could be unbelievable, sometimes.

I'd left Mitchell to pay her and walk her home while I went to check on Missy. Her bedroom was next to ours, with an adjoining bathroom in between. I'd frowned as I'd reached it and seen that the door was closed.

Jade knows better, I thought, making a mental note to have a word with her. How could she have heard Missy if she'd woken up, if the door was shut? In fact, I couldn't imagine how she'd gotten Missy to sleep with the door shut. It had only been a few months ago that Mitchell and I had managed to get Missy to sleep in her own room.

A trickle of unease had swept over me as I'd turned the knob. Call it women's intuition, or just plain paranoia, but I'd known that something was wrong before I'd even opened that door.

The bed was empty! I'd stared at it for a long, terrified moment before checking her closet, and under the bed. There was no sign of my precious little girl.

Okay, I thought, taking a deep breath and fighting panic. She probably got scared and crawled into our bed.

Nearly running, I'd raced into our bedroom and switched on the light.

The bed was empty, still made from that morning. Our walk-in closet was empty, too, and she wasn't under the bed.

"She could be hiding anywhere," I muttered. But my mouth was dry and my heart was pounding. Systematically, I'd turned on all the lights as I'd checked every inch of the house. Missy was not hiding in the big cabinets in the laundry room, as she sometimes did. She wasn't hiding in the hallway linen closet, or in the spare bedroom. And she wasn't in the computer room, or the kitchen.

I'd returned to her bedroom, almost numb with panic by that time. Like a woman on the edge, I'd checked everything again, telling myself that she had to be there. She had to be somewhere in the house!

When I'd ripped her curtains aside to check the windows, I'd screamed.

There was a neat hole in the glass just above the lock on the window, and Missy's favorite stuffed animal, a soft brown bear, was resting on the ledge.

Missy slept with the bear. She wouldn't go to sleep without it. The implications hit me with the force of a cement truck.

Someone had taken Missy from her bed! Someone had cut a hole in the glass, unlocked the window, and stolen my baby girl from our house.

I was breathing hard, as if I'd been running. I was unwilling to accept the enormous, horrifying facts. The bear stared at me with empty eyes. I'd picked it up and clutched it to my chest, but the soft, worn feel of my daughter's favorite toy had only increased my terror.

I'd heard the sound of the front door slamming in the distance. It had sounded miles away, and I'd sensed that I was about to faint. Mitchell's voice came from that far-away distance, as well. A tiny part of me that had remained sane knew that he was coming closer.

"Honey? Where are you? Sorry I took so long, but Jade was trying to get me to take her down a dark, dirt road—"

I'd sensed, rather than seen, Mitchell coming to a halt in the doorway, his teasing words dying on his lips. "Simone? Where's Missy? Did she wake up and crawl into our bed again?"

My lips formed the words, but they wouldn't come out. Saying them out loud would make them more real, and I wasn't ready for reality. My baby was out there in the night somewhere with a madman. She might already be dead.

"Simone?" His voice came closer. He put his hands on my shoulders and turned me around slowly. "Simone?"

I'd tried to focus on his concerned face, but I couldn't. I'd shut my eyes, squeezing burning tears through my closed lids. The stuffed bear was crushed beneath the force of my clenched hands.

"Oh, my God," Mitchell whispered. Obviously, my expression had told the story without my having to say a word. "Are you sure, Simone? You've looked everywhere?"

With an extreme effort, I'd opened my eyes. Screams were building inside of me, filling my chest. I'd managed to nod. I was afraid to open my mouth for fear that I'd never stop screaming.

Mitchell had refused to accept what had happened. "I'll look again. Maybe you overlooked her. She's good at hiding. I should know. After all, I taught her." His voice cracked on the last words. "Stay right here, honey. I'll be back in a moment." He'd led me to our daughter's frilly bed and forced me to sit down. I could only imagine how pale and terrified I'd looked.

It was nothing compared to the way that I'd felt. I wish I could have explained my terror. I wished that I could have found the right words to verbalize how I'd felt at that moment, but there were no words to express my utter fear. There were no words that could possibly have come close to explaining how terrified and empty I'd felt, knowing that my daughter was gone. Only a parent who had experienced that type of horror could have understood.

Finally, Mitchell had returned, after what had seemed like hours later. I'd refused to look at his face. I didn't want to see the confirmation of my worst fears reflected there.

"Simone—" he began slowly.

When I didn't look at him, he'd approached the bed and gently tilted up my face. I'd kept my eyes lowered. I was in shock.

"Simone, honey. We have to call the police," he said firmly.

I shook my head wildly. Didn't he know that calling the police meant that it was true? That someone had taken Missy? No—I couldn't be a party to such disloyalty. My baby was hiding somewhere. She had to be. Or, perhaps Jade was playing a sick joke—not realizing how petrified I would be.

Clutching his hands, I'd pleaded with him. "Find her, Mitchell. Find my baby! I have to have my baby back. She's tired, and I need to put her back to bed."

Mitchell's eyes filled with tears. He looked agonized. "Honey, she isn't in the house." He'd stared at the window—at that horrible hole in the glass. His face had crumpled for an instant. Then, he'd clenched his jaw and regained control. I think he knew that if he fell apart, I'd be hopeless, too. He'd pulled me up, gently trying to remove the stuffed bear from my hands.

I wouldn't let him have it, though. "Don't touch it!" I snapped. "You can't take it from me. You can't have it. Missy loves this bear, and I have to make sure that it's here when she gets back."

He'd given up instantly. "Let's go into the kitchen and call the police together."

I didn't want to leave Missy's room, but Mitchell was relentless. He'd practically pulled me down the hallway and into the kitchen, then pushed me into a chair.

"If you think you're going to faint, put your head between your knees," he instructed in a hoarse voice.

Faint? Not a chance. Not while my mind was spinning with questions and horrible thoughts about what might be happening to my baby. "I'm not going to faint," I insisted, almost belligerently. I'd felt like a shattered windshield—as if the slightest touch would send me scattering into a million pieces.

Where was my baby? What kind of monster would take a three-year-old child from her bed? From her loving parents?

I could ask myself the questions, but my mind backed away from even hinting at an answer. That was something that I couldn't face—not yet.

"They're coming right over," Mitchell told me as he hung up the phone. "I'll make some coffee." He'd hesitated, as if he didn't know quite how to handle me in my fragile, unsteady state. "Maybe I should fix you a stiff drink, honey."

"No!" I shouted, clutching the bear and rocking back and forth. My heart was pounding. "I don't need, or want, a drink. I want my baby back!"

Mitchell knelt before me. His face was creased with worry, and his eyes mirrored my own horror. "We'll get her back, Simone. I swear it."

How can he be sure? I'd asked the question to myself, then discarded it. I didn't want to doubt him, so I'd tried to believe him. A tiny flare of hope had flickered inside me, but it had died before I could grasp it. How could he get her back, when he didn't even know who had taken her? I wasn't stupid—not even in the state that I was in.

We'd waited in the ear-splitting silence for the police officers to arrive. I could hear my heart pounding wildly, and I could hear the rush of breath in and out of our lungs. Every sound seemed magnified—especially the sound of my teeth chattering. I'd even heard the patrol car pull into our driveway, and the slamming of the car doors. It had sounded like gunshots.

Mitchell went to answer the knock. Then, he led the officers back to the kitchen. He'd offered them coffee, as if they were just our neighbors, stopping by for a visit. For one, wild moment, I'd nearly launched myself at him, claws and teeth bared. How dare he act normally! How dare he think about coffee at a time like that? Somehow, I'd managed to constrain myself as the officers had taken out their notebooks and begun to ask questions.

"I'm Officer Murphy, and this is my partner, Officer Granger. Have either of you noticed anyone suspicious hanging around the neighborhood?"

After a brief hesitation, Mitchell shook his head. "No. I haven't."

Both officers had stared at me. I shook my head, my gaze straight ahead, unseeing, thinking about my baby in the clutches of a madman. "No." My voice was a tiny whisper, but they'd obviously heard me.

"Okay. I need each of you to answer this question: When was the last time that you saw your daughter? Mr. Sloane, we'll start with you."

Mitchell had briefly told them that he'd seen her only a moment before leaving the house to meet my father for dinner.

Then, it was my turn. I'd swallowed hard several times, wondering how I'd speak without sobbing. I knew that I had to try; though. My daughter's life was at stake.

"I left her in front of the television watching a video while I gave instructions to the baby-sitter. I kissed her before I left with Mitchell to meet my father for dinner," I said.

"So, she was with the baby-sitter when she was taken?" Officer Murphy asked sharply.

We both nodded. "Her name is Jade Cranston. She lives on our street, and she's fifteen. She's watched Missy for us often."

Both officers had scribbled in their notepads. Officer Granger looked up after a moment. "Did your baby-sitter have anyone over? A boyfriend, maybe?"

"No. Jade knows that's against the rules," Mitchell told him.

"What about ordering out? Do either of you know if she ordered any kind of delivery—pizza, Chinese food—while you were gone?"

That time, I'd answered. I was working on autopilot. "I don't think so. She was complaining about not having any lunch money because she'd just bought a new jacket. We didn't pay her until we returned."

Officer Granger scribbled again before asking the next question. "Can you tell me what she was wearing when she went to bed?"

Jade had dressed her for bed after her bath, but I had laid out Missy's pajamas on her bed. "She was wearing pajamas with pictures of princesses all over them. They were purple." Missy loved to pretend that she was a fairy princess.

I squeezed the stuffed animal harder and ground my teeth to hold back an anguished scream. Where was my baby?

"Ma'am, can you think of anyone who would have taken your daughter?"

"No!" I shouted the word, then bit my lip hard enough to taste blood. Tears flowed down my face. I knew that I wouldn't be able to keep it together much longer.

"Mr. Sloane?" The officer turned to my husband.

Mitchell shook his hand, staring at the floor. "No."

"What about a kidnapping? What's your financial situation?"

"We don't have any money," Mitchell told him. "Nothing that would interest a kidnapper." His voice cracked.

I'd hated him for saying that. It had brought home the very terrible probability that a crazed maniac had taken our daughter for reasons other than money. And those reasons had paralyzed me.

"We can't completely rule out a kidnapping," Officer Murphy told us. "Kidnappers know that parents will do anything to get their children back. Take out a second mortgage, borrow from family or friends—things like that. They don't always target the wealthy." He paused.

"I'll need a list of family and close friends—anyone and everyone you can think of. Try to include everyone that you've known in the past, and in the present." Officer Murphy hesitated, just long enough to get our attention. "I'll also have to fingerprint both of you, and get blood samples."

I'd gasped. "Why? She's our daughter!" The insinuation itself was insulting and demeaning, and it had enhanced the surrealism of the situation. "You need to get out there and find the lunatic who took our daughter!" I knew that I was losing control, but I couldn't stop myself. Their ugly, ridiculous insinuations had caused me to crack. "And stop wasting time. Stop asking stupid questions."

The police officers continued to stare grimly at me. "I'm sorry, ma'am, but we're just following procedure. When the special task force gets here, they're going to tell you the same thing. It's hard to consider, but often when a child is taken, the perp is a family member, or a friend—someone that the child knows."

"But we weren't even here," Mitchell muttered, sounding as disgusted as I'd felt.

The police officers focused their stares on Mitchell, as if trying to see inside him. "We just wanted to prepare you for what lies ahead during this investigation. You want us to do everything we can to find your daughter, don't you?"

By midnight, our house was crawling with a team of specialists. No stone was left unturned—no question left unanswered. I was exhausted and so was Mitchell, but I knew that neither of us could have slept, even if we'd had the opportunity. Not without our baby home, safe and sound.

Since they hadn't completely ruled out a kidnapping, the officers put a recorder and a tracer on our phone so that they could trace any suspicious calls, if the unlikely possibility arose.

I was faced with calling my father, and I dreaded it. Although his heart attack the year before had been mild, I was afraid that the terrible news would trigger another, more massive attack. So I did something that I hadn't thought that I could do: I'd pulled myself together and tried not to sound as if I were one step away from the edge of a steep cliff.

"Hello?" Daddy's voice was groggy from sleep, but understandably edgy. Like most parents, he knew that any call in the middle of the night would most likely bring bad news.

"Daddy? It's Simone." Despite my resolve, my throat had burned and ached from a fresh surge of tears. I'd swallowed hard, reminding myself of his fragile health. I couldn't bear to lose him, too. "Something terrible has happened. Can you come over?"

"What?" Daddy barked into the phone, making me jump. "What is it? Is it Missy? Has something happened to Missy?"

He had zeroed in on the one thing that mattered most in his world, other than myself. And since I was talking to him, he'd made the obvious deductions.

"I can't tell you over the phone, Daddy. I don't want you to be too upset to drive."

There was a long pause. "Give me fifteen minutes," he said curtly, with the weary resignation of someone who knew that he was about to face a crisis.

"Be careful, Daddy." I'd hung up the phone quickly, before I'd broken down completely. When I'd turned around, Officer Murphy was standing behind me.

"You scared me," I told him.

"Sorry." He'd looked at the phone, then back to me.

"That was my father. He's on his way over," I explained.

"Was he asleep when you called?" he asked.

My stomach lurched at the hidden insinuation in his voice. I knew that it was his job, but that didn't make knowing any easier. "Yes, as a matter of fact, he was," I told him through clenched teeth. I didn't add that my father worshipped the ground that my daughter walked on—that the news might kill him. I didn't shout that Daddy would be the last man on earth other than Mitchell—that would harm one tiny hair on Missy's head—or mine, for that matter.

I didn't say anything because in my heart, I knew that he was just doing his job. I didn't want to hinder the investigation in any shape, form, or fashion.

"Tell me, Mrs. Sloane. Did you enter your daughter in any beauty contests?" he asked.

I should have been used to his lack of subtlety by that point, but I wasn't. My emotions were too raw for rational thinking. "No," I told him. "Missy's too shy with strangers. And, besides, I don't believe in exploiting children that way."

Officer Murphy had sighed at my tone. "It's not what you're thinking, Mrs. Sloane. Sometimes sexual predators hang around places like beauty contests, searching for their next victim."

He must have noticed how pale I'd become. I'd felt as if the blood had drained from my body at what he'd said. Yes, I had thought the same thing myself. I'd thought about the chilling possibility that Missy's kidnapper might be a sexual predator, or a sick psycho, but to hear the words out loud—well, it was just too much.

I'd slapped Officer Murphy hard enough to make his head jerk back. I wasn't sorry for my actions, either. Officer Murphy might have been good cop, but in my opinion, he had the sensitivity of an assassin.

Before he either of us could respond to my shocking reaction, I'd looked up to find Jade standing in the kitchen doorway. The moment that our eyes met, she'd burst into tears and come rushing toward me. Wearing grim expressions, her parents had hovered protectively behind her. It was as if they'd feared that I'd physically attack their daughter.

The thought had crossed my mind. After all, Jade had been asleep while baby-sitting my precious little girl. But what had kept me from taking out my grief and terror on Jade was the fact that the special team working in Missy's room had found traces of ether on her pillow. My daughter had been drugged, so the chances were slim that Jade would have heard anything, even if she had been awake.

"I'm sorry," Jade murmured, burying her face in my shoulder. "I'm so sorry! I'm so sorry!"

Her mother moved forward and wrapped her arms around her daughter's shoulders, trying to pull her away from me. I'd just stood there, stiff as a board. I was too distraught to give the teenager the comfort that she needed.

"Come here, darling. Mrs. Sloane doesn't blame you." Jade's mother had shot me a cold, pointed look. "She knows that you would never let something so terrible happen if you could prevent it."

With great effort, I'd mustered my strength to comfort and reassure Jade. I'd realized that I was the only one that could.

"She's right, Jade. They said that he used drugs to make Missy unconscious." I'd grabbed the cabinet as the room had seemed to tilt. I'd had to force the words out through my constricted throat. "You wouldn't have heard anything, anyway. It's not your fault." My words had sounded dull and without conviction, but I was doing the best that I could. I'd wanted to blame someone, but Jade's mother's guarded look had reminded me that Jade was young and hysterical.

Throughout the night, friends and neighbors had arrived to join our vigil. Daddy was a rock, constantly assuring me that we would find Missy, safe and sound. He'd told me that he felt it in his bones. His face was strained and pale, but I hadn't sensed any frailty, thank goodness.

Somewhere along the way, I'd let go of Missy's precious bear, and suddenly, I'd wanted it back. I'd searched the house like a robot until I'd found the stuffed toy in a chair that was occupied by my next-door neighbor, Ken Hodgkins. Ken and his wife, Rosemarie, along with their two teenage boys, had moved into the neighborhood about six months earlier. Mitchell and Ken had immediately hit it off, and Ken had came over earlier in the night to find out what was going on.

He and Rosemarie had stayed, apparently unperturbed by the special team of officers that had given them a grilling, asking them personal questions about themselves and their sons. Their calm acceptance had made me ashamed of my previous reaction. Had I sounded guilty? I'd thought that I had. But, I knew that I couldn't undo what had already been done.

The phone rang at three in the morning. The twenty or so people that were still milling about the house had frozen in unison. All conversation had stopped abruptly. Officer Granger had motioned for Mitchell to answer the phone. Another officer had placed his hand on the extension phone, carefully coordinating his movements with Mitchell's.

I could see Mitchell's hand shaking as he'd picked up the phone. "Hello?" he asked anxiously.

I'd held my breath, my hand over my mouth to stifle any involuntary noise I might make. Daddy's arm had tightened to an almost painful degree around my shoulder.

After a brief moment, Mitchell had hung up. He was frowning. "They hung up. Whoever it was hung up the moment they heard my voice."

The disappointment made me weak. Had I really thought that the kidnapper would call? We had no money—and we wouldn't, at least, not for another few years.

"Do you often get hang-up calls at three in the morning?" an agent asked us.

"Just occasionally," Mitchell answered. "No more than anyone else probably does."

I'd refused to believe that it was a coincidence. Officer Murphy picked up the phone and dialed the number that was listed on the Caller ID. He'd listened for a moment, then replaced the receiver.

"It was a pay phone. Some wino answered. I told him to stay put until we can get a man to him to ask him if he saw anyone. But I wouldn't hold my breath." He'd nodded at me. "Just in case it was the perp and he wanted to talk to you, Mrs. Sloane, you be sure and answer the phone—if and when he calls back."

At that moment, the front door opened and two men came in.

"We've got a footprint outside her window," one man said. "Look's like a sneaker. Probably a woman's footprint."

A woman's footprint? I couldn't wrap my mind around the information. Daddy had asked the question that I hadn't had time to form.

"Are you saying that a woman took our little girl?" he asked, his voice sounding harsh from exhaustion and worry.

"We're not saying anything," Officer Murphy told him. "But it's the first real lead that we've got."

Maybe I should have felt a tremendous relief at the possibility that Missy's kidnapper was a woman, but I didn't. My little girl was gone—alone with a stranger, for only heaven knew what reasons.

One of the special agents, Sergeant Prentiss, appeared at my side. He spoke in a low voice.

"Can I speak with you in private, Mrs. Sloane?" When Daddy had stood up to go with us, Sergeant Prentiss shook his head. "Sorry, sir. We'll only be a moment—I promise."

He'd led me into the spare bedroom and closed the door. Another special agent stood there, silently, by the window, frowning into the dark night. A shiver of premonition had swept over me. I felt something in the air—a charged tension, expectation, maybe.

They know something, I thought, my hopes rising so sharply it made me dizzy. They know something, and they're afraid to tell me.

"What is it?" I demanded. "And why isn't my husband here with me?"

The agent at the window had turned toward me. His expression wasn't what I'd hoped for. He'd looked grim—very grim. "I'm Special Agent Harrison, ma'am. I need to ask you a few questions, and they won't be easy ones. Are you up to it?"

"Will it help with the investigation?" I countered.

"It might," he answered evasively. He'd motioned for me to sit on the bed. I did, but only because my legs were wobbly. "The officers have spoken with you about the possibility of your daughter having been kidnapped by someone close to her—or, at least, someone she knows and would recognize?"

"Y—yes," I whispered. I'd wanted to say more, but I'd forced myself to wait for the questions.

"Can you think of anyone that you know who's desperate for money—someone who would know about the trust fund that you stand to inherit when you turn thirty?"

I'd sucked in a sharp breath. I supposed that I shouldn't have been shocked that they knew about my trust fund. They had talked to Daddy for almost an hour—alone. "My trust fund isn't a big secret," I said, my voice trembling.

"I need names, Mrs. Sloane," Agent Harrison persisted gently.

My throat had locked up. I'd had to swallow twice before I could answer, and even then, it was difficult to say aloud the names of those I knew and loved. People that I knew in my heart couldn't have done something that terrible.

"My husband knows," I began. "My brother knows, and I'm certain that a lot of people on Daddy's staff know about it. My brother was working for our father when he turned twenty-five and got his money.

He bragged about how much Mom trusted his judgment more than she trusted mine."

I'd thought about Garrett, and I'd forced myself to consider his unstable nature. Could he have masterminded something so horrendous? And, what about Gavin, Daddy's ex-assistant? He was surely a disgruntled employee, and he would have had a motive for revenge against my father.

As for Mitchell, I'd absolutely refused even to consider the possibility—even though we'd just had an argument that morning over money.

But, someone had taken my daughter, and Agent Harrison seemed far too certain for it to have been just a hunch that it was someone that I knew.

"You know something," I said. The moment I said it, I knew that I was right. They did know something, and if they knew it, I was bound and determined that I would know it, too. "Tell me, please! We're talking about my baby—my little girl. If there's anything that you know—" I broke off.

"It's not so much that we know something, Mrs. Sloane," Agent Harrison began. "It's the unanswered questions that we have: How did the perp know which room was your daughter's room? There's there no evidence that he came into the house through any other entry than the window. Also, if you made plans to meet your father just this morning, how did the perp know about it? How did he know that you and your husband would be gone?"

I'd sat there, absorbing his very logical questions—questions that I would never have thought of on my own.

But, he wasn't finished. He'd pointed to the stuffed bear that I'd held in my hands. "And that. Didn't you say that you found it on the windowsill?" When I'd nodded, a flash of satisfaction had flickered in his eyes. "If the perp drugged your daughter, she wouldn't have been able to hold onto the stuffed animal. I think that he or she was planning on taking it with them, but they dropped it when they were going through the window."

His theory had made sense.

"I don't think that this is really the work of a—" He paused delicately. "—disturbed person. I think that your daughter was kidnapped, and that we'll be getting a call soon. It isn't likely that someone with devious intentions would worry about comforting a little girl with her favorite toy."

The agent had approached me then, and I could tell by his reluctant expression that he'd hated to say whatever it was that he was about to say.

"Mrs. Sloane, I know that you find it hard to consider, but just for a second, humor me, okay?" he asked.

"Okay," I whispered. I'd squeezed the bear tightly, aching for my little girl—for my baby.

"Are you and your husband having financial problems?" he began.

A totally inappropriate, shaky laugh burst out of me. "You're joking, right? You can't possibly think that Mitchell would kidnap his own daughter, just to get Daddy to pay up with my trust fund, do you?"

"So, the thought did cross your mind," he observed.

"No, it did not!" I protested. "What crossed my mind was that you guys might be thinking it. But, I can assure you—you're wrong. If anyone would have a motive and the gall to do something like this, it would be my drug addict brother, Garrett. He's in town. Why don't you pay him a visit?"

"He's on our list, along with the disgruntled employee, and your next-door neighbor."

"Ken? What reason would he have for taking Missy?" I was shocked.

"Money," Agent Harrison muttered grimly. "When you're in our profession, you learn that it truly is the root of all evil, Mrs. Sloane."

I'd absorbed his words. "Do you know something about our neighbor that we don't know?" I asked hesitantly.

"We know that your husband told him about your trust fund. We also know that Ken moved from across the country to get away from a loan shark who wanted to break both his legs. He has a gambling problem, Mrs. Sloane. Didn't you know?"

I shook my head. Ken was Mitchell's friend. Rosemarie had always worked the night shift as a nurse at the hospital, and she'd slept during the days, so we hadn't had much time to get together. "Did Mitchell tell you all of this?" I asked. And, if he had, why hadn't he mentioned it to me?

"Yes, he did. He didn't want to implicate Ken, but he also understands that we have to look at every angle." When I'd tried to stand up, he'd put up a stalling hand. "You have to keep quiet about this. It could be any number of people, right beneath our noses, but we don't want them to know that we suspect. It's crucial that you keep this conversation to yourself—do you understand?"

"Or—" I'd swallowed a hard knot of fear. "Or, they might panic, and do something rash." I'd watched enough movies in my lifetime to pretty much sum it up. Agent Harrison's nod hadn't come as a surprise.

"That's right—they could. And, Mrs. Sloane—" He'd paused to put a warning hand on my shoulder. "That includes your husband. Until we prove differently, everyone's a suspect."

Even me? I wondered. Had the two agents pulled Daddy and Mitchell aside, as they had done to me, and filled their heads with suspicions about me? I knew that it was a possibility. And, what did it matter? I had done nothing wrong, and neither had Mitchell. I should have been thankful that they were taking their jobs so seriously.

The next few days passed in endless waiting. I'd camped out in the recliner in our living room, refusing to move from the phone. Sometimes, I'd dozed, but not for long. When I had managed to fall asleep, the nightmares would haunt me. I'd wake up in a cold sweat, shaking and crying, with Missy's pitiful cries echoing in my ears. Was she okay? Was she frightened? Were they treating her well? Was someone taking care of her? Feeding her? I have imagined that the same questions went through the minds of any parents whose child had been taken.

On the third day, Mitchell went back to work. "If I keep sitting here, I'm going to go out of my mind," he told me. Daddy had agreed that it was a good idea, and he'd agreed to stay with me.

By the fourth day, we were down to two agents, waiting for the call. On day six, there was only one agent. Finally, he'd packed up his equipment and told us the bad news.

"Chances are that the kidnappers would have called by now. We've interviewed everyone, and we've taken blood samples and fingerprints, but after that, we've hit a dead end. I'm sorry," he said solemnly.

He was sorry? They were just going to forget that my daughter existed, and he was sorry? The days of waiting, wondering, and praying had taken their toll. I knew what I'd looked like. I had glanced at myself in the mirror that very morning when I'd washed my face. There were black circles under my eyes. My skin was almost translucent, and I'd lost weight. I couldn't eat, knowing that my daughter might be dead, or starving—or worse.

I was so weak that I could barely walk. Daddy had threatened to bring me to the hospital if I didn't start eating something soon.

"We're not giving up, ma'am. We'll keep the investigation going, and if you stumble upon anything, give us a call right away. We'll keep you informed as best as we can."

"As best as you can?" I'd stared incredulously at the agent, my hollowed eyes burning.

"Ma'am, we've got over thirty pending cases involving missing children. You're not alone."

When he was gone, Daddy had taken me in his arms as if I were still a baby and held me as I'd cried my heart out. I was drained and beaten. But I hadn't given up hope. I could never give up hope.

Finally, Daddy had grasped my shoulders and looked at me. His eyes were wet, and, for the first time, I'd noticed how gaunt his face had become since Missy's disappearance. A pang of guilt had hit me. What was I doing? I was being selfish—ignoring my husband's pain, and that of my father. Daddy looked as if he were on the verge of a breakdown as well, and yet, I was still clinging to him.

I'd taken a deep breath and tried to get hold of myself. I knew that crying wouldn't do Missy any good. Trying to figure out who might have taken her would help, though.

"Daddy, would you make us some soup while I freshen up?" I asked.

Daddy looked hopeful. "That's my girl! I'll do that, honey. I sure will."

When he'd disappeared into the kitchen, I'd made my way to Missy's bedroom. I'd sat on the bed and stared at the window where some crazed maniac had carried out my daughter, after drugging her. What if they'd given her too much? What if that was why they hadn't called asking for ransom—because they'd already killed her?

Stop those negative thoughts. Think, Simone. Think! I ordered myself.

Who had known that Mitchell and I were meeting Daddy for dinner? Garrett, Daddy, myself, and the baby-sitter. Who else had Daddy or Mitchell told? Gavin probably knew, too, because Gavin usually knew every move that Daddy made. Had Daddy said something before or after he'd fired him? Had Daddy's firing Gavin pushed the man over the edge?

Ken! Ken lived next door, so he could easily have seen us leaving. I didn't think that Mitchell had had time to talk to Ken that day for him to have mentioned having dinner with his father-in-law, though.

Shoving my knuckles into my mouth to hold back the sobs, I turned on the bed to retrieve the stuffed animal that I'd placed there earlier.

It was gone. I frowned. Obviously I'd forgotten where I laid it last and had only thought I'd put it back on the bed. I rose and went to my bedroom, searching for the bear.

I couldn't find it. The phone rang. I'd jumped, freezing, as I had each time the phone rang. I could hear my father's deep voice, but I couldn't understand what he was saying.

Slowly, I'd approached the living room, my body on guard, my mind praying that it was someone with word of Missy.

Daddy stood there, his face so pale that I'd thought he'd die right on the spot. He'd held a hand over his chest.

"It was the kidnapper, honey," he whispered. "They've got Missy, and they want one hundred thousand dollars."

One hundred thousand dollars. The same amount that I'll be getting when I turn thirty. So, it is about the money, I thought.

Then his words had hit me. I'd realized the implications of his words: Missy wasn't dead! She hadn't been taken by a sexual predator. She had been kidnapped for money! I was almost giddy with relief. I knew that might have sounded strange, but after all of the horrible things that I'd been thinking, kidnapping had sounded much better to me.

"Oh, Daddy," I whispered, tears filling my eyes and brimming over. Daddy was crying, too. We came together in the middle of the room, hugging and laughing as if we'd truly gotten good news. I'd certainly felt as if I had.

Eventually, life had intruded into the fragile moment. I didn't have any money—not yet. I knew that I must have looked terrified when I'd stared at Daddy.

"Daddy? We're going to get Missy back, aren't we?" I asked.

Daddy didn't hesitate. "Of course we are, honey. If I have to sell everything that I have, we'll get her back."

"I want to use my trust fund. I don't want you to use your own money. That money's for your retirement."

"Now, honey—" he began.

"No, Daddy, I mean it," I insisted. I'd felt my strength miraculously returning. Even my voice had sounded stronger. "Did they give you a time and place?" Then, I'd realized something. I'd realized that whoever it was had waited until the police had cleared out before they had called, which meant they must have been watching the house the entire time.

A cold shiver had swept down my spine. More than ever, I'd wondered if it was someone we knew who had been behind the awful torture. I hadn't realized that I had dug my nails into Daddy's arms until he'd winced.

"Sorry, Daddy. You don't look too well. Won't you sit down?" I asked.

"You don't look too well yourself," he mumbled gruffly, but even still, he sat on the sofa. He'd patted the seat beside him. "It was a woman."

A cold, dark rage had filled me. I'd believed that I was, at that moment, capable of murder. "Who, Daddy? Whom do we know that might have taken Missy? I've tried and tried to think of any women that I know that would do such a thing, but I can't come up with a single one—not even remotely."

Daddy sighed and patted my shoulder. "Me, either, honey." He'd hesitated, then continued in a low voice. "She said that if we went to the police again, she would kill Missy and bury her where we'd never find her."

I'd closed my eyes and clenched my teeth, my previous terror—which was never far away—returning full force. I'd had no doubt that that monster had meant every word that she'd said. Since I didn't have a clue about who she might be, I'd had to believe that she would do it.

"I don't want to take any chances, Daddy," I told him. "Let's just pay her the money, and get Missy home."

"She said that she'd call back later to give us the details," Daddy said wearily.

"I'll call Caleb and start the ball rolling." Caleb was our attorney. I knew that if anything could be done to get my trust fund released, Caleb would be able to do it.

"I'll have to sign a waiver."

Money was the last thing on my mind at that point. I'd had a brief, ugly thought about what Mitchell would think about me losing my trust fund, but I'd quickly pushed it away. What was I thinking? I was obviously overwrought even to consider that Mitchell would be worried about the money. He loved Missy as much as I did.

That thought had reminded me that I had yet to call him with the news. I'd quickly picked up the phone and dialed his office number. His secretary had answered, politely telling me that he'd taken a long lunch and wouldn't be back for another hour or more. When I'd asked her where he'd gone, she was evasive, stating that she wasn't certain.

I was frowning when I'd hung up the phone. When I'd looked at Daddy, I'd seen a flash of guilt in his eyes before he'd hastily turned away. I'd started to tremble uncontrollably.

"Daddy? That was Mitchell's secretary. She told me that he'd gone to lunch, but she didn't know where. I can't believe, with everything that's been going on, that he wouldn't let someone know where he was at all times."

Daddy was still avoiding my gaze. "Maybe he just needed some time alone to think."

He was lying. I could feel it in my bones. My trembling had turned into an all-out shaking—a reaction, I was sure, to the news that we'd gotten, and to the news that I was certain I was about to get. "Something's going on, isn't it? I thought—" I'd bit my lip and swallowed hard. "I suspected that he might be having an affair. Is he, Daddy?" It had hurt me deeply to think that my father might know something that important, yet kept it from me. But then, he didn't like hurting me any more than I liked hurting him.

"I only saw him with the woman briefly," Daddy told me, after a long silence. "That doesn't mean that he's having an affair."

But I'd heard what Daddy hadn't said. "Who was this woman?"

"I didn't recognize her. That's why I thought it was odd," he admitted.

"Where were they when you saw them?" I asked.

"Outside a hotel, on the sidewalk," he confessed reluctantly. "He kissed her good-bye—and it wasn't a friendly kiss."

A moan had escaped me. How much more could a person take? I'd licked my parched lips. "When were you planning on telling me? Or, were you planning on not telling me at all?" I'd suspected the latter, and it hurt, even though I knew that my father was just trying to protect me.

"I didn't want to hurt you, honey," Daddy confirmed. "Besides, I wasn't certain of anything."

"I'm a big girl now. You can't shield me from everything in life," I reminded him.

Daddy had smiled slightly, his eyes glistening with tears. "But I can try, can't I?"

I'd laid my cheek on his knee, my throat aching with the words that I was about to say. But they had to be said, and I knew it. "Daddy, the night before Missy disappeared, Mitchell and I had an argument. It was about my trust fund." Daddy's hand had tightened on my shoulder. "Do you think—" I'd faltered, unable to finish.

"Do I think that Mitchell would be capable of kidnapping his own daughter to get that money?" Daddy's words had sounded so brutal that I'd flinched. "I don't know, honey. I'd hate to believe it, but if he's involved with another woman, anything is possible."

And the call had confirmed what the cops had already suspected—that Missy had been taken from her room by a woman.

"I haven't completely ruled out Garrett," Daddy went on, sounding pained.

"But we have to consider Mitchell, too. I'm going to tell the police about the woman."

"You don't know anything for certain," Daddy reminded me.

"Daddy, you told me that he kissed her. That's pretty certain, as far as I'm concerned."

"What about the money and the ransom instructions?" he asked.

I was silent for a moment, forcing my exhausted mind to think. If Mitchell was behind the whole thing, then he would know the moment that the police became involved again. I couldn't bring myself to believe that he would have hurt Missy, but I couldn't speak for the woman. I knew nothing about her.

Also, if Mitchell wasn't behind the kidnapping, then bringing the cops back into it would further jeopardize Missy's safety. I couldn't take that chance.

"We pay her the money, then tell the police about our suspicions. I want to get Missy home safe and sound before we do."

"I agree, honey," he told me.

Moving on autopilot, I'd kissed my father good-bye, warning him to try and take it slow. I didn't like his gray pallor, but at that moment, I'd felt helpless to do anything about it. I couldn't make him stop worrying, any more than I could stop worrying.

After Daddy left, I'd had to throw up. I'd sat there on the bathroom floor and thought about Mitchell with another woman. Either I was numb from all the stress, or I truly didn't care, because I'd felt nothing—not as far as the affair.

But I'd vowed that it if turned out that Mitchell had placed our daughter in jeopardy, just to get his hands on my trust fund money, then I was going to kill him.

The drop-off place was at an old, abandoned schoolhouse, about five miles out of town. Daddy and I had parked there and killed the engine, taking a moment to get our bearings. Both of us were nervous about the amount of cash that we were carrying in an old, battered suitcase.

The old schoolhouse had been vandalized time and time again. In fact, I could remember at least one time in high school when I'd met a few friends out there to party. The windows were either gone or broken, and the doors were warped and beaten. The long steps leading up the front doors were pitted with holes and rife with rotten boards. It looked to me as it had always looked—spooky, dead, and dangerous. When I was a teenager, it had intrigued me, but, as an adult, it had repulsed me.

But I'd had to admit grudgingly that if I were a kidnapper, it would be the perfect place to leave the ransom money. The old schoolhouse was set right out in the open, and it was almost impossible for someone to sneak up on it. If the police were around, they'd find it hard to hide from someone who was watching.

"Wait for me here," I told Daddy. I didn't want to risk him breaking a leg or a hip walking up those steps. So nervous that my teeth were chattering, I'd grabbed the suitcase and opened the car door.

The dome light that came on in the car was the only light that I could see for miles and miles, in all directions. Everything else was pitch black, making me glad that I'd brought a flashlight.

The woman on the phone had been precise in her orders. I was to leave the money in an old sink in the girls' rest room. Carefully, I'd managed the steps without falling through. I wasn't exactly keen on going into that spooky old building by myself, but what choice did I have? I wanted my daughter back.

I'd made it to the rest room without mishap. My flashlight had picked up the faded, mold-covered picture of a girl on the door of the rest room, confirming that I had found the right one. The doorknob fell off in my hand, so I'd used my foot to push the dirty door open. I'd shone the flashlight all around, then squatted to look under the stalls.

If someone was hiding, then he or she were standing on top of a commode. The thought had made me shiver. With more haste than grace, I'd placed the suitcase in the sink and backed out, probably moving far faster than was safe.

Daddy had started the car the moment that he'd seen me emerge from the house. We'd wasted no time in getting out of there. According to the woman, while I was dropping off the money, she would be leaving me a message on my answering machine, telling me where I could find Missy.

That was the excuse that I'd had for leaving Mitchell at home. He'd been a great actor, ranting and raving, and insisting that I call the police. He'd even gone so far as to accuse me of recklessly endangering our daughter's life by taking the matter into my own hands.

I hadn't believed him for a moment. It wasn't anything that he'd said or done to make me more convinced than ever. No, it was the very fact that he was so quick and perfect in his reactions—as if he'd rehearsed them. Still, there was a small part of me that believed I could be wrong about Mitchell. Understandable, I supposed, considering that he was my husband and the father of my child.

The house was ominously silent when I'd opened the door. My heart had begun to pound wildly. I glanced back at Daddy and was terrified to find the same look of foreboding on his face.

Something was wrong. The house was too quiet.

"Mitchell?" I called out. I'd had to try again because my voice was cracking. "Mitchell? Are you here?"

There was only silence.

"Maybe they've already called and he couldn't wait for us to get back." I'd tried to sound hopeful. "Maybe he went to pick her up." But even as I'd said the words out loud, I'd had a terrible suspicion that I was wrong.

My feet had felt as if they'd each weighed a ton as I'd walked down the hall to our room. I'd gone into Missy's room first. Everything was the same, except that her closet door was ajar. I'd pulled it open and found it empty. All of her clothes were gone.

Moving in slow, robotic movements, I'd headed into our bedroom and into our walk-in closet, conscious of Daddy behind me.

Mitchell's clothes were gone. All of them—along with the new luggage that my father had given us for Christmas two years before.

I'd swung around, my voice flat. "It was him. It was Mitchell and his new girlfriend, and now they're gone. They've taken Missy with them."

"Honey—" my father began sorrowfully.

Daddy had opened his arms to me, but I'd pushed past him. I'd never felt so murderous in my life. Mitchell had kidnapped his own daughter for my trust fund! Then, he'd headed out of town, and not only taking my money, but our daughter, as well. And he'd been with another woman!

That part didn't bother me as much as the horrible betrayal that I'd felt. How could I have lived with someone, and not know that they were capable of such a horrendous act? How long had he been planning it? How long had he been having an affair with a woman that he'd planned to run away with, after he'd stolen my trust fund—and my daughter?

In the living room, I'd paced back and forth, ignoring Daddy's concerned gaze. Of course, he was concerned. I'd probably looked exactly like a woman driven to the point of murder.

"We need to make a call," Daddy said, attempting to sound stern. But I knew that he was just as furious as I was—or close. I don't think that anybody could have been as furious as I really was.

I'd leveled a cold gaze upon my father. "What was the name of the hotel that you saw them at?" I demanded.

Something in my face must have alerted my father to the fact that I had completely lost the ability to think rationally. He wouldn't tell me, at first. "You need to let the police handle this, Simone. He'll go to prison for this."

"He'll die," I announced with conviction. "He has to die. I have to kill him for what he's done to me and to Missy—to our life. You understand, don't you?" At the time, I didn't feel irrational at all. What I had to do was crystal clear in my mind: Mitchell had to die, and at my hands. I had to be the one to kill him.

Daddy was beginning to panic. His hands were trembling as he'd reached out to me. "Come here, honey. Come here. We'll call them together."

I didn't budge, and my resolve didn't waver. "The hotel, Daddy. I need the name of the hotel," I insisted.

"They might not even be there," Daddy told me desperately.

"Maybe. Give me the name, Daddy." I supposed he'd finally realized that I wasn't going to give up.

"It was the motel on Highland Road, near the airport."

"Do you still have a gun in the glove compartment?" I asked.

"Yes, but—" he faltered.

"Give me your keys," I demanded.

"Honey! You can't go after him with a gun! You'll go to prison."

At the moment, I didn't care. "The keys, Daddy. Now!" I repeated.

"I'm going with you," he announced.

"No. You stay here and talk to the police when they arrive. That should give me enough time to do what I have to do."

Reluctantly, Daddy had pulled the keys from his pocket and handed them to me. "What good will it do Missy if her mother's in prison?"

"She'll have you," I murmured dully, heading for the door.

I didn't think you could have called what I was experiencing "temporary insanity." It was lasting too long. For six long days, I had died a thousand deaths, wondering if my baby daughter was being raped and tortured—or, if she were already dead.

And, all along, Mitchell had known where she was. He had probably seen her, and spent time with her. He'd probably assured her that everything was all right. My mind was made up: Mitchell was a dead man.

The drive to the airport had passed in a blur of dark, boiling rage. I'd probably come very close to dying in more than one aggressive move on the interstate, but I didn't care.

I'd left Daddy's car parked outside the motel and slipped the gun into my purse. The clerk at the desk had looked up as I'd approached, smiling.

"Can I help you?" she asked.

"I'm meeting my husband, and I've forgotten his room number." I knew that the instant I'd said the words, I'd made a mistake.

The clerk's smile had slipped from her face. "I'm sorry, ma'am, but I'm not allowed to give out that information."

Without hesitation, I'd opened my purse and pulled out the gun. The clerk had frozen, her eyes wide. "Check for a Mitchell Sloane," I ordered.

She did. A few minutes later, she was shaking her head. She'd looked as if she would faint.

"Check for a single listing for a woman," I persisted.

Moments had ticked by. Finally, the flustered clerk had looked up anxiously. "I've got four listings for women in single rooms."

"Write the room numbers down," I insisted. "And if you call security before I leave this hotel, I'll start shooting people. You don't want that on your conscience, do you?" I'd probably sounded like a gangster from an old movie, but I didn't care, not at the time.

She'd scribbled down the numbers on a piece of paper. I'd snatched it up, placing the gun back in my purse, and giving her one last, warning look before I'd started walking toward the elevators.

An elderly woman, perhaps in her seventies, had answered the first door that I'd tried. I'd apologized and moved on.

The second door that I'd stopped at had revealed an attractive woman in her early to late thirties. "Do you know Mitchell Sloane?" I snapped. I'd figured that, with surprise on my side, I'd know whether or not she did.

She'd looked blank. "You must have the wrong room," she told me.

That time, I didn't bother with apologies. I'd gone on to the next room, and knocked on the door. I'd waited a full three minutes before I'd realized that the room must have been empty. The gun in my purse had tugged heavily at my shoulder as I'd trudged down the all to the last room number on my list.

A pretty young woman had answered the door. "Do you know Mitchell Sloane?" I demanded, watching her expression carefully.

She frowned, then called over her shoulder. "Honey, do you know a man named Mitchell Sloane? There's a woman at the door who wants to know."

The man that answered was definitely not Mitchell.

Which meant that Mitchell had been behind the third door. My fury had nearly blinded me as I'd realized that somehow, he'd gotten away. I'd suspected that Daddy was behind it. Daddy wouldn't want me to go to prison for killing someone as worthless as Mitchell, so it sounded like something he would have done.

There was no sign of security as I'd stopped at a pay phone and called home. I wasn't surprised when Agent Harrison answered the phone.

"Come home, Simone. We'll handle this," he told me firmly.

"I can't." I'd shouldered my purse and taken a ragged breath.

"Come home. We caught them at the airport, trying to catch a plane out of the country. My partner's bringing your daughter home as we speak."

I didn't believe him. I couldn't believe him. I was afraid to believe him. "No," I whispered, feeling myself began to crumble. "You're lying, just to get me to come home."

"I'm not. In fact, just stay there. Your father should be there any moment now to get you," he told me.

I'd hung up, leaning against the wall as the strength had left my legs. I'd slid to the floor and begun to sob.

Some time later, I'd felt a tender hand in my hair. I'd looked up and seen my father through blurry, unfocused eyes. "Daddy?" Was I hallucinating?

"Yes, honey, it's Daddy. I've come to take you home. Missy's waiting for you."

"No she isn't." I'd slapped at his hands weakly. "You're lying."

"I talked to her on the phone, Simone. I talked to my granddaughter, and she sounded fine. She said she'd been on vacation with her daddy and Melanie."

Melanie. So the witch's name was Melanie. The witch who drugged my daughter and stole her from her bed, I thought.

I'd felt physically sick. I'd staggered to my feet and let Daddy lead me to the hotel entrance. We'd passed the clerk, and I'd remembered my awful threats with more shame than I would have thought possible. I hadn't felt shame at the time.

When I'd looked at the clerk, she'd quickly turned her back to me. Maybe Daddy talked to her, I thought. Or, more likely, he paid her to keep quiet about the crazy woman with the gun.

Missy—my baby girl. Missy would be at home, waiting for her mommy.

The drive home was quick. The moment Daddy stopped the car, I found strength that I hadn't known that I'd had. Otherwise, how could I have run to the house that way?

She was waiting for me at the door, grinning and jumping around like an excited puppy. "Mommy!" she cried the moment she saw me.

I'd closed my arms around my daughter, deeply inhaling her little-girl scent of shampoo and childhood sweat. My arms began to tighten. My baby was safe. My baby was home. Then, everything went black.

Mitchell was convicted of kidnapping and child endangerment, and is now serving thirty years without parole in a maximum-security prison. His girlfriend, Melanie, received fifteen years after convincing the judge that the kidnapping was all Mitchell's idea. She'd claimed that he'd threatened her that if she didn't go along, he would kill her.

He writes me and claims that he's a changed man. But I haven't answered, and I don't intend to. As far as I'm concerned, my husband is dead. The love that I once felt for him is gone forever. In my heart, I feel only hatred for Mitchell. And I can't help but want him to suffer, every day, for the rest of his life.

THE END

HUSHED CRIES
Who is taking the babies?

Years have passed, but I still can't get the scent and feel of baby Emily out of my mind. She was beautiful and sweet. When I held her in my arms, I thought everything was wonderful. Then she whimpered—just a little baby cry—and all my dreams ended. . . .

Years have passed, but I still cannot get the scent of baby Emily out of my mind. She was beautiful and sweet. When I held her in my arms, I thought everything was wonderful. Then she whimpered, just a little baby cry, and all my dreams ended. . . .

It has been more than forty years, but it still feels like yesterday. I can still remember a young, handsome Devin.

Devin handed me a small, fragrant bouquet of violets. "These will be orchids by the time I become a doctor," Devin said. Those were the same words he had used every year. The same diffident, appealing voice, but this time I couldn't smile.

Near me, a boy had his arms around his girlfriend. They looked barely twenty. She was laughing up at him. He stole a kiss and she flushed, glancing shyly around. They might have been Devin and me four years ago. Every year Devin gave me violets on my birthday, but every year marriage and children seemed further away.

I felt miserable tears fall on the fragrant flowers. I bent my head to hide the shame I felt. I didn't want my tears to be seen.

When Devin Caldwell and I met, we fell in love. It was as simple as that. I was eighteen; he was twenty. It was one of those clearly defined things that happen sometimes. There was nothing wild and tempestuous about it, just steady and channeled deep, like his goodness. Even then, his eyes were troubled when he asked me to wait for him.

"It'll be years, honey, before we can marry. Years before I graduate, then struggle for a long time! You know what a doctor's life is! You'll lose that little girl roundness in your cheeks, and I'll become a short-tempered lout. And when will we have those kids? You'll have to keep working at the dry cleaner!"

I knew. I did want children. I didn't care about having lots of money, or a grand house; I wanted only Devin Caldwell, and a home for my babies. It was a longing all the deeper because I had been an orphan. I wanted a child of mine to have all the love my mother had never had the chance to give to me because she died in childbirth. Apparently, my father loved her so deeply, he was a lost cause after her death. He couldn't care for himself, not to mention a newborn baby. My father was institutionalized and died shortly afterward. Unfortunately, neither had parents or family who could take care of me.

I laid my mouth against Devin's. "I love you, love you, love you—" I whispered. "Nothing else counts!" At eighteen, it had seemed so easy. I was sure that love was the whole sum and substance of existence!

But at nineteen, twenty, twenty-one, twenty-two—it's different. Devin worked nights to pay for his tuition. When we saw each other one night, or sometimes twice a week, his eyes were often heavy with needed sleep. It's difficult to be romantic and fun when you're working and studying for eighteen hours per day. Yet his temper hadn't become short—mine's had. And the little girl roundness in my cheeks had already given way to a slim oval. We wanted each other more and more, and we couldn't have each other in the way that would make it right for us.

Now, on my birthday, Devin slipped his arm around my shoulders. "Honey, some day I'll give you—"

I jerked my shoulders away from beneath his hand. "Someday," I echoed bitterly. "We've been saying that for four years! Devin, let's get married! It'll be easier. We needn't have a baby for a while, but at least we'd have each other!"

"Honey—" Devin's hand was strong on mine, his voice grave and quiet. "Don't let's argue today, on your birthday! I don't want my wife supporting me, but I'll tell you what I'll do. If I go south, like some of the other guys, I can gain six months on my time. Then we'll be married when I graduate next June. I've already got an internship lined up here with Dr. Smithson. He likes me. Interns don't make money, but, at least, I'll feel as if I'm doing a man's work."

I caught his hand. "It would mean not seeing each other for so many months, Devin," I began. I looked at the thin line of his cheek, the steady brown eyes, the firmness of his dear mouth, and a wave of contrition swept over me. "You're worth a dozen of me, Devin," I whispered. "I'll be patient, I promise."

"It'll only be ten months, Thalia darling!"

"It'll seem like ten years, Devin!"

The night Devin left for Mississippi, I cried myself to sleep. It was dawn before I slept. Perhaps that was why I woke late. The Clean-Rite, the cleaners, was strict about its hours, and punching a time clock makes you nervously aware of the minutes. It was a cleaner that did a lot of industrial jobs. We handled a lot of job for the restaurants and hotels. We did linens for beds and tables.

Breakfastless, I raced to the bus stop. I was quickly walking down the street, when the heel of my right shoe caught on the step. I heard it crack, and I slipped, hurtling to the bottom. The excruciating turn of my ankle and the crack of, my head against the concrete floor were the last things I heard before I lost consciousness.

"She'll be all right now," I heard a cheerful voice say, as I struggled back to awareness. I looked up into the eyes of a white-coated interns. "We're taking you to the hospital for an X-ray of that ankle and maybe of that head, miss! Taking a dive like that into anything but a swimming pool is dangerous!" He grinned. "Hey, Quentin, help me get her into the ambulance!" he called.

A blond giant swaggered over. "Hey, if I can't lift that alone, I got cheese where my muscles live!" He lifted me like a feather and put me carefully into the ambulance. Our faces were close together for an instant. He gave me a once over and softly sang the lyrics from a song about a hot-looking woman.

"Quentin Favre's the name, baby," he whispered as he took me into the hospital. "I'll be driving this bus around wherever you live any time you say!"

For an instant, through the throbbing in my head and the excruciating pain in my ankle, I managed to get my breath. "I'm engaged to be married!" I got out, just before he put me down.

Quentin Favre was waiting to take me home in the ambulance when they were through X-raying and setting my ankle. And he telephoned me every night. And, some nights, he passed by in his ambulance. He'd ring the bell and tell me he was just checking on me.

When my ankle was feeling better and I could return to work, he began asking me to go out with him.

"But I'm engaged to be married to a man I love, Quentin!" I tried to explain. "As soon as he gets back, in June, we'll be married! Go find yourself another girl!"

"That's easy," he retorted. "Girls are waiting wherever I wave! But you, you're something special. He's a fool for leaving you alone. You could bet, I wouldn't. I certainly wouldn't have you waiting at home. You gotta have fun. He's not expecting you to live like a nun in a convent. I'm sure he's having a good time wherever he is. I know how men are; you don't. Because if you did, you'd be down there with him or he'd be here with you."

But I only laughed at him. You don't know Devin!" I defended him warmly. "Devin's different."

I persisted in refusing him until the day Devin's first despondent letter came. Until then he had been steadily cheerful. But now his letter sounded so sad.

It may be another six months, honey. I guess working so hard at night makes me dull. I don't know whether I passed the exams, and my marks are pretty low. Maybe it's because I can't get you out of my mind. Maybe I oughtn't ask you to wait, Thalia! God knows when I'll make a living for you! I love you but if you want to go out with anybody else, go ahead. I'll understand.

I should have known it wasn't Devin speaking, but that it was only his despair and loneliness. I didn't stop to think of how noble he was, lonely, driven, but still thinking of me. I was full of a hopeless bitterness. Maybe he'd never get where he wanted to!

I didn't want to go out with Quentin. I longed for Devin with a fierce need. But the next time Quentin asked me to go out with him, I went. It was harmless enough. We sat at a little table in a club and between dances he told me tales—racy and glamorous. He had been in the military and had lived a bunch of different places. He had been trained to work in the medical corps.

He said, "We worked hard and played harder. It's the only way to survive everything you have to see on a daily basis." He was as different from Devin as a brilliant comet is from the steady stars.

"Don't let it get you down, kid! You gotta laugh! I drive an ambulance and I see plenty. It makes me grateful and want to live life to the fullest. You never know what's going to happen!"

That was his creed. He lived by it. He really lived. I never knew anyone who wanted to cram as much as possible into every single moment.

But things raced ahead too fast in my memory. I remember how once he pulled a ring off the ring finger of his left hand.

"See that?" The ring had covered a small, diamond-like birthmark. "That's the way my family'll know me if I anything ever happens. I left home at seventeen, and I've never been back. There was too much despair, doom, and devastation—too much responsibility for anyone to bear. Those people wouldn't know fun if an amusement park ran over them. That's why I'll never marry any girl, even you, gorgeous!"

"Nobody asked you to!" I scoffed at him. He put a finger under my chin and tilted it. And, still laughing, brushed his mouth across mine. Then he stopped laughing. His mouth came down again, slowly. I felt it pulse against mine with a hot, desiring pressure. I pushed him back, angrily.

"I guess I deserve that for going out with you, Quentin. I won't go again if you do that. I'm engaged to Devin. I'm marrying him. I don't want any romances on the side. Let's laugh—that's what you want, isn't it?"

He was staring at me, intently. "Sure, I thought so. Sure, that's what I want!" But he didn't laugh. "Maybe I'm falling for you, kid, at that. The laugh would be on me, wouldn't it? Quentin Favre, the guy that always gets away before the noose tightens! Maybe I want that noose!"

I smiled at him. "No, you don't, Quentin. Neither do I. If it's a noose, it's not the real thing. We're not fooling each other, Quentin. We're going out with each other because I'm lonely for the man I love, and you're after excitement and fun. Let it stay that way."

"Okay by me, baby!"

But he didn't come for ten days after that. I missed him because the days were dull with nothing to look forward to. Then I got Devin's next letter. There was little hope of his graduating in June. He couldn't make it. He couldn't afford the fare to come back and see me, either, for the summer.

I was staring with blind, angry eyes at the letter when I heard the familiar clanging of the ambulance. Quentin! I ran down, the letter still in my hand. Quentin looked curiously from it to my tearstained face.

"Get in," he said abruptly. I'd never ridden in the ambulance with him, and I hesitated. "The doctor is around the corner attending to a woman that's having a kid. It'll be an hour or so at least. Come on. We'll take a ride. It's against the rules, but rules are for breakin'!"

He wasn't cocky or laughing now. And my heart was aching so, it hurt me like a wound. He stopped just outside the park where the cemetery lay still and quiet beyond.

"What you crying about?" he demanded.

I began to weep in earnest, then. He slipped his arm around me, and held my cheek against his shoulder.

"That guy of yours gives me a pain, Thalia. What's he waiting for, somebody to pick you up? What the devil a guy wants to be a doctor for is beyond me, anyway. You gotta work all hours of the night; only the big ones makin' any dough—" He stopped, then laughed, shakily, "Say, what am I talking about? An ambulance driver ain't any better, but then I ain't marryin'!"

I was huddled against him, and he lifted my face. And then, suddenly, the words poured out. "Listen, Thalia, I want to get married. I want you to marry me, Thalia! I never met a girl that I cared anything about but you. You're under my skin! You'll be rustin' out your years, waitin' for that guy to put out his shingle! Marry me now. I'm nuts about you. I guess I was the first time I saw you in the ambulance."

My face was lifted to his, my eyes seeing only the dark blur of him above me. His mouth came down on mine in a hungry, passionate kiss. I should have denied him my lips. I wanted to, but I was bruised and defeated, wanting Devin and furious at life for keeping us apart. I felt guilty, too, that I had sent him away from me, to make our marriage come sooner. All of it went into the need of being comforted. Quentin didn't wait for me to answer. His arms were hard around me. Beneath the dark shadow of the trees, with the quiet dead sleeping beyond, we forgot time and honor and restraint.

Quentin wasn't comforting me. He was covering my face with bruising, harsh caresses; his arms were like steel, his lips hungry . . . and then, even though I struggled at first, such waves of hungry desire washed over me that I was drowned in an emotion too overwhelming to escape from—that shook me to the very depths of my soul.

"I'm a louse, Thalia," Quentin cried later. "I deserve to be shot! But

I mean it. I want you to marry me! I'll make up to you for—for this—and—"

But I was staring stonily ahead. I couldn't speak. My heart and body felt dead, as if I'd lost something that made me move and feel. Devin. Devin!

"Kid." Quentin touched me and I shrank away. He saw it. "Well, I guess I got it coming to me, Thalia. Let's get back." He peered at his watch. "Good grief! The doctor will be mad—" He swung the ambulance around, the motor roaring. "Hold tight, kid. We gotta make time! Lucky I'm driving an ambulance and don't have to wait for lights!"

He put it into high, and we swung madly around a curve. Excitement was keying him up again. "Close, that! Hold on! I'm going to cut across that street. Bet I make it before the lights change anyway." He was laughing now at the thought of danger. He flashed a pleading look at me. "Don't be mad at me, Thalia! I—"

Still laughing down at me for that brief instant, he heard the shout of the policeman, the gnashing of gears. Just before the huge vehicle loomed up before us, Quentin's hands left the wheel. He lifted me, flinging me out to the roadway. Mercifully, I didn't see what happened after that.

But I saw the papers, the next day. Pictures of Quentin crushed behind the wheel, his body in the fantastic, horrible posture of sudden death. Me, lying where he had thrown me out of danger. My eyes were closed, but the likeness unbelievably clear. There was a great cry for an investigation as a result of the accident. The newspapers shrieked about ambulance drivers joy-riding while on cases. Reporters, health officers, investigators, all came to ask me questions at the dry cleaner. It cost me my job.

But all I could think about was that I had cost Quentin his life. If it hadn't been for me, Quentin would have been alive, laughing. If I hadn't given myself to him, he wouldn't have been late, or driven so recklessly. He had loved me—and it had brought him death.

I couldn't stand the whispers in the boarding house. I took a room in another part of town, slipping out at night for food I didn't touch. I couldn't eat.

And I was always tortured by my regrets and my thoughts of Devin. Had he seen the pictures? Why didn't he write? Time and again I began a letter to him, trying to explain, to tell him the truth. But the futility of it stopped me. I wanted to say, "I love you, Devin! I've never loved anyone else! That Quentin was a moment's madness!" What man, loving a girl as Devin loved me, could be expected to understand or believe that? Yet I had to tell him. I could never marry him with a lie, and Quentin's memory silently between us.

I wrote it, finally. It was a page and a half of a confession that might have been written in blood. I didn't try to spare myself. I didn't ask him to forgive me; I only begged him to try and understand and give me another chance.

I'll give him one week, I told myself—one week to answer. If he doesn't, I'll know he's through with me. And I won't blame him. I'll deserve to lose him.

I knew I had lost Devin, when weeks passed and only silence answered. And added to that was another certainty. When I found out that I was carrying Quentin's child, I knew that I was to bear my punishment to the last bitter end

I was having the baby I had always yearned for—but it wasn't Devin's. The baby I had vowed would never know the cold austerity of an orphanage. That baby that should have a father's and mother's love that would wrap it securely against coldness, would be born fatherless, in poverty because of its mother's weakness.

Tearlessly, I sat remembering my own bleak childhood, my small face pressed enviously against the tall gates of the orphanage, seeing babies wheeled by in carriages by loving mothers or careful nurses or happy sisters. Seeing small girls kissed and fondled and soothed by loving hands and lips.

I had missed all that. My baby would miss it all—and more. I remembered the children who had never known whose name they bore. Even orphanage children can be cruel and remorseless to those more unfortunate than they were.

That night I walked the long street to Oceanview Drive. I stopped at the piers where the houseboats and yachts were tied. On one houseboat, a party was in progress. I could hear the band blaring as I saw the girls in light dresses dancing on the smooth deck. I heard their laughter and the deeper laughter of men. A couple came along, and the man unlocked, the gate of the pier. I slipped in after them. I followed them as they walked, the girl clinging to the man's arm. When they stopped to kiss each other, I couldn't bear it.

In a sudden frenzy, I shoved past the girl, and raced down the dock to the end. I heard the man shout and the girl's cry, and hand shot out and caught my arm. It was a watchman.

"Say, sister, what's the idea? You can't spoil that houseboat party by committing suicide here!" The tone was half jocular. I jerked madly at the big hand, but it was like steel. I bent and bit into his thumb, and with a savage roar, he slapped my face so that I reeled as he swore at me, and then blew whistle.

Men and girls were running toward us from the houseboat, the policeman came up. I stood there, debased, the object of curiosity and comment, while the watchman shoved me.

"Better put her in the cell, officer! Trying to commit suicide and murder! Bit my thumb clear down to the bone, the she devil!"

I went numbly past those curious eyes, feeling as if I had died already. Nothing could hurt me anymore. Automatically, I went to the sergeant's desk. I answered his questions.

Suddenly he bent forward. "Say, you're the kid that was in that ambulance with Quentin Favre, aren't you? You're a glutton for trouble! Cool your heels overnight. I think you need to think about what you're doing."

I followed the matron. Only when the key grated outside the door of the detention room did I look around. A girl, not much older than I, was leaning back on a cot, her half-closed eyes measuring me.

"What did they pull you in for, kid? You ain't in my business or I don't know my job." I looked at her dully.

"Job?"

She came over to me. "Soliciting." Her voice went hard "Either that or the river. And you got to have guts for that."

I stared up at her. Hysteria rose in my throat, a gurgle of laughter stopped at my lips. "I had guts for it, but there was a boathouse party—I couldn't spoil it! They stopped me and—"

My face went into my hands. And for the first time since Quentin's death, I began to cry, long, torturous sobs. The matron came to the door.

"Stop that noise, will you? People are trying to sleep!"

But I couldn't stop, though I crammed my hands against my mouth. The girl came over to me. She didn't touch me, but the voice was kind.

"Trouble, kid?"

I nodded.

"I guess you ain't married, then. You got any money to see a doctor?"

"Not enough for something like that." I managed to get out the words.

"Listen, kid, I'm giving you a tip. Take it for what it's worth. I know a house in Suisse County. The woman who runs it is a hellion, but it's no worse nor better than any other like it. They keep you there till it's time for you to have the kid. You've got to work for your board, and they make you get medical attention. Then they either give up the kid for adoption or you can keep it."

Even through my weariness, something about it confused me. "Why should they run houses like that? What do they get out of it?"

She smiled cynically. "Money, kid. The girls who don't want their babies leave them there, and there are always people who do want babies for adoption. Betty Swanson makes out all right, don't you worry!" She patted my shoulders. "Anyway, it's better than the river, kid!"

Looking back, with Betty Swanson's face clearly before me, even after all this time, I wonder. Betty Swanson was about forty-five. She looked like a schoolmistress, with graying, thin hair pulled back from a shiny, taut forehead. And her eyes were the bleakest, coldest eyes I have ever seen. Like soiled, crusted ice. Her mouth was small and tight. I never saw it smile in all the months I was there. Nothing that girl in the cell had told me could have prepared me for the reality that was Betty Swanson.

"Name?"

"Thalia Pryor," I said dully.

"Your own?" Her tone was skeptical.

"Yes—I'm not married." I felt my face burn. She drew her lips together.

"So I gathered. But most girls come here under assumed ones. Not that it makes any difference. Got any money?" I shook my head. "Then you'll have to sleep in the dorm. We have private rooms for those who can pay. What work can you do?"

"I used to work at a dry cleaner," I answered.

"Then we'll put you in the laundry. Dr. Wallington will give you an examination. We make them periodically. You don't want the baby, of course?"

She spoke like that hard, fast, with no intonation at all, not looking at me. I might have been a log of wood. Before I could answer, she shoved a printed sheet and a pen into my hand.

"Sign this. It gives us the right to put up the baby for adoption."

For some obscure reason, I hesitated to write my name. She looked up, frowning above those cold, opaque eyes.

"Do I have to say so, now?" My voice shook with nervous exhaustion.

"Make up your mind, girl!" Her mouth twitched impatiently. "You want us to keep your secret. You don't want to go out of here with a baby and let the world know, do you? Girls like you should be grateful for the chance to hide your mistakes!"

"I'll wait till my baby comes." I drew a long, difficult breath. "Maybe I'll want it afterward!"

I didn't really want the baby; only I didn't like being intimidated. Her mouth became pinched, and for an instant the impact of her will hit me like a blow. I grew frightened, then. Suppose she told me to get out? Involuntarily my fingers tightened on the pen.

But she snatched the paper from beneath my hand. "Very sentimental!" she sneered. "However, we don't coerce!" She pulled another sheet out of a cubbyhole. "Sign this."

I read it. It was a few lines, typewritten, specifying that the signer was to work for board and get medical attention until the birth of her child. Five days after, she was to be discharged. The amount of the fee was three hundred and fifty dollars, this amount to be worked out on the basis of so much per week.

"If you're too sick to work for any length of time, you will be expected to stay on and work afterward to make up the loss," she warned.

She touched a bell, as I put my name at the bottom of the page. A door opened, and a tall, heavyset man with a pale face and a full, sulky mouth came into the room on rubber-soled shoes. He wore a white hospital coat and behind him I caught a glimpse of hospital paraphernalia.

"Please witness this, Dr. Wallington." Subtly, her tone had changed. There was something placating, almost appealing in it. A spot of red appeared on each of her cheekbones as he bent down and wrote his name, his arm touching hers. I glanced at his hands, and a queer repugnance swept over me. They were white—dead white, and as soft looking as a woman's. Hers looked dried and hard by comparison.

"Go in with Dr. Wallington for an examination," she ordered. I went through the connecting door into his office, and he followed me.

There was nothing I could have taken exception to in his brief perfunctory examination. Yet I shook with loathing when he was through.

"You'll be fine," he stood up, towering over me. His smile gave his face a strange, womanish roundness, oddly at variance with his great height and breadth. "Don't hesitate to come to me if there's anything I can do." He put those pallid hands on my shoulders, and I felt my skin crawl with a violent repulsion. "And don't mind Mrs. Swanson's manner. Her temper sometimes gets the best of her."

I hadn't heard the connecting door between their offices open. Suddenly, it was ajar, and Betty Swanson came in. She must have heard, because her look flickered from him to me. He dropped his hands, and I went to the door leading into the corridor. As I passed her, she moved aside, deliberately, as if, my touch would soil her. Weakly, I leaned against the other side of the closed door. Her voice came through, harsh, yet curiously pleading.

"I heard you, Leonard! I—"

His words cut across hers. "One of these days, Betty, you won't hear me! Nor see me either! You mind your end of this business and I'll mind mine!"

That was my entry into the Swanson Home. Home! It was like a prison. We muttered about escape, but there was none.

"The other places are no different, except maybe worse!" was the cynical comment of the girl who was angrily shooting off her mouth. It was in her high cheek-boned face with the hollows beneath the eyes, in her wide mouth with its cynical twist. "I've been through it before," she told me, in her flat, dragging voice. "The other time I waited on table. Them trays did for me."

"Didn't you want the baby?" I asked.

"I did but he didn't." She stared down at her hands with the broken nails. "It's just as well it died. And this one—" She coughed suddenly and pressed the back of her hand to her mouth. "I'm sick but nobody will tell me that. I know it, though. I've got the signs." Suddenly she shut her eyes. It ain't as bad as Betty Swanson. It ain't wars that show we're still savages. Talk of man's inhumanity to man! What about woman's to woman?"

We did all the work, the laundry, the cleaning, scrubbing, waiting on table, washing dishes, in that big house. At a time when every bit of comfort is craved, when we ached for a little kindness, we were harried like beasts of burden to pay for the wretched food, the hard beds, the indescribable bareness and poverty of the dormitory where twenty of us slept. For the privilege of hiding our mistakes from a condemning world, we became veritable slaves.

Daily, despite nausea, wrenching backaches, and a deadly weariness from too little rest, I had to go down to the laundry with its steam, its clamorous, insane churning of mangles. The specter of having to remain to work out our time after our babies were born, kept many a girl at work when exhaustion claimed her. And too often, nature, goaded mercilessly, hurried those babies into the world prematurely.

Though I brought myself to a dulled acceptance after a while—seeing girls, sixteen, seventeen, eighteen, with frightened children's faces over bodies too rapidly maturing into coming motherhood, seeing a girl stagger beneath a tray too heavy was so difficult. I never became hardened to the sudden, sharp outcry that meant only one thing. I smoldered with a wild, loathing and impotent rage at the way a girl doubled to her knees or collapsed beneath an onslaught of unbearable pain, and her callous, swift removal by the two nurses. I remember huddling beneath inadequate covers, stuffing my fingers into my ears to shut out the muffled cries that often pierced the night for hours.

And hovering like a vulture over us was Betty Swanson's hatred. It was incredible, that stark hatred for those unfortunate girls who found miserable haven in the big, rambling four story house that must once have been a home, with compassion and love ruling it.

"Sure she hates us. Why not?" Colleen muttered, staring after her with hostile, bitter eyes. "Old and dried up—never had a man make love to her! I'd still rather be me than her!"

It was true. Life had deprived her of things we had known, through love or despair or weakness. And she was in a position where she could make us pay for that deprivation of hers. Jealousy of us was the whip that drove her—and she used it mercilessly.

I don't know when it became clear to me that she hated me most. She never let a chance go by to goad me, reminding me why I was there, but I learned to face those opaque eyes without visible quivering. The click of her heels was like a drum major's. She loomed through the steam like a figure of doom.

"Wasting time again, eh? Here, turn it this way!" She said as she moved the machine. It caught my fingers. Involuntarily I screamed, and then shut my lips tightly as Colleen darted her eyes in my direction.

"The—" Colleen said viciously, "you'd better go and see Wallington about that finger, or you'll be laid up and have to make time afterward. She'd like nothing better."

I went slowly upstairs. His look at my hand was comprehensive, but he asked no questions, bandaging it with professional efficiency and speed. But when he was through, he kept my hand between his. Those apparently soft fingers were deceptively strong. He bent near, and I caught the smell of whiskey on his breath.

"When you're out of here, come and see me, Thalia. I'll have a job for you. You can always reach me at the Bluehill in Wiltshire." He smoothed my hands. "A girl like you needn't pay too much for one mistake."

I withdrew my hand and mumbled my thanks. I had barely closed the door behind me, when Betty Swanson came down the corridor.

"You couldn't wait for an excuse to see him, could you?" she said in a fierce whisper. "If you didn't owe me so much already, I'd kick you out. You're a—" A string of vile, unprintable names slid off her lips. I put my hands to my ears and ran down the corridor as if a devil were after me. When I turned to look back, she had opened the door of his office, and he was standing, staring at her. Before the door closed behind her, I heard her say, "Drinking again! You can't leave it or women alone, you—!"

I would have left, then, but I didn't know where to turn. And you don't get up enough guts for the river more than once. It was Dr. Wallington who left, and I knew why. Knew, too, why those pale eyes of Betty Swanson's followed me always with a watchful stare. In Dr. Wallington's place came Dr. Gaslaphz, a small man with a hard, thin mouth, and a professional manner that covered a violent temper. Yet I felt I would rather have had his nervous, thin hands take care of me than Dr. Wallington's.

In that place, where all kindness seemed to have deserted us, Dr. Wallington was forgotten. If I remembered the promise he held out to me, it seemed too far away. What awaited me was a dreary, dark future.

But Betty Swanson remembered him. The endless months stretched away like a path to Calvary. Sometimes I thought of Quentin and his laughter. There wasn't any laughter in the world anymore, it seemed. Sometimes I thought of Devin, with a terrible crying need for the comfort of his hand, his nearness as my time drew close. I had said good-bye to him in my mind, but my heart clung to the thought of him with a tenacity all the more fierce when I tried to put him out of it. How I must have broken those high ideals of his, that he couldn't bring himself to write and forgive me!

By the time Heather Spellman came to the Swanson House, I was as dulled as an animal is to suffering. But from the moment I saw her waxen face, her dark blue eyes nearly black with fear, I knew a surge of pity and affection. She was so slim and little, with her dark, cloudy hair damp with rain, clinging to her cheeks, her beautiful hands clutching the cellophane raincoat about her. The outlines of her figure were already blurred and coarsened.

"It's so different from this—" she whispered, showing me the advertisement that had brought her. My lips curled as I read it.

"Comfortable, homey surroundings for convalescent girls of the better class. Reasonable payments. No cash needed. Personal care and complete medical attention. Betty Swanson, Box 218."

"It is different," I told her gently, "but don't let her frighten you. There's nothing she can do, really, except hate us."

But I was wrong. When Betty Swanson realized I was championing Heather, she showed no mercy. It was against the rules for us to assist each other. If a girl got too sick to work, she could stay in bed but the Swanson House demanded its pound of flesh later.

If there had been more menial jobs than we had to do there, Betty Swanson would have found them for Heather. And as I daily watched the girl's increasing pallor, her fragility evident, I felt the lashing of Betty's whip. She was always there when I tried to help Heather, mocking, hindering me.

"A female Sir Galahad, eh, but not so pure? Let her do her own work! If she can't, she can always make up time!"

But Heather, looking after her, shuddered. "No, no. I've got to get through quickly. And out—with my baby."

"Are you taking your baby when you go?" The irony of that question came back to haunt me, but I didn't realize it then.

Heather turned to me. Those big eyes were soft, luminous.

"Of course. That's why I'd endure anything." She hesitated. "I've never told you, but I want my baby. I'd never gives it away. I have to have something I can care for. Something I can love. Neither of my parents cared about each other."

Now that she had begun to talk, the dam was broken. Words spilled over her pale lips. "My mother and father had too much to do, hating each other, divorcing each other, to care about me. Six months of the year I'd spend hearing my mother telling how rotten men were. The other six months my father would poison my mind against women. Each one pouring their hate into me."

She shivered. "I guess that's why, when Raymond asked me to elope with him, I said yes. But his father found out, so he had it annulled. He didn't like the fact that my parents were divorced. Raymond is twenty; I'm seventeen. His sister Cara and I were schoolmates. When I found I was having a baby, after the annulment, I had nowhere to go. Cara was overseas. I was ashamed to tell my father, and my mother is traveling with her new husband. I had a little money. I stayed at a farm until—until they saw and thought I was bad—"

I put my hand on hers, strongly, "When we get out of here I'll help you. We'll help each other," I comforted her, though the bleakness of that "afterwards" held so little hope.

It comforts me to remember how she turned her hand, palm up, into mine, trustingly.

That night Colleen went upstairs. I heard her moaning to herself, sometime during the night. Heather heard her, too.

"So long, kids!" Colleen tried to grin as she reached the dormitory door, her hand clenched on my arm so that the nails bit deep. "Tomorrow I'll be out of this damned place and some romantic fools will have my baby—" She bent. I could feel the dampness start in her palms. "She'll tell them I was a good girl—good family—give my kid a pedigree so they'll pay big bucks—" She grimaced and stopped for an instant. "But I'll go out without carfare. I don't care. Let somebody pay for what I—went through. Society owes me something. My kid'll pay back for me—" She stiffened. I pulled the bell again frantically, for the nurses. "Sure is a great big laugh—" she whispered. "They won't know the father was—was a—" She went heavy against me with a groan of unbearable pain, as the two nurses came down the hall, grumbling at being waked before morning.

I didn't see Colleen again. Not till many months had rolled by. We never saw a girl after she went upstairs. Soon again, a car would drive up at night, and a couple would leave with a bundle, and the girl who should have known radiant motherhood would be weeping with bereavement or smiling with relief. We never knew.

Our ranks never emptied. Another girl would come to take her place. Another recruit, with bitterness and fear lining her face. It was just another girl whose baby might be prematurely born, unless she had money to pay for surreptitious motherhood.

Soon—I totalled the days—another fortnight and my turn would come. I would be out, free of Betty Swanson, free of that burden Quentin's passion and my own weakness had laid on me. For I had determined I would leave alone when I went. I wanted no tie with the past, as Heather did. I meant to keep my promise and help her when she came out, but privately I thought she was a fool for wanting so passionately to keep her baby. I never said it, though.

Her pallor frightened me, but her indomitable courage seemed to overcome any momentary weakness. Yet she seemed so soft, so made for loving and being loved, for protected motherhood, I remember thinking, watching her toil up to the dormitory after a grueling day. I stood below, breathing with difficulty. It was becoming increasingly hard to climb the stairs.

Heather turned to speak to me, one thin hand pressed to her side. I never knew what she meant to say. The ghastly whiteness of her face as she clutched blindly at the staircase. Her voice mingled with the screams of girls as she toppled over and came down the whole flight, thudding—thudding

I think I shall hear the sound until I die. In a mist, I saw the nurses race down the stairs, heard Betty Swanson's crisp, unmoved voice giving orders.

I went temporarily mad. I caught hold of her and twisted her around. She pulled back, but my hands were like steel, hardened with my hatred of her.

"If she dies, I'll tell the world when I get out what happened! How you worked her like an animal—the way you work us all. Somebody will listen—"

Her palm lashed across my mouth, silencing me. The girls stood like automatons.

"The world doesn't take the word of girls like you or her," Betty Swanson said, breathing hard. "There's no health officer ever been here who could find anything to tie a handle to or complain about. You make your bargain when you come here, and work never harmed anybody but lazy devils like you! Now get upstairs, all of you, and stop gawping! I'm expecting visitors!" She went down to the kitchen.

I know now why men and women commit murder. I could have murdered Betty Swanson then. I made my way upstairs, while the girls muttered. "Visitors! Guess it's Colleen's baby she's selling now! You're next, Thalia. If it wasn't for my mother knowing, I'd cheat her out of mine!"

I scarcely heard them. My lips were swelling from the blow. At the tops of the stairs, I paused. The girls went before me into the dormitory. Up beyond—on the top floor, the hospital floor, was Heather, going through her hell of pain and horror a month too soon. And she had no comforting hand near her. Only two indifferent nurses and a hard-mouthed doctor.

I crept up the next two flights, like a thief. There was utter silence—a silence that clutched at me with awful foreboding. Why wasn't Heather crying or screaming?

I was at the top of the flight when I heard it—the weak, protesting cry of the newborn, coming into a world I hated just then with a consuming, bitter hatred. And as I stood, staring, waiting, Dr. Gaslaphz came out.

"Heather," I whispered, through dry lips, "how is she?"

"You've no right up here," he said as he came toward me, drawing off one rubber glove. "It's against rules."

"Rules! Rules!" I tugged at his arm. "I want to know!"

He shook my arm off, his eyes evading mine. He began to walk down the stairs. "I'd advise you to go downstairs now, before you cause any trouble," he said, without turning his heat again. His footsteps went on like measured steps of doom.

I knew. Heather was dead. All her hopes gone now. Seventeen, and paying a penalty for a broken home, for a boy's desertion. But more—for Betty Swanson's cruelty.

I remember saying to myself, clearly, like a promise I must keep. "Someday I'll make her pay for it. Somehow. Somewhere." Below, I heard her voice at the door of the big pink-and-white nursery where babies were shown off to prospective parents.

"You're very fortunate to get this precious little girl child. The mother has an exceptionally fine background in spite of her—mistake. Just fourteen days old. I'll leave you in here until you decide. I'll be in my office down the hall when you want me."

Colleen's baby! Her way of getting even with the world that had turned its back on her!

I went downstairs, slowly. This was one sale Betty Swanson wouldn't make. I'd tell them of Colleen, her sickness, her family—

I got down and pushed open the nursery door. Neither of the two young people standing over a crib, heard me. The man's back was to me, but I saw the face of the girl yearning over the baby.

"Such a lovely baby," she touched it gently. Her plain little face was illumined with happiness. "But, Mike, we know nothing of its father and that's an awful lot of money to pay!"

I clung to the door. One thousand dollars! And Colleen had thought it was five hundred dollars. What a price to put on their little souls!

"I know!" The man was speaking impatiently. "But that's cheap. The Darlings paid the other place more for their boy. Sure they got the father's pedigree, but look how long they had to wait! Anyway, who knows how a kid turns out, even your own! And what's the sense of waiting a year or two for a baby just to make sure its father came from a good family. Let's not quibble anymore, honey. Look at her eyes, blue, like yours! I'll bet she even grows up to look like you!"

The girl's eyes filled with happy tears as she bent over. "Oh, Mike, if we could have had our own! I'm sorry for the girl who had to give her up but I'm glad, too!"

I couldn't let Betty Swanson fool them! Maybe it was true—you didn't know how your own turned out—but you started with a decent chance! Maybe a girl, born of good parents would do what I had done but usually what you were, was in your blood. I wasn't condemning Colleen. It wasn't her fault if her father was no good and her mother left them periodically, coming back whipped looking. Only this girl with the fine eyes wasn't going to have to combat that in the baby she was holding—and paying for!

The thought of the sums that were pouring into Betty Swanson's pockets through the suffering of the girls, who came to her to hide from the eyes of the world, filled me with a new, hard determination.

She wouldn't get my baby, either. She wouldn't sell my baby to pad her pockets any further. And Heather's—

What was the name of that boy she had loved? Raymond—Raymond Lassiter. I'd write and tell him, smuggle the letter out some way. He'd have some feeling of responsibility toward Heather's baby, even if his parents hadn't.

I was filled with the violence of determination. At that moment, as if she must have seen through the door with those pale eyes, Betty Swanson opened her office door.

"Thalia!" Betty's voice rang out like a pistol crack of authority. The man and his wife came to the door of the nursery. I opened my mouth to speak, but I couldn't. For the eyes of the man swept me up and down, with a scornful look, and he caught his wife's arm. They went past me down the hall into Betty's office, and Betty came down the hall to where I stood.

"What are you doing here?" she demanded in a harsh undertone. Behind us, in the nursery, Colleen's baby set up a whimpering. It made me quiver. I thought of Heather, lying upstairs, and the thin wail I had heard.

"I know what happened to Heather," I said heavily. Her breath came sharp and hard. "I suppose you'll try and sell her baby—" I couldn't go on. I could feel tears for Heather rising in my throat.

She turned to go to her office. "Don't go dramatic," she said icily, "and get down where you belong. Heather's baby died."

We have all read stories in which the young mother wakes to tender words, weakly smiling as she listens for the cry of her new born. But I woke to a stern, harsh reality that even now has the power to fill me with impotent terror, as it did then.

Betty Swanson's was the first face I saw, wavering in the mist above me.

"It's a girl," she answered my faint question.

"Let me see her!" I forgot all about the hours of pain. Suddenly, it seemed worthwhile to have struggled through that awful eternity, to hold her in my arms. I forgot that there had ever been a time when I hadn't wanted that baby.

Betty Swanson came near to smiling as she answered, slowly "You can't see her. That's the rule here, and you know it. Any child that's signed away for adoption when a girl enters, is our the minute it's born."

"Signed away?" My scalp prickled. My voice was weak, but I seemed to get superhuman strength to cry out, "I never signer her away! I said I might want her—"

"Be still," she said inflexibly, "screaming won't do you any good. Look."

I knew by the facility with which she produced that sheet of paper I had signed, that she had been prepared for this. I stared below the typewritten lines in which I had contracted to work for the months until my baby came. That other paragraph had not been there before. It had been inserted—afterwards. I read it while my breath suffocated between my dry lips.

"And I, Thalia Pryor, do hereby relinquish all claim to the child I am to bear, giving Betty Swanson the sole right to give it out for adoption to worthy parents."

"I never signed that." My voice was almost inaudible.

She folded it contemptuously. "And it was witnessed by Dr. Wallington, as you may recall. It won't do you any good to cry."

I didn't cry anymore. All of me tightened to a ball of hard implacable will. "I'll pay you back some day," I remember thinking. "For everything."

But hatred can't fill you to the exclusion of hope. I knew that in five days I would be sent away at night, as the others had. I began to plan, cunningly; I pretended I was resigned. On the fourth night I got up, after midnight. I pulled on my clothes, tied my shoes to my belt. Barefooted, dizzy with weakness, but somehow blessed with unbelievable good fortune, I got to the stairs There seemed a million of them, but I reached the bottom, finally and crept to the nursery. Had they given her away yet? I pushed open the door. A dim light burned in a corner, and I went in.

She was there. I bent over the crib. She was sleeping, unbelievably lovely, with none of the redness of a new baby. Two small fists were bunched inside the long sleeves of the nightgown. I was trembling with exhaustion. Gently, so as not to awaken her, I pulled her up.

I had forgotten Quentin—forgotten it was his baby, too. But as I looked at my little daughter's face—incredible as it may sound to you—I could see Quentin's face. She had the same bone structure. Oh, an unmistakable resemblance! And as I touched the soft, satiny skin, the baby's eyes opened. I had a glimpse of her eyes, Quentin's eyes, too! They were so big that they dwarfed the tiny, rosy face, and then the pink mouth opened and she wailed. I caught her against me, holding her face pressed to my cheek, but the wailing continued, like doom drumming in my ears. I was at the door when a sleepy nurse opened it and snatched the baby from my arms.

I heard Betty Swanson's order. "Put her out!" and someone's arms gripped mine.

I clawed and bit like an animal deprived of its young, but they were too strong for me. The baby's wailing was shut off as they closed the doors of the Swanson House behind me, and I heard the key grate in the lock.

I lost track of time, then. I remember the stark outline of trees above my head on the desolate road I traveled. Cars swept by as I plodded on, not even moving out of their way, hoping against hope that one of them would run me down

It must have been nearly dawn when a big vegetable truck came toward me slowly, and the driver leaned out.

"Want a lift, kid?" He was heavyset and red-faced, and though I couldn't see him clearly through the haze before my eyes, the kindness in his voice reassured me.

"If—you don't mind—" I gasped, stumbling toward him, but the truck blurred.

He slid down and came toward me as I fell, and, lifting me, I heard him say, "Pete's sake, you're skin an' bones! What the—" before I lost consciousness.

That dim unreality was still wrapped around me when I woke again, and I couldn't lift my eyelids.

"What's the matter with her, Dr. Miseleman?" It was a womanly voice, fretful but concerned. Then the doctor's answer, in a vigorous, hearty voice invested now with honest indignation.

"Matter? That girl recently had a baby. She may have a fever! I'll bet it's that damned Swanson House again. Same place that girl came from last year, that suicide in the Big Pond. She's lucky you picked her up, Warren. The other girl wasn't so lucky—" His voice fell significantly.

The woman's voice came again, shocked and angry. "It ought to be closed. What's the matter with the county that it can't do anything about it? You're on the board, Dr. Miseleman, why don't you start an investigation again?"

"What good would it do—any more than the last one?" The doctor spoke testily. "You can't get these unfortunate girls to testify. They're ashamed—afraid they'll be ostracized if it's known they had illegitimate children. They won't be able to get jobs, afterward, except one kind. Nope! Without their testimony, it'll go the way the other investigation went—nowhere!"

My eyes seemed weighted with lead. I couldn't open them, but I heard the man say heavily, "Am I glad my girl's already married, Doc! A kid like that!"

But it was the woman's sharp answer that hit me like an unintentional slap. "Our Emily had a good upbringing, Warren."

The doctor's tolerant reply was reassuring. "It isn't always upbringing. I'll be here tomorrow, and move her to the hospital." I lost the rest of their conversation as the door closed behind them.

I was too exhausted to resent anything they had said or to be grateful to Dr. Miseleman for having defended me. My head felt light as a balloon. Sleep came as a boon to me, comforting me with the thought that I was somewhere away from the Swanson House and its horrors. Tomorrow I'd tell them about the baby. Tomorrow—

But it was many tomorrows—three weeks of them, to be exact, before I could tell them anything coherently. The bare white outline of the hospital room was what I saw when I came out of the fever.

"Well, she finally knows she's alive, Doctor." A woman's voice spoke with satisfaction. I focused my eyes on her plain, square face with its small, faded blue eyes and kindly smile.

Turning my head with difficulty, I met the doctor's quizzical eyes behind the glasses. The long, humorous face with its strong chin looked back at me reassuringly.

I tried, weakly, to speak, but I began to cry instead. "I'll get her some good broth." The nurse hurried out of the room, leaving Dr. Miseleman with me.

He sat down and took my hand. "My poor child, you've been through hell. But now you're with friends. Get strong and rested."

"Doctor," I whispered, "how long—have I been—like this?"

"Only three weeks," he patted my hand, "and your sickness certainly did its good turn for this community anyway. Mrs. Nelson was so worked up over what had happened to you that she's got the town rocking with it. They must have smelled a rat, because—"

I stared at him through eyes widening with fear.

"Don't look so scared, my dear. They can't harm you anymore. They've disappeared. The house was emptied, lock, stock, and barrel, two days ago."

My fingers dug frantically into his hands.

"Doctor—" The words scarcely sounded past my dry lips. "Doctor, I'll never find my baby now!"

Days later, when I was stronger, Dr. Miseleman came to me with his plan.

"We've got to get girls to testify, Thalia,"—Dr. Miseleman was pounding out his point with his square, efficient hands—"so no other girls will go through."

"I'll testify," I told him dully. "I'll do anything to get my baby back." My lips twisted with the sullen hatred of Betty Swanson. "And to get even with Betty Swanson!"

He looked at me pityingly. "Your testimony isn't enough. We must have the testimony of other girls. Didn't you keep any address of your friend, Colleen?"

I shook my head. "She said she'd go to Darawheel some day. She was sick." I looked up at him through lackluster eyes. "Dr. Miseleman, even if I had Colleen's address, she wouldn't talk up in court. Her guy didn't want marriage, for other reasons. Reasons that would come out, if she told about him. Maybe he'd leave her if she turned that spotlight on him. She cared about him, I know. And the other girls—some of them have families they've got to live with afterward. And others—well, they know if they talk there's only one thing left to them. You know what that is."

He nodded brusquely and leaned forward, one hand on my knee. "You can save a lot of them from that kind of job, Thalia," he said meaningly. "Are you willing to help?"

I nodded, and he smiled approvingly.

"This Leonard Wallington who offered you a job," he began, his eyes oh me, while his words sank in, "you say he told you to get him in Wiltshire? He may have a connection in a hospital there, too. He's probably a small fry in the obstetrics field, or I'd have heard of him. He's probably little better than a quack. You can't pin them to any of those homes on any counts at all. But they do often get on the staffs of decent hospitals. Their records are kept hidden—and when you find them, they're more twisted than corkscrews. A rotten business! Some of it smells to high heaven!"

His face showed his disgust. There seemed no end to the way the tentacles of this vile racket of shanghaiing babies spread —blackmail, thievery, even white slavery.

"We've got to get at records." He said each word slowly. "Once we get those, we may be able to force those girls to speak up. And you can get those records if you take the job he promised you."

"No! He'd remember how Mrs. Nelson started the investigation because of me, and you know the kind of job he would offer me. He's horrible! His hands—" I shuddered. "I'm afraid, Dr. Miseleman. I couldn't!"

"But think of all the girls who won't let us help them because they're blinded by fear! Help me and them and yourself, Thalia, won't you? You're courageous. You can hold him off. He's too much of a coward, if I know his type, to try anything that can be directly pinned on him. You'd be safe, physically at least. Besides, he'd never connect you with the girl who was put out of the Swanson House. We didn't know your name then. It didn't get into the papers at all."

"I wish I were courageous like you," I said.

Dr. Miseleman smiled a trifle sadly. "I'm not really courageous, Thalia, believe me," he said soberly. "I'm a practical, unsentimental man. I'm forty-five, and I've never been able to afford even the sentiment of letting myself want a woman enough to marry her." For an instant a shadow crossed his face. "There's only one thing I care about now. That's helping humanity where it needs help. They call me a crusader, and the doctors who smudge their sacred oath hate my guts. But this is one racket I can smash if you'll only help me. Stop thinking about the past, Thalia. We all must. I'll find out if this Leonard Wallington has any connections with hospitals and you go to him and remind him of the job he promised you."

He lifted my face when I didn't speak. "You have your baby to think of, and I've the babies and the hundreds of girls who go to these places to think of. You'll do it, Thalia?"

I didn't look at him as I whispered, "I'll try to help. But it's for my baby's sake. She's all I care about! I don't care anything about the world. I hate it!" I hid my face in my hands, and Dr. Miseleman held my head against his shoulder until my sobs lessened.

It was a month later that I went to see Dr. Wallington at the Memorial Hospital, whose head was Aaron Smithson. The name brought a pang of memory to me. This was the doctor who had promised Devin his internship long ago.

I went quickly down the corridors, my heart pounding. Here in this hospital, Devin had planned to begin the practice of medicine. Interns in their white suits, nurses in their starched uniforms—a world of pain and death—but clean pain, clean death, clean life. A place where an idealist like Devin belonged. When I thought of Dr. Wallington and the dual role he played, I wanted to turn and run out into the sunshine. If I had not turned down that next corridor, with the need of escape driving me, the rest of this story might never have been written. In front of the glass enclosed nursery, a young father and an old, gray-haired woman waited to see a baby.

I stood there while a nurse held up a blue eyed, red-faced baby, it's small fists blindly crowding its yawning mouth. The young father pressed his face against the window as if to get nearer, and the grandmother wept in quiet happiness.

I ran past them, tears obscuring my sight, my heart like a leaden weight, weighing me down with despair I stood behind the turn of the next corridor until I could stop the tears and my shaking body could steady itself. Then I went doggedly on to Dr. Wallington's office, the memory of my own black-eyed baby seeming to lie gently against my heart to remind me of my promise to Dr. Miseleman.

It took Dr. Wallington a long minute before he recognized me in the little black suit and black hat Mrs. Nelson had given me from her daughter's wardrobe.

"Not Thalia!" Dr. Wallington's voice had that same, too smooth silkiness, his great height loomed over me the way it had ages ago, it seemed, in Betty Swanson's office. He put those pallid hands that had so revolted me on my shoulders in a gesture that held a curiously subtle insult. I didn't let him see me cringe. "You're so different. I scarcely knew you! You've grown even prettier! And softer! You looked so hard then!"

I ignored his last words, and looked up at him through veiled eyes.

"I am different," I said slowly. "Life does things to change one. I came because I remembered your promise of a job, Dr. Wallington," I said determinedly, but my lips trembled.

He stared down at me for a moment, his eyes blank. I knew he had forgotten that promise if he had ever meant it. As he lifted his hands from my shoulders, his palm brushed my cheek, seemingly without intent. But I knew better.

"What are you doing now?" he asked blandly.

"Nothing." I sat down because my knees felt weak. Now was the moment when I had to act the role Dr. Miseleman had outlined for me. I looked at Dr. Wallington with the frightened eyes of a timid girl. "Nothing, because I can't get work. You will help me, won't you?" I pleaded, leaning forward. "I remembered so often how you offered to. I'd take anything—anything." I stressed the word as his eyes flickered. "The only thing I've been grateful for, out of all the mess I went through, is that I have no baby to look out for. If ever I was sentimental enough to think I wanted it, I'm grateful to Betty Swanson for making me see the light. There's only one thing I want now—to make money!"

I could almost see the tenseness melt from him. I knew then he had suspected something about my baby when I came in. Now he smiled reassuringly.

"I think I have just the thing for you," he said in a lowered tone. "As you know, we must observe, ah—certain protocol—regarding the unfortunate girls in our care. When prospective parents come for babies, we have to remember that the girls, who give themselves into our care until their babies are born, do so in order that we may keep their secrets. But people who adopt babies pay more for babies when they have a feeling of confidence."

He smiled again, more widely. "I need someone who can meet prospective parents. Someone who looks"—his eyes swept me consideringly—"likes you. Young and soft and seemingly untouched, who will have my interests at heart." Beneath his words I could almost read his mind.

"You were one of those girls, once. You bore a child, nameless. You hid away in shame, like a mole burrowing into the earth but you are fair bait for me now. You aren't an innocent any longer—"

I knew it was not me he wanted. I intrigued him merely as another girl who would eventually capitulate and feed that inordinate vanity of his.

Yet I kept my eyes on his and that eager, attentive look on my face, as if he were a prophet and I a disciple. I couldn't—I must not—let bitterness invade my eyes or my face, or let it twist my mouth. Not until I had done the job I had come to do, for the sake of other girls and the baby I longed for so unceasingly.

It worked. He got up and came close to me. "If you look at anyone else with that look in your eyes, they'll believe anything you tell them. How on earth can a girl like you do it? You could make Lucifer believe he was an angel, Thalia!"

"You could make a girl believe anything, Dr. Wallington!" I said softly, as he opened the door. "You've given me new hope with this job! I was ready to give up!"

He opened the door for me, his hand in that familiar gesture on my shoulder. I was smiling at him, when a door down the corridor opened and an interne came out, his head bent over a chart. The smile stiffened on my lips, and my heart stopped as if a bullet had found its mark there. That brown head—the walk I remembered so well—

He was abreast of me when he raised his head and looked at me, blankly at first, as if he didn't believe his eyes. Then his gaze traveled from the hand Dr. Wallington still kept on my shoulder, up to the blandly smiling face of the physician. He didn't look at me again.

"Hello, Caldwell!" Dr. Wallington's voice was agreeably smooth, unperturbed. "How's the patient in 104?"

"Just looking over her chart." Devin's voice was as mechanical as a robot. He looked at Dr. Wallington, ignoring me as if I were the door. "Fever's down two points."

"Like to see that chart a minute, Caldwell—" Dr. Wallington put his hand out. "We'll, see you tomorrow, Thalia!" His hand slid familiarity round my shoulders before it dropped.

I died a thousand deaths as I walked down that corridor to the exit. My legs moved woodenly. My mind was saying, Slowly—go slowly, give him a chance to catch up. Maybe he didn't want to show that he knew you— But all the time I knew. I knew. Once, nothing on God's earth would have kept Devin from me. Now, a million worlds divided us.

It was possible, then, for a man to cease loving a woman. Possible for eyes that had been filled with love, to look at a beloved face and not see it. Possible to find it too hard to forgive—

But that was not what pounded through my heart, jolting it to unbearable pain as I went home. It was the realization that after all, Devin had graduated in June! And Dr. Smithson had kept his promise and taken him into the Memorial Hospital. That despairing letter of his, which had sent me for comfort and disaster into Quentin's arms, had only been his fear of failure, not the certainty.

Only one certainty crystallized for me during that long, hideous night—the knowledge that I had lost Devin, forever. If only I had waited, Quentin's life would never have been sacrificed to that mad, brief dash against time, and the terrible months at the Swanson

Looking back now, it seems to me as if a giant stamping pad had been dipped in ink and smeared across my life a second time. A stamping pad that had the Swanson House on it, with its black memories clear, its steam, clattering laundry.

The Haven, in which Dr. Wallington was now interested, was different only in three things. It was bigger; it had a huge nursery instead of the small one in the Swanson House, and a luxurious top floor that might have been lifted bodily out of some fine mansion. I knew little of the worth of good paintings and fine rugs, but Dr. Wallington's office, his sitting room with its big couch, and the two luxuriously fitted rooms for patients who could pay. They were fitted with rugs and pictures and silver with the undeniable stamp of authenticity on them. It was as different from the drab lower floors and the bare delivery room and the sick rooms adjoining it, as a penthouse from a poor house.

In one of those two rooms lived Alyce Hatton, reading the latest novels with which Dr. Wallington supplied her. She was twenty, with all the earmarks of decadent riches. Sleek black hair, black eyes with enormous lashes, and red lipsticked mouth splashed against a pallid skin. Her hands were exquisite, tapering and rosy tipped.

Even her approaching motherhood took nothing from that hard cynical look in her eyes. I was in Dr. Wallington's office when she stopped at the door. She looked me up and down as if I had been a prize mare or a dog in a blue ribbon show.

"So you're the newest Wallington addition," she remarked in her husky, cynical voice. "There've been four since I came six months ago. I hope you last longer than the others if it means anything to you. You're the best looking of the lot, but you don't look as if you know your way around much."

Suddenly below in the delivery rooms we heard the faint, muffled cry that meant another life being brought into the world. She stiffened.

"Crying doesn't help, does it?" she said in a thin, scornful voice. "Men hate it and women see through it. I'll be darned if I'd let them hear me scream." She crushed her cigarette out on the tray, moved indolently toward her room. Despite the difficulty of moving quickly, she had a high headed, aristocratic quality that marked her with the stamp of wealth. The velvet negligee she wore trailed behind her.

Looking at her and realizing that very soon she would go through the same agonies of the unknown girl downstairs, I felt a pulsation of common sympathy. But I knew she neither wanted it nor would give it. She must have lived hard and loved hard, young as she was—and so she would suffer hard; but I knew nobody would hear her complain.

She went to the window, stood looking into the bleak yard.

"They've let them out again," she said, dispassionately, as if she spoke of a herd of cattle. "Look at them. They sit there the whole hour not talking, like animals. Every day it's the same."

Swift anger surged through me. "They work like animals," I said slimy. "They do all the work in this house because they've no money to pay! They'd have no choice, otherwise, but to have their babies in some barn, or the open fields, or take their chances at the hands of some quack! And most of them haven't even the money for that!"

She turned to look at me with studied insolence, but I had the feeling that under her cool, arrogant exterior she was ashamed of what she had said, but too proud to admit it. I was still smarting beneath her words when I went down to the nursery.

As I passed the delivery room the door opened. Nurse Fenter came out, carrying a small bundle whimpering weakly in her arms. Behind her I caught a glimpse of Dr. Wallington, rolling down his sleeves, his mouth sullen and compressed. He looked up and saw me, but before he moved, I had turned and was walking quickly into the nursery before Nurse Fenter, my heart thumping at the temporary escape from the daily, hourly need of evading him. Each day the tentative touch on my arm, my shoulder, grew more and more assured.

"Dr. Wallington's been at it again," the nurse said curtly. "This kid's lucky to be here."

I knew what "at it again" meant. Since the day when Betty Swanson had taunted me with trying to attract Dr. Wallington, I had never forgotten her shrill voice shouting at him, "Drink and women."

In the three weeks since I had come to The Haven, I had seen him pour more than one stiff drink from the bottle in the big leather covered desk. It made my aversion to him more violent and the necessity for concealing it more difficult.

I escaped to the nursery whenever I could. The Haven was in reality a huge clearinghouse for babies sent from many other places. Each day new arrivals were added, and almost every day the number lessened. I never looked at a new baby without my heart beating to suffocation with the eternal hope of finding my own baby for I was pathetically sure I'd recognize her by her resemblance to Quentin.

These babies, ticketed with only a number, like so much baggage, came and went in a ceaseless stream. Where they came from, was never disclosed. I reasoned, bitterly, that many were stolen from girls and sent through devious channels until their bereft mothers had given up hope of tracing them. Some of them were scrawny, some fretful. Under Nurse Fenter's expert care, they bloomed.

Emma Fenter was big, ungainly, and completely without sentiment, but efficient and capable. Watching me yearning over the babies, she made no secret of her impatience.

"You're a sentimental fool," she scolded without rancor. "They're just so much cargo to be shipped out to bring home the dough."

But to me they were babies—soft, pink, helpless.

In my first three weeks in The Haven, seventeen babies were sold. I recorded the name and address of each purchaser. These were the only tangible bits of evidence I could mail to Dr. Miseleman as yet. These, and the word pictures I gave him of the men and women who came, some furtively, some openly, for the babies they bought. None of them seemed to care what blood ran in the veins of these bits of humanity. None asked for the heritage or were asked for more than their own names and addresses as guarantees that the babies would have worthy homes.

I can see some of them now so plainly—the big, blowsy woman and the thin, sickly man with her, looking the small baby boy over with kind but impersonal eyes.

"Guess he'll do," she said after a moment, "maybe give you something to think about instead of Freddie. I tell him you can't live your life in the past," she said to nobody in particular. "We lost ours—" She choked and stopped.

Then there was the sharp voiced, well-dressed woman with the man in the loud checked suit. "This one'll looks to me like that nursery fixed us up, hey, Liz?" He pinched her cheek, and laughed loudly, dragging out his pocketbook with a flourish. "Have a fine life, too, that kid—traveling around."

The woman looked at him with weary disgust. "By the time he's ten, he'll probably know more about horses than I know about where you spend your time—if he gets your education."

But the man's loud good nature didn't abate. "Give you something to occupy you, Liz, so you don't gripe all the time. Anyway, pot calling the kettle black. You got a good swift thumb for dealing, ain't you?" He said it without rancor, but I saw the red veins swell on his cheeks, and I had a pang of pity for the tiny boy they carried off that night. Drinking, card playing, horses—

And so it went. With love or with calculating motives at which we could only guess—the babies In The Haven came and went, their pasts as obscure as their futures. "Out of the nowhere into the nowhere," I remember thinking with grim pity.

I had been there three weeks when No. 106 was sent out. We knew them only by numbers. No. 106 was two months old, a pink infant with a fat, contented smile and eyes like cornflowers. She had been there before I came and I wondered that nobody had asked for her. But I knew better than to question. Nurse Fenter never answered, and Mrs. Broughton who managed the house turned a blank, hard gaze on me as if she were deaf.

She was a heavyset woman with a mannish face and a deep voice. She had none of Betty Swanson's viciousness, but she conducted The Haven as if it were a business from which she had to exact the utmost in returns. Yet in them both, I knew, lay the same vast contempt for the unfortunate girls who came and went in an endless dreary succession.

"Took us a long time to satisfy this Cradish woman, but she'll be here in ten minutes with a fat check," she said in that drum major voice. "Get No. 106 ready."

I turned soberly back to Nurse Fenter. "I wish they'd leave No. 106 here a little longer," I said. The baby gave me a toothless, contented smile, and I put my cheek against hers.

Nurse Fenter took her from me with a gesture of impatience. She stripped the small pink body and began rubbing olive oil on it. "The plumper they are, the more they bring. This one's expensive—two thousand dollars. That's why we kept her three weeks." She turned the baby over. "Any fool who pays that much just to have the baby the right color blue eyes and blond hair and a dimple in her chin must have a reason for it!" she snorted, wrapping the baby in a clean undershirt. "Maybe she'll pay them back by growing up to show her father was a thief and her mother a street walker. They usually are that when they do without the marriage license."

Her callousness drove me to speak, though I could have bitten my tongue for it. "Not always," I said, breathing fast.

She raised her glance and her eyes swept me up and down, a knowing look that made me flush. "Oh, well, there may be exceptions," she conceded, "but I doubt it!" She was wrapping the baby in a pink-frilled robe. "There you are, miss, ready for your trip!" She put the baby in my arms. "Dr. Wallington knew what he was talking about," she said with a cynical lift of her mouth. "It adds to the asking price when there's a pretty frame around the picture. You look as if a kid belongs in your arms!"

The woman who came in ten minutes later had once been pretty, but her face was lined now with marks of harsh temper and dissipation. A sullen boy of ten sidled in and stopped just inside the door. Mrs. Cradish looked at the baby in my arms and beckoned to the boy, who came forward reluctantly.

"I don't want any baby. I'll hate it," he said with vicious emphasis. With a gesture of uncontrolled anger, she jerked his arm and the boy cried out. I had seen such a shrewish, vitriolic look on Betty Swanson's face, but never anything like the strange queer shine in this woman's eyes.

With a terrified cry the boy flung his arms around her.

Don't be mad," he whispered. "I'm trying to like it. Honest I am, but you always say if I'm bad you'll take me back where you bought me and get somebody else. I want to stay with you."

The look on her face passed as quickly as it had come. She smiled at him, and I could see how the boy could be coaxed back to her by this sudden reversal to affection. I thought with a sudden, swift pity that no child could remain normal long in that abnormal atmosphere of violent temper and as violent outbursts of affection. Not even a grown person could bear it.

Involuntarily I clutched the little soft body in my arms more closely. What would this baby know of normal love with a woman like that? And again, as always, I thought with a pang of my own baby. Supposing some child, hating the intruder, were to stare at my baby with that steady, unchildlike resentment.

My eyes blurred as I watched the check pass into Mrs. Broughton's hands and saw Nurse Fenter wrap the baby capably in a warm blanket and follow Mrs. Cradish out to the car. I didn't realize I was crying until Nurse Fenter came back.

"Stop being a fool," she said gruffly. She was staring at the empty crib. For the first time I saw something humane in her eyes. "But this time it's got me, too. That woman's taking drugs. Did you see the gleam in her eyes? The boy's adopted, too. A kid's got no chance in a home like that. If I know my reform schools, he'll be a first-rate candidate the way she handles him. Crazy about her, too. That's funny, isn't it?"

Funny? I remembered that long afterwards.

In the week that followed, something like a heavy, menacing shadow hung over the house. Wallington drank incessantly, and I caught Alyce, the society-type girl I met the first day, watching him with the first shadow of fear in her eyes from the end of another. Piles of half-used cigarette butts mounted on her table.

Despite her hard shell, I had the feeling that she was desperate for some word of comfort. In all these weeks, not a word had escaped her of her past, nothing of the man who had been part of that moment of yielding which had ended in her being at The Haven. As her time drew near, I could sense a growing tension in her. The small room I slept in was below hers, and often during the night I heard her pacing the floor with heavy, slow steps.

The day before she knew she was to go down to the delivery room, she called me in to her room and shut the door. Dr. Wallington had just come in. I could guess what was happening behind the closed door of his office.

"Is he the only doctor you can call when we need him?" Her eyes were black-circled, her mouth looked pinched. "I'm having this baby because I didn't want to chance dying, by taking another way out. But I don't want to die now, either. Or have the baby die, even though I don't want it."

"He's never had an accident—" I began, but she cut me short.

"There's always a first one! And he's drinking constantly." She looked at me with an intent gaze in which pleading struggled against her pride. "I'm—scared. I've taken hurdles and done crazy things for excitement, but I've never been frightened like this. If I weren't afraid of being found out, I'd go away now. But I can't risk it." She bit her lip hard. "But I can't risk having him attend to me, either. I've seen his hands shake when he's been drinking—when he examined me last week." She shuddered.

And then she leaned forward. "You—you have influence." The way she said it made me cringe. There was a note of unconcealed contempt in her voice mingled with the anxiety. "If you're in love with him, the way you seem to be, will you try and keep him sober. At least till after I'm over it?"

In love? My heart seemed to stifle with the memory of Devin that the word always brought The impulse to wipe out that contemptuous look went as quickly as it came. I couldn't tell her what my errand here was.

"I'll try," I said dully. "I'll go in now."

Dr. Wallington's door was open: He was standing with his back to the room, looking out of the long French windows that opened on a small wooden balcony with a fragile, delicately carved balustrade. I never see a bit of woodcarving or a balcony without that hideous memory returning.

Before Dr. Wallington turned, I had time again to look about that rich room. Somewhere in here those records were hidden, but in all these weeks I had seen nothing but a box of cards with girls' names on them. And I knew that many of the names were assumed. Not a certificate—not a nurse's chart. It looked like a rich man's library, soundless with rich rugs, hung with velvet hangings for the first time I felt a hopelessness about Dr. Miseleman's plan. I stared at Dr. Wallington's thick, heavy neck, the vast shoulders in the long white coat. Something in my silent gaze must have reached him, for he whirled, glaring at me with congested eyes.

"What the devil do you mean, playing—" he began, and then made an effort to change his tone. He came toward me with that long, heavy stride. "I'm edgy today. Had a bad day at the hospital." He reached down into the drawer of the desk and pulled out a bottle of whiskey. Though I knew he drank, I had never seen him toss off one drink after the other until the bottle shook in his hand and some of the whiskey slopped over onto the leather covered desk.

I watched him with distaste that mounted momentarily.

With a sudden gesture I could not evade, he pulled me toward him. "Listen, Thalia," his voice was blurred, "you know I'm crazy about you. This business of playing innocent's gone on long enough."

I stood still within the hard pressure of his arms, trying to down the sickness at the closeness of his face, the loose mouth and the look in his eyes.

"Not just now," I pleaded softly. I forced myself to put my hand to his cheek. "Dr. Wallington, you ought to stop drinking for your own sake. Or—for mine," I whispered.

"I'd do anything for you," he said thickly. He bent and put his mouth to my throat, and I stood there, fighting the sickness that curdled inside me. His eyes held mine. "You're lovely." He tightened his arm around me. "No wonder Betty hated you. Jealous as the devil of every woman I looked at."

His fingers slid down my cheek to my throat. Rigid, my heart suffocating me with its pounding, I endured the insufferable touch of his fingers.

"Betty Swanson," I repeated her name slowly. I had to divert him, as one would divert a drunkard from a dangerous corner. "She hated you, too!"

He laughed, throwing his head back. "Betty? Betty's nuts about me, always was. Never let me out of her sight till I shoved her dust off my feet!" His face bent to mine again.

I strained back from him.

"She said you left because you were scared—"

I was prepared for anger, but not for the swift red rage that darkened his face. He let me go and his hands braced themselves against the desk. "The devil with her! What should I be scared of?" he demanded, but his voice shook.

My mind was whirling, but out of somewhere I found the right words to say, not knowing they were right, only following some blind instinct out of that hatred of Betty Swanson and my fear of him.

"I knew she was jealous. I didn't believe her. But she said—you forged contract for the girls about them and their babies—"

It went home. His face paled until the line about his mouth was a greenish white. Its ugliness was appalling.

"She's mad—" He said the words slowly, groping for them as if he were blind. "Mad—as a hornet! Some day she'll be put where she belongs!"

If I feared him before, now I knew terror that turned my blood to water. His eyes were red with rage and fear—and something else. He caught my shoulders in a vicious grip.

"She lied, see? A jealous woman—she'd say anything! Anyway, she can't do anything to me. A wife can't testify—" he stopped, and his mouth shook.

For a long moment we stared at each other, while pictures clicked into place in my mind. Betty Swanson—Dr. Wallington. Swanson—Wallington. Their offices, opening into each other . . . Betty, agonized with jealousy, accusing me of trying to make him notice me. A wife can't testify against her husband.

I drew out of his arms. Instinct acted for me, put words into my mouth.

"So you're married to her. Then that's why you've always said you were crazy about me but never spoke of marriage. I made a mistake once, Dr. Wallington. I won't again. It's marriage—or nothing."

His lips curled. "Marriage?" He caught my shoulders in a hard, hurting grip. "You've got your nerve!"

I remembered the role I was playing. I'll always believe any woman has it in her to be an actress. I drew his head down toward mine.

"Why?" I asked softly, my eyes holding his. "Why? Betty Swanson loved you and you married her."

"To keep her mouth shut, that's all. There never was anything between us." The words shot out before he could stop himself. The drink and desire was clouding his caution again. But he was still cunning, still shrewd.

"She's lied before—she will again," he said savagely. "She'd fight like a demon before she'd give me a divorce. She'd try to put me on the spot with her lies." He was drawing me against him, but I resisted.

I smiled at him, slowly. "No court would believe the testimony of a mad woman. You're too big a man to be wasted on Betty Swanson. I knew that the first time I saw you! We could go far together, make a lot of money—travel. . . ." I kept that wide eyed look on my face as I whispered, "You said I'm lovely—"

"Lovely!" He crushed me against him. "Lovely and clever as they come!" he whispered. Suddenly his mouth was on mine, hard, the brutal, possessive kiss of a man who knows nothing of love except sensuality. It sickened me, but I held myself still, letting his hands move over my shoulders. This was the moment to tie him to me with the promise of what I might give him. Only my eyes closed to conceal the look that would have betrayed me. When he released me, he was shaking.

"I'll divorce Betty," he promised.

It was during that night that I heard Alyce's footsteps, but now they seemed to stumble across the floor in a kind of blind terror. I knew what it meant. I had known that terror, too. Then I heard her voice calling, "Dr. Wallington! Dr. Wallington!"

With shaking hands, I pulled my robe around me and raced out into the hall, up the stairs. She was standing against the door, her face blanched and drawn with agony. The hard shell had cracked. She was like every other girl going through an unknown terror with agony companioning her. Her teeth chattered as I caught her, wrapping her in a blanket I snatched from the bed.

"I'll get you downstairs," I comforted. "Just hold to me." I guided her stumbling steps down the stairs to the delivery room, and rapped at the nursery door for Nurse Fenter. She came sleepily, resentful at being awakened.

"All right. You go up and get Dr. Wallington. I'll be there in a minute," she yawned.

I sped back up the stairs, knocking at the door of his sitting room. There was no answer. I opened it, knowing somehow before I did, what I would find. He was lying, half dressed across the couch, his lounging robe trailing. I shook him, called him, but he was suddenly asleep.

My mind zigzagged frantically. I had to get a doctor for Alyce. I had no authority to call any other doctor—neither had Nurse Fenter. Any physician would become a dangerous question.

"Fine fix we're in!" Nurse Fenter's voice whirled me around. "She needs a doctor now and from what I can see, it's not a case I'd touch alone, though I've helped bring babies into the world before, heaven's knows. It's Mrs. Broughton's night off, too!" From downstairs, Alyce's scream came, bitten off. "She's got courage, that one."

"Go down," I said rapidly. "I know a doctor I can trust. He'd do anything for me."

I sped down past the nursery, down past the dormitory where girls tossed on their hard, narrow beds, down to Mrs. Broughton's office. I rang Dr. Miseleman's number.

"Dr. Miseleman's out on a maternity case," a woman's voice told me sleepily. "He won't be back for a few hours. Who shall I—"

But I had hung up. Who now? The memory of Alyce's words, "If I weren't afraid of being found out—" stuck in my mind. I couldn't betray her secret.

I don't know what sent Devin's name into my mind. He hated me. He despised me—but I couldn't believe he would refuse to come if I needed him. Interns were never allowed to go out on cases. I remembered Quentin telling me about hospital routines. But I hoped desperately that at this hour of the night, he would be off duty. The sound of his voice stopped mine for an instant. When I spoke again, it was in a tremulous voice he didn't recognize at first.

"Devin, Devin, I need you. I'm in trouble! This is Thalia—"

I heard the click as he hung up. I hadn't expected that. In that moment, I hated him. I rang again, frantically. "Operator! I've been cut off. This is an emergency!" For what seemed a thousand years I waited until the hospital operator called his name in her flat, mechanical voice, "Dr. Caldwell—emergency. Dr. Caldwell—emergency—" At last he answered.

"Devin, you must come now! There's nobody else I can trust. Please, if you ever—"

His voice was hard, unyielding. "I'll send the ambulance with an interns."

"Nope. My voice was hoarse with nervous exhaustion. "You must come alone, Devin, please!" There was an interminable silence until he spoke again.

"Give me the address," he said in a monotone. I heard the scratching of his pencil on paper before he hung up.

Then I was back in the delivery room, holding Alyce's hand. "I'll have somebody here in a few minutes."

A shadow of fear crossed her face. "Somebody I know. We can trust him!" I tried to smile, but my lips were stiff. Nurse Fenter was doing things with hands that seemed efficient and calm, but her eyes kept going to Alyce's bloodless face and back to the watch on her wrist with a look that sent a cold premonition through me.

When the sound of wheels crunched to a stop on the gravel outside, I ran downstairs. My heart hurt me with its clamorous beating as I saw Devin's cold, set mouth.

"What's the matter?" He looked me up and down, at the thin wrap I had flung about me, my bare feet thrust into sandals. I saw his look go comprehensively around the hallway, and then rest on something behind me.

I looked up. The door of the dormitory was open, and frightened faces showed over huddled, heavy bodies. I saw his gaze sweep over them—seeing the evidences of motherhood on those young, appallingly apathetic bodies.

He whispered a hoarse curse, but he wasn't really cursing. His look swept over me in that same fashion, and I shrank from it, but I had no time to think of anything but Alyce.

"What's wrong with you?" he asked harshly again.

"Not me, Devin. A girl upstairs—"

I went before him, my feet seeming wooden. The old need of him was filling me in a bittersweet flood. No matter what I did, I knew I'd always love him.

As we neared the delivery room, Alyce's voice rose in a scream of unbearable pain. She turned her face as we came in, and its twisted, agonized features seemed to have no semblance to the face I had known.

Devin asked no questions then. He sent orders to Nurse Fenter with a certainty that brought a look of reluctant respect to her face. If I had ever doubted that he would reach his goal, I knew better that night, with dawn seeping into the room in a gray, miserable tide while Alyce's daughter was born.

I had never seen a baby born, though I had gone through the agonies of childbirth. Watching Devin, his tenderness, his swift, sure hands, I was bound in a sense of irremediable loss. I remembered Dr. Gaslaphz's nervous hands, his barked orders to me, the callous indifference of the nurses. I envied Alyce even in her agony, because Devin's hands were bringing help to her, his voice pleading gently, urgently, for patience, helping her bear each pain.

When it was over, he turned to me. "Get me a basin of hot water and cold—quickly! The baby's blue—"

Automatically I obeyed, watching him fascinated as he plunged that small body in first one, then the other, rubbing, blowing into the baby lungs, pressing and patting and urging, almost coaxing in a voice that had all the old, loving timbre that I remembered.

It seemed ages while I supplied hot water, over and over. But when Nurse Fenter took the baby after its first weak cry, I saw that only ten minutes had elapsed since he had cut the cord that bound Alyce's baby to her.

My eyes were blurred and my head ached, but I stood upright as he put on his coat and picked up his bag.

At the door he turned, speaking over my head to Nurse Fenter, giving her some last minute directions. He ignored me as I walked down the stairs beside him.

"Devin—" We were at the outside door. I put my hand on his arm with a sudden, unconquerable need to touch him. He drew away with a brusque movement. Up above a door opened, but I didn't heed it. "Devin, I must talk to you! I must tell you—"

He was pulling out a pad and pencil.

"All I want to know is the name of the girl in there. I have to report the birth to the authorities."

I was staring at him, wide eyed. "You mustn't—" I whispered. "You can't, Devin!"

"What do you mean—I can't?" he asked me. A muscle twitched at the corner of his mouth. "I came because I thought you needed help. If I'd known it was anything like this, I'd be darned if I'd have come! I'm going to report it!" And then with a contempt that twisted his mouth, he said, "I guess I should have expected to find you in something like this after that letter."

We stared at each other like enemies. Suddenly, I hated him, his smugness, his sure conviction that I was bad. I was filled with a maddened recklessness. I had to tell him even if he wouldn't listen, even if I never saw him again.

I spoke in a harsh, violent whisper.

"You—you can stand there and tell me that! What do you know of what I went through when you didn't answer my letter? I told you the truth about Quentin, but all you knew was that I'd done something shameful! Quentin wouldn't have turned me down the way you did! He was crude, but he had a kindness in him that couldn't be turned bitter and hard as iron!"

His face turned chalky white.

"There is no need—" he began, but I rushed on.

"There is need! I've gone through hell since then! I tried to commit suicide. I was dragged to the police station! I had a baby—Quentin's baby—in a house like this, worse than this! They stole her from me!"

All the pain and frustration and hatred of Betty Swanson was in my voice, all the deep, deep need of love and kindness that had gone from my life when Quentin had diet and Devin had rejected me.

"All you had to face was a broken dream of a girl you though above those things, and you couldn't face that! I could have lied to you, but I was honest. I wrote you that letter before I knew I was going to have a baby! I wanted to start out clean and you; threw me out of your life! You're so holy!"

He reached out and caught my arm, but I twisted away from him. A new look was struggling into his face, but just then I hated him too much to have him touch me.

"You saw those girls up there. They have to hide! They come here hoping not to be found out, so they can go on living when they get out. Burdened and worked like animals till their babies are born, kicked out five days after, while their babies are sold for money they never see—" I stopped for breath. "If I could get girls to tell the truth, testify for Dr. Miseleman—"

"Don't you listen to her, Doc!"

I whirled. A tall girl with eyes like agates was coming down the stairs from the dormitory. She shot a harsh, searching glance from Devin to me.

"Sneak!" she said clearly. "Letting that drunk up there make love to you! Oh, we ain't blind, us down here! You with your cushy job, like all the others Doc Wallington brings here!" Her look swept me disdainfully. "Testify!" She put acid into the word. "We got enough to go through without letting the world know! If you try and make us, well, you got another think coming, see? It suits us all right, don't it, girls?"

She turned. Behind her a dozen girls were coming slowly down the stairs. All my life I will remember the faces of those girls, menacing, hating, and facing me on the stairs. For a fleeting moment I remembered myself, facing Betty Swanson so, hating her for what she stood for.

Behind me the outer door opened and closed. Devin was gone. I didn't have to turn to know it. An immense hopelessness filled me as if I had gone through all I could bear; there was only one thing I now had to do.

I looked straight ahead at the girl who had spoken. My eyes were as hard as hers and my face was just as grim.

"Listen," I said slowly, distinctly, "I'm telling you the truth, all of you. I went through what you are going through. I had a baby. I wanted it but it was stolen from me. I got my finger caught in a wringer—" I lifted my hand, showed them the scar with its long white ridges. "The woman who did that—Betty Swanson—"

"Swanson, Betty Swanson?" A girl came toward me. She pushed up the sleeve of her nightdress. Above her elbow was a vivid, ugly scar. "See that? She pushed me against the boiler because I didn't stoke the furnace quick enough—the last time. She's crazy!"

"I know!" I raced on against time, against the dawn now paling through the window blinds, against Mrs. Broughton's return.

"But until we talk up, the Betty Swansons will go on. Until some of us will be plucky enough to face the world, you'll keep on enduring it—or other girls will!"

"Pluck!" a girl choked. "My brother's wife would kick me out if she knew, and Teddy's all I got in the world. He thinks I'm working in Chicago—"

I heard the babel of their voices, crowding one another, and I broke in hushing them. At any moment, Dr. Wallington might awaken.

"I know! I know all about it. We all have our reasons. That's what they trade on, reasons for hiding ourselves away like moles in the ground. Reasons for stealing our babies, selling them for five hundred—thousands of dollars!"

"My God!" The word was like a prayer from the tall, gaunt girl. "And we slave our guts out here! A thousand dollars for my kid! And I signed her away so I could scrub floors until my back's breaking!"

"There are places where you could have had your babies without breaking your backs, where you'd get the money for your babies when they were sold! They're state agencies," I raced on.

"Yeah, and where you got to tell every last thing that ever happened to you. Let the world know you're a—" The girl who spoke wasn't more than sixteen, but she had the knowledge of sixty in her eyes. Even her voice sounded old.

"Yes," I retorted, "but they keep it silent, too! They only want to know those things so they'll know where to put your baby, who its father was, what sort of blood it had. That way they can put a kid in the right home, and get the right parents for it. It's not only us we have to think of but also the babies we bring into the world! I wish I'd known before I had mine; before I ever met Betty Swanson!"

I looked around at them. It was light now. I could see their faces clearly—haggard, pallid faces, worn and too old for their years. A vast pity clogged my voice.

"There's nothing any of you can do now. But when you get out of here, if you'd go to Dr. Harris Martin at the District Hospital, and tell him you'll testify at any investigation—"

I couldn't read their faces or their eyes, but I had a feeling I had reached them. I spoke straight to the girl who had accused me in front of Devin.

"Sure I let him talk nice to me." I looked at the circle of pale faces. "It's the only way I can stay here and maybe find my baby. Perhaps I'll never find her, but I wouldn't like to give up yet."

That was all the appeal I made for their silence. I went up to the nursery where Nurse Fenwick was wrapping Alyce's baby into a blanket, ticketing it with a number.

"It would be better not to tell Dr. Wallington and Mrs. Broughton that we brought a strange doctor in," I said quietly. "We can say you did what was necessary, Nurse Fenter. I don't believe the doctor we called will report the case. I asked him not to."

Five days later, Dr. Wallington called me into his office. "I've started divorce proceedings," he told me.

There was a nervous twitch to the big shoulders, and his hands played constantly with the paperknife. But he smiled that loose, wide smile at me.

"Betty can shoot off the fireworks, if she likes. Thank heavens, this state permits it on grounds of incompatibility."

He stared at me. I felt as if a noose were tightening around me.

"You glad?" he demanded, when I stood silent. I forced a smile to my face.

"I'm only afraid for you?" I said softly. "Betty's ugly. I wouldn't want anything to happen to you."

He got up and came around to me, lifting my face and staring into my eyes. "I'm a rotten doctor. I'm sunk up to my ears in things no decent physician would touch. You've got looks and you're decent. Yet you want to marry me. Why?"

"I guess I'm like you a lot," I said slowly, my eyes on his. "They say water seeks its own level."

I endured his kiss as I had endured all the others. I was thinking triumphantly, soon—soon Betty would be free. She would be forced to speak against him, tell what she must know of the things he had done in that vicious house that bore her name. Tell, perhaps, where my baby had gone, so I could claim her. I could be patient till then.

I went into Alyce's room. She was facing the window, reading a newspaper. She turned, her usual reserve broken.

"Look, did you read this?"

I took the paper from her. First I saw the picture—a boy with a sullen, resentful face beside a woman who looked vaguely familiar. Beneath it was the caption:

Boy kills baby sister in a fit of jealously!

The name leaped out at me below it. "Todd Cradish, adopted son of Nancy Cradish, is in the custody of the court today, pending decision of Judge Mahrle on a case unparalleled in newspaper history. The boy has apparently no criminal tendencies. He readily admitted that he was jealous of the baby, recently adopted by Mrs. Cradish. He told how, when Mrs. Cradish left the house, he took a pillow and held it over the baby's face to stop her crying. Mrs. Cradish wept frantically when accused of taunting him with loving the little girl more, and threatening to send him back to the place where she bought him."

The whole sickening tale unwound as I read. The woman had been taking drugs steadily. Neighbors testified that the boy wept and screamed hysterically in fear, often long into the night. But it was the last paragraphs that stunned me.

"Nancy Cradish broke under steady questioning. She admitted that she had waited many months for a baby with blond hair and blue eyes who resembled her, so that she might palm her baby off on James Cradish, her divorced husband, in order to collect alimony. She had adopted the boy for that same reason and had been successful in collecting alimony until she married James Cradish.

"Judge Mahrle," the paragraph continued, "is one of the men who has steadfastly and courageously moved for new legislation on adoption procedure. His denunciation has started a storm of protest over the heartless sale of babies—"

"I never wanted the baby," Alyce was saying. The brittle mask of sophistication was cracking. "But when I think of her going into the hands of a woman like that—" She shuddered.

"You've got money," I cried. "Why don't you keep her? You wouldn't have to go out to work to feed and clothe her, like me—like those girls downstairs—or Colleen—or Heather—"

I stood up to go. "Keep your baby, Alyce," I pleaded. "You can really take care of it."

She shook her head. "I just couldn't—I went through all this so it wouldn't be found out!"

I pointed to the newspaper. "You'll live with fear, if you give her away," I said grimly. "Every time you see anything like that —and it'll happen again and again in one way or another—you'll feel as I do now. Wondering if your baby—remembering—" My lips quivered. "Even if your baby gets into a good home, you'll never know it."

Her eyes were wide with fear and uncertainty.

I turned and went out. I couldn't help her—nobody could. Any more than one could be helped down that dark road of agony to bring a baby into the world. You had to do it alone. I was swept by that vast loneliness like a black wave as I went down the stairs to the nursery.

At the foot, I stopped. Two men were being shown upstairs by Mrs.

Broughton. Her usually impassive face had a queer, strained look.

"Dr. Wallington is upstairs in his office," she said, glancing at me.

They looked at me, too, expressionlessly, their eyes hard and smooth as agates. Mrs. Broughton stared after them for a moment, and then went downstairs, her steps hurried and uncertain. Probably reporters, I thought, on the trail already.

I went into the nursery. Nurse Fenter turned, and I saw the newspaper in her hand. She was pale.

"No wonder Mrs. Broughton's worried," I told her.

"It'll be a fine smell," she said heavily.

I had my doubts then, only you can't say anything." She bit her lip. "That poor baby."

I'd never heard a word of sentiment from her in all these weeks. I would have sworn she was beyond it. She seemed hardly aware that she was talking to me as she went on, "Some day that bunch'll get wise to themselves. They'll hang themselves with one of those loopholes they're always talking about in the adoption laws."

"Who?" The word shot out before I could stop it. She looked up and the old hard screen slipped down over her eyes.

"Let's get the babies ready," she said brusquely. "There'll be two going out today."

But my mind was racing. That bunch. She didn't mean Wallington, then. There were others beside him caught in this vicious intrigue! How would I ever find out? I looked at the cribs, each one with its tiny occupant, going blindly into a world that had its own cunning uses for it, and a kind of desperation began to seep into me.

The house telephone rang and I answered it.

"I want to see you right away," Dr. Wallington's voice came over, harsh and domineering.

The two men were gone, and he was alone. His face was pasty, his mouth loose with fear. On the table there were three glasss, two of them half-empty.

"Listen, Thalia, I've got to get out quickly. Judge Mahrle's ready to try and get some legislation passed. He wants to go on some sort of a crusade," he said viciously.

Dr. Miseleman's words flashed into my mind. "They call me a crusader, they hate my guts, those men who smear their holy oath."

"You didn't know she was a drug addict," I said cautiously watching him. "You can't be personally responsible for everyone who adopts a baby!"

He smiled stiffly. "Sure, but these crusaders think we should investigate every one of them, kick 'em out if they're not perfect. Should be puritans with a church record long as a yardstick! But I know these investigations. You have to lay low till they die down. They can't find a thing on me, but I'm not waiting till they get on my trail!"

He had been drinking again. I saw the same uncertainty in the movements of his hands, the glaze that was beginning to cover his eyes. He came over and caught my arms, his face horribly close to mine.

"You're coming with me, Thalia. That way they won't get you for questioning, either."

"Of course I'll go." My heart was pounding, but I kept my eyes steadily on his. "Just make sure you leave no incriminating evidence behind—no records—"

His mouth twitched. "Smart girl, Thalia! But those records have already gone where they won't be found. We burn 'em when the fire gets too hot."

I remembered those two men with their hard mouths. Those records had gone with them! I would never find them now. I couldn't let him see my face. I walked to the little balcony, leaning against it, with my back to him, drawing great lengths to breathe of the cool air. He came behind me with heavy steps, and put his arms around me.

"This is a nice place," I forced the words out, fighting against time. "I'll be sorry to leave it."

"I know better ones," he said thickly. "We'll open our own place somewhere, take the profits ourselves. This business of splitting five ways—"

"Leonard—"

At the sound of that voice, he whirled, his back to me. As if carelessly, he swung the big French window to, its heavy drapes shutting me off from sight of the room, so that I couldn't be seen. But it couldn't shut out the sound of that voice I had never forgotten. Every nerve in me was shrieking. Suddenly, a violence of hatred and remembered fear. I loathed myself for that fear but I couldn't control it. Betty Swanson's voice seemed to bring back to me each moment of that awful year. Now it had a curiously dead flatness, as if she willed it to be quiet.

"Leonard, I've come about the divorce papers."

"You're a fool, Betty, if you think you'll gain anything by coming here!" His voice was smooth, but beneath it there was uncertainty, and she must have felt it.

She laughed, a high-pitched, curious sound from her. I had never heard her laugh before. There was something strange and eerie about that humorless, sharp sound.

"Maybe not. But I came to tell you a few things. Things you forgot, I guess. A wife can't testify against her husband, but once she's divorced, she can! She can tell a lot! Things like a girl who died because the doctor was drunk. A lot was paid to hush that, but he can't hush me if I want to tell it. And about forged papers, and about keeping money from Keager and Walsh and Tidwell, and marking different amounts on the records!"

She stopped for breath. I could imagine his heavy mouth, the temper pulling it sideways. Thieves falling out—ugly, damning.

"You can't pull me in without pulling yourself in! If you don't know that, you're crazy." His voice was so cold and vicious that I scarcely knew it. "Anyway, they'll never believe the testimony of a crazy woman. Besides, when you burned those records it let me out! When I left the Swanson House I left it clear."

It was as if all these months had drawn to that fine point of was all over. The thing that had kept me alive, despite Devin's loss, despite the ugliness of my life was gone. I knew that Betty Swanson had destroyed my last hope of recovering my baby.

In the tide of despair that rose and choked me, the memory of those blank faces of the girls downstairs seemed to mock me with their futility. They would go out when their time came, as full of fear of detection as Alyce was, anxious only to burrow into their dark corners until the world had forgotten them. They would never come forward to testify, any more than she would.

Suddenly, rage began to fill me. Murderous, deep rage. Once before I had wanted to kill Betty Swanson, when Heather had fallen down those stairs. Now again that red tide obscured my vision. I hated Wallington, but it was Betty Swanson I wanted to kill.

I stood there, taut, waiting for the moment when I could control my voice, the shaking of my body. I heard her laugh again, deep in her throat the laughter of madness.

"Those records are burned, but Keager has others! The Shedville House and the Barrister House, and the—"

"If you don't shut up, Betty—" he said in a low, deadly tone, but he didn't finish. I heard her cry out in the frantic voice of a woman who was possessed of only one desire. In the mounting violence of hatred that consumed me, I knew a fierce joy.

"Leonard, I'll keep quiet! I swear it! They could burn me, but I'd never say a word against you, only don't throw me over! I know you never cared, but someday you'll get tired of these young fools and I'll be waiting—"

I heard the sharp slap of his hand against her cheek.

"You're mad, Betty—" The repetition seemed to bring a fearful satisfaction to him as he said it. "Mad as a March hare. You know why I married you—it pulled us both out of a hole, not being made to testify against each other. But it's over now. I don't need you any longer." He stopped. I could imagine them staring at each other, poisoned hatred rising like a miasma between them. "Sure you'll be waiting—in a nut house, where you belong."

In the momentary silence I put my hand on the knob of the French window. I was ready now. I stiffened myself for the moment when I would face her.

In that instant I heard her voice. It stopped me. It wasn't human. It was saying things that had no place on a human tongue. In an appalling, deadly stream it poured out, disconnected phrases, senseless, hideous words. And before I could move I heard him cry out, sharply, "Keep away from me!"

Then with incredible swiftness for so big a man, Dr. Wallington was on the balcony, trying desperately to close the other French window. Behind the one he had closed to hide me I stood frozen in the horror of a nightmare where you try to run but cannot. At the open window, Betty Swanson appeared. With the desperation of madness, she flung herself on him. He slipped, tried crazily to regain his footing on the narrow wooden floor of the balcony and clutched at the low balustrade.

Beneath their combined weight, the delicate carved posts cracked and gave way. The last thing I heard was his scream and hers, mingled in a frenzy of fear—and before darkness came down over me, I saw his white hands clawing vainly at the empty air.

It is far behind me now. Once again I have come to a wholesome belief in the goodness of people, in their innate courage. The girls whose courage I doubted came—reluctantly, I know—to testify. The tragedies and sacrifices that must have resulted from their shrinking testimonies are things I can only guess. But they came, a sorry, dreary, heartsick stream swelling the tide of evidence against Keager and the others who shared the enormous profit of the traffic in babies.

Alyce, facing the storm of censure, testified, too. And, so did I. I wanted it on record. I wanted the homes to be shut down—forever.

And finally—Devin. I heard him tell the story of that night when he came to The Haven, and admit he had not registered Alyce's baby. That took courage, too. Our eyes clung, his telling me he loved me, mine full of a tremulous happiness that the black cloud between us had been swept away.

It was Dr. Miseleman who had told Devin the truth. I have never found out what happened between the time he found out what happened between them, but it was a chastened, white-faced Devin who flung himself down beside me and pleaded for forgiveness.

"I wanted to forget you—I tried, after your letter came. It made me work like a savage to get through in June. I knew I couldn't live without you. I looked all over for you—everywhere—after I graduated. You'd moved. Nobody knew anything. Then I saw you with Wallington in the hospital. I knew his reputation—and his arm was around you." I remembered my heart cringing. "And then I saw you in The Haven, and that girl said you were one of Wallington's—"

I put my hand over his mouth. "It's behind us, Devin, for always. I never want to remember it," I told him.

But I've never forgotten it. Those homes did close down, but others opened, too. They were more careful. Nowadays, those places don't exist.

At least, I hope they don't. There isn't the same stigma to illegitimate birth. I never found my child, but I was fortunate to have others. Devin married me, and we've been happy most of the time.

There's a place in my heart that will never be whole. I still miss the little baby girl I got to hold the one time. And I'll never forget her.

THE END

HELP ME!
MY SON IS MISSING
I left him in the car for a minute and he was gone

The day started as any other day. My husband, Ted, finished his coffee and grapefruit, kissed Teddy and me good-bye, and strode out to his car. So he didn't kiss me as passionately as he used to, he was still with me, and we had our darling Teddy.

Ted and I had been married eight years when Teddy was born. I have to admit we'd been growing apart before his birth because Ted wanted a son so badly. Ted always had the idea that having a son was the only way to validate himself as a man. Me, I just wanted a little one of my own to love and care for and I didn't care whether we had a boy or girl.

So, being pregnant was a magic time for me. I worked as a salesclerk in a huge department store until I was six months along, and then Ted insisted I quit so nothing would happen to the baby. I did as he wished because I wanted to please him.

We'd just gone through a bad time that almost tore our marriage apart. I learned that Ted was having an affair with one of the junior partners in the law farm where he worked. Sarah Robertson was a beautiful woman, with long black hair and ivory skin that needed little makeup. She'd joined the firm long after Ted had worked his way up in the firm until he was one of three partners. It had been a long, hard climb for the both of us. Ted was proud of his accomplishments and always needed to be complimented for them.

Ted and I met when we were in college. He was a jock and I fell madly in love with him when I first saw him. He was surrounded by pretty girls and barely noticed me. But I stayed close and eventually he asked me out. It's not that I wasn't pretty, I just wasn't among the popular crowd. But I stuck it out and he finally asked me to marry him. I was ecstatic. I walked down the aisle on a cloud and started my marriage with the fantasy that we would live happily ever after. It was a shock when I realized I was wrong.

We had a rocky road in the beginning, because Ted was going to school and trying to earn a living working for a law firm. He wanted his own firm. He wanted to be in charge, but it never happened. Eventually after graduation he had to join another firm. He took a lot of his frustration out on me, but I understood. I worked hard to help pay the bills and keep him from worrying. Our sex life was wonderful and we both expected me to get pregnant as soon as we stopped using protection. But it wasn't to be. He was sure it was my fault because he was such a big, handsome man. He worked out regularly and had the muscles to prove it. Even now there was no sign of a bulge in his stomach. He was still as hard and flat as he had been in college.

When I found out about Sarah Robertson, I was sure I was going to die. How could he cheat on me? I'd always been a loving wife, doing everything in my power to make him happy. The only person in my life was my mother. She was a wonderful woman whose only goal in life after my father's death was to make sure me and my younger brother got an education and were happy with our decisions. She was totally supportive of me, even when I couldn't get pregnant during our first chaotic years.

"Having a baby won't fix your marriage," she told me on a few occasions. "You have to love and respect each other before the marriage can be fixed. Having an affair is not the way to promote love and respect."

"He said he was sorry, Mom, and now that we're having a child he realizes it was wrong. I've forgiven him and things are wonderful between us."

And that was true. Ted began coming home every night on time. He was loving and tender, insisting I quit my job when I began to get big. "Don't want anything to happen to the little guy," he'd smile, patting me on my stomach. My delivery was hard and he was there through every minute of it—holding my hand, coaxing me to be strong, and then telling me how brave I was after it was over. He was so proud of Teddy that I thought I'd burst with pride. He was healthy, happy, and cried very little when we brought him home.

Ted couldn't wait to get home after work to play with him. He didn't mind changing him, fixing his bottles, and getting up in the night when it was necessary. Any little sniffle or cough threw him into a tizzy, and he would yell at me to get him to a doctor to make sure it was nothing serious. I though he was a little paranoid, but it was sweet, too. The baby had a wonderful disposition and his presence truly made our house a home.

On this gray, dreary morning I was glad I didn't have to get outside. I'd spend the whole day playing with my son and cleaning house. I knew I would probably have to go back to work one day, but right now I was grateful to be indoors with my darling Teddy.

"Come on, sweetie," I said, picking him up out of his high chair and taking him to his room to give him a bath and put on clean clothes. It was such a joy to bathe him. He loved the water and we always had a good time. I felt a little sad when I thought I might not get to do this when he was too old for me to come into the bathroom with him. Sooner or later I was going to have to go back to work and leave him with a baby sitter. Ted had hinted as much but realized the longer I could stay home with him, the better off we all were.

Later he played in the den while I cleaned up the kitchen and fixed us some lunch. I sang as I worked. After that we played his favorite game about the little tea pot. We would sing it together and he would stand there on his sturdy little legs with one hand on his hip and the other hand a spout. Afterwards, he would fall on the floor laughing. He was such a joy. How can one person be so happy? I thought to myself.

It was still raining after we ate lunch and I was preparing to put Teddy down for a nap when the phone rang. Probably Mom, I thought. She usually calls to say hello and sometimes drops by for a visit.

"Hi, honey," Ted said when I picked up the phone. "I got a little problem. Do you think you could help me out?"

"Sure," I said. "What do you need?"

"I need you to go in my office and look on my desk. There should be a file folder there with name Judson on it. Go see while I hold."

I laid down the phone and went into the small room Ted had turned into an office. Sure enough, the file lay on the desk.

"It's here," I said, picking up the extension.

"I need it," he said. "Could you bring it down to the office? Park around back and come in that way. You won't have so far to walk in this weather."

"It's raining, Ted," I said, dreading going out in it.

"I know," he said regretfully. "But I really need that file this afternoon. The client will be here in an hour and I can't leave the office and I don't have anyone to send for it. I hate like the devil to ask you to do it, but I need it."

"Okay," I said. "I'll get us some rain gear and we'll be there soon."

"Be sure and wrap the baby up good," he said. "Don't want him catching anything."

"I'll do that," I said, then hung up.

It was a terrible day. Lights were on all over town to dispel the gloom of the rain and fog. I was glad we had a garage so we wouldn't have to go out in it, but when I pulled into the parking lot behind the offices, it seemed to be raining even harder. I turned to take Teddy out of his car seat, and then hesitated. How could I carry him and the folder without it getting wet? And why should I take Teddy with me? He was safe and dry here in the car. It was only a few steps to the door and then down the hallway to Ted's office. "I'm going to leave you here, sweetie," I told him, as his arms reached for me. I leaned over and kissed him on his chubby cheek and reassured him I'd be right back. Looking carefully at the parking lot, all I saw in the rain were empty cars and dim street lights. I shoved the file folder up under my raincoat. Taking the keys, I locked the car door behind me and dashed for the door. It opened under my hand and I breathed a sigh of relief. I raced down the hallway to Ted's office and pushed the door open. His secretary was on the phone and smiled at me. "Just a moment," she said, placing her hand over the mouth piece.

I lay the folder on her desk and told her to give it to Ted. "Just a moment," she said. "He wants to see you."

"I can't stay," I told her. "I left the baby in the car."

Annoyed, she told the person on the phone to hold and went into Ted's office, shutting the door behind her. Anxiety made me nervous and I picked up the file folder and started toward Ted's office. His secretary came out. "He'll be with you in a moment," she said, picking up the phone.

"Wait?" I told her. "I can't wait. The baby is in the car by himself. I can't wait."

Just as I turned to go, Ted strode out the door. "Hi, honey," he said, kissing me on the cheek. "Thank you so much for bringing the folder down. It was really important or I wouldn't have asked." His hands were on my shoulders and he was looking at me with such love and appreciation. I felt guilty about wanting to get away so soon.

"That's okay," I said. "I left the baby in the car by himself. I have to get back."

He frowned. "You locked the doors, didn't you?"

"Of course," I said, pulling away and starting toward the door.

"Kiss him for me," Ted called, lifting a hand.

I hurried to the car and stuck my key in the lock, but it was not locked. Jerking the door open, I peered inside. The car was empty! Even the car seat was gone. I couldn't believe it. I crawled in and looked in the backseat and on the floor board of the front seat. He wasn't there! I jumped out of the car and ran around the parking lot, calling his name. Everything was silent, with only the sound of the rain dripping off the trees. My stomach churned and fear ripped through me. Where was my baby?

I raced back into the building and down the hallway. I ran past the secretary and into Ted's office. He was on the phone.

"Teddy's gone!" I screamed. "Somebody took him out of the car."

He said something into the phone and hung up. "What the hell are you screaming about?"

"Teddy's gone. Somebody took him out of the car."

He came around the desk and took me by the arms. "How could that be? You said you locked the car."

"I did. I did." I sobbed. "But somebody came and took him."

"How could they take him if you locked the car? You're the only one with a key to that car."

"I don't know." I cried. "But we have to do something. He's gone. He isn't there anymore. I left him in his car seat and I locked the doors."

"If you'd locked the car doors, he'd still be there."

"Please call the police so they can help find him," I said desperately. "Please get somebody to help us find him."

"I'll go look," he said, pushing me into a chair. "Knowing you, you might've looked in the wrong car." He strode out the door and slammed it shut.

I sat in the chair, staring straight ahead, hoping to God he was right.

Hoping beyond reason that I somehow missed him.

Ted was back in a moment. "He's not there. I'll call the police."

After that everything was a blur. The police came and questioned me. I felt so guilty and there was no way I could explain why I'd left him in the car all alone. What seemed so sane at the time now seemed like something a crazy woman would do. Ted kept asking me why I'd left him in the car with the doors unlocked, and no matter how much I protested, nobody believed me. After a while I began to doubt my own sanity. I knew I locked the doors, but the more I protested the more nobody seemed to hear me.

The night dragged on, but there was no sign of a little boy in a rain coat. The police finally convinced me I should go home. Ted said he'd stay at the police station in case anything happened.

I called my mother and she met me at the house. Taking me in her arms, she led me to the couch. "I did lock the doors, Mama," I kept repeating. "I know I locked the doors. I wasn't gone but a few minutes. How could he get out of the car so quickly?"

"Somebody took him, darling," she said. "Somebody stole him in the few minutes you were gone."

She tried go get me to go to bed but I couldn't. I was waiting for the phone to ring and someone would tell me they'd found my baby. "Come on, Angela," she begged. "You've got to get some rest. When they find him, they'll let us know. Now come sit down."

"I can't, Mama." I cried. "He's out there somewhere, maybe in the rain and cold. Why didn't I take him in with me? It was so cold and I was only going to be a minute." I answered my own question but I knew it wasn't good enough. I was responsible for my baby being stolen.

Ted came home at dawn. His face was drawn and tired. He just shook his head and brushed past me as I tried to talk to him. I heard him in the shower and knew he'd talk to me after that. But he didn't. In fact, he never talked directly to me after that horrible day. He told me he didn't blame me, but I knew by the way he treated me that he did. I was solely responsible for our son's kidnapping.

The word came over the radio and on the local television the next day. The reporters came to the house but I couldn't talk to them. The phone rang with people who had harsh questions until I quit answering it. How could they think I would ever deliberately do anything to harm my child? They wanted to know if I'd killed him and hid his body somewhere to get rid of him. The horror of such a thought drove me to take to my bed, a pillow over my face. The horror of it all was more than I could bear.

Everybody used everything at their disposal to find Teddy, but there was never a trace of him. We did everything we could personally—posters, interviews, but it was all for nothing. There were no leads. Nobody had seen anything. It was if he disappeared off the face of the earth.

Weeks passed and I kept hoping, but other people went back to their own lives. Ted went back to work and I was left all alone in an empty house with a baby's room that had no baby. I felt as if someone had reached into my soul and turned off the light.

Six months passed, and Ted hardly spoke to me when he did came home. He usually didn't come home for dinner and Saturdays were spent at the office, Sundays at the golf course. He looked right through me if I insisted that we talk.

"He blames me," I told Mama on one of my many trips to her house. "I don't blame him, but doesn't he know I love Teddy as much as he does? I wish he would talk to me about it. Accuse me or something."

"Ted has always been a bit self-absorbed," my mother said. "He feels that this was done personally to him. He doesn't have room in his heart for forgiveness. I hope he changes, but I doubt it. You're going to have to learn to deal with this on your own."

"I can't deal with it at all," I told her, tears springing to my eyes. "I spend hours in his room just remembering him as he used to be. I know he's changing, wherever he is. Getting older with somebody else shaping his personality. Oh, Mama, how I pray that whoever has him is taking good care of him! I can't even think that he might be dead."

"I know, dear," she said, cradling me in her arms like I was six years old again. "I wish I could tell you something different than the authorities have told you, but I can't. It just doesn't make any sense that someone would take him without leaving a clue, but that's what happened. I think you should think about finding a job. Something to occupy your mind. I know you will never forget him, or quit looking for him, but a job would help with the time. There is an opening down at the children's center."

"I couldn't!" I cried through a fresh batch of tears. I couldn't work with children. It would hurt too much. Every little boy around three made my heart pound and my palms wet. After staring at them a few minutes, my eyes would fill with tears and I would turn away.

But the more I thought about the job at the center, the more I thought I might go. I wasn't accomplishing anything laying around the house except feeling sorry for myself, so I went by the center to talk to the director.

She knew who I was and encouraged me to come in and help out a few days and if I could do it, maybe it would be healing for me. I didn't think so, but I decided to give it a try.

A year to the day when Teddy was taken, I went to work in the children's center. When I told Ted, he just stared at me. "Do whatever you like," he said coldly. He'd moved his things into the guest room and we didn't sleep together anymore.

"Give him some time," everybody said. "He's had a terrible shock. He'll come around."

But our home life never changed. I worked all day, laid awake most every night thinking of Teddy and where he might be. I automatically kept the house clean, including his room. I did the washing, shopping, and cooking, but Ted never seemed to notice. He just took it for granted that he'd have clean clothes and something in the refrigerator to eat whenever he did decide to come home.

The job at the center was the only thing that kept me sane. I was put in charge of the babies under one. I could hold them and love them all I wanted. They didn't mind like the older ones did. We cared for children from three months to twelve years. Those going to school were brought to the center after school for the parents to pick up. We had a strict check-in, check-out program to keep the kids safe. Each worker eventually was expected to care for every age at one time or the other. By the time I graduated to the ten year olds I was able to handle it.

Another year passed and things at home hadn't changed. I'd lost so much weight that my clothes just hung on me and I hadn't been to a beauty shop in years, so it didn't come as any great surprise to me when Ted came home one afternoon and told me he wanted a divorce.

"We have nothing left," he said.

"You mean all we had was Teddy?" I asked, willing him to look at me.

He didn't have to think about it. "That's right," he said. "All we had was Teddy, and you took that away from me."

"He got taken away from me, too!" I cried. "Don't you think I miss him as much as you?"

"No," he said coldly. "Or you wouldn't have left him alone in the car."

I started to protest, but I could tell by the look on his face that nothing I said could penetrate that wall he'd erected between us.

"I'll move into an apartment and leave the house for you. I'll finish paying it off but after that, it's your responsibility. I'm not going to pay you any alimony because you have a job. My lawyer will get the papers to you in a few days."

He stalked from the room, leaving me in shock. I sat down at the kitchen table, putting my head in my hands. I cried. I cried for Teddy and Ted's inability to understand and forgive me. Perhaps Mom was right. There was no forgiveness in him.

I sat and waited until after he packed his bags and left. The house was empty, but it had been empty since Teddy was kidnapped. I picked up the phone and called Mom.

"I'll be right there," she said.

She sat beside me as we talked. I poured out all my hurt and frustration to her. Toward morning, she put me to bed and crawled in beside me. I thanked God that I had a mother who loved me and believed me when I said I had locked the car before I left him that day.

The next morning while we were drinking coffee, she asked me what I thought about Ted refusing to pay me alimony. "Your job doesn't pay enough to really support you, does it?"

"No," I told her. "But I guess I can find a better job or get a second job."

"Why?" she asked. "Ted makes good money. There's no reason in the world why he shouldn't pay alimony. I have a friend who's a lawyer. Let me talk to her. Let's see what she thinks."

I wanted to object, because I felt in my heart I'd let Ted down when I'd allowed Teddy to be kidnapped. I could understand why he hated me. But the reality was that Mom was right. My salary would not cover the household expense. My car was over three years old and was already beginning to require repairs.

Mom's friend was named Joyce Rubin, and she was appalled that I would let Ted get away with not paying alimony. "Let me handle this," she said. "Bring the papers by when his lawyer sends them to you. After that, leave everything to me."

Needless to say, Ted was infuriated when he heard from Joyce. He stormed in the door, his face red and his eyes blazing. "What the hell do you think you're doing?" he yelled. "We agreed that you would keep the house and I wouldn't pay you any alimony."

I just stared at him. I was finally getting a good look at the man I married. His clothes were smart and the latest fashion. He wore a flashy watch and a big diamond on his little finger. He'd driven up in what looked like a little foreign car. And he wanted to leave me destitute.

"My lawyer told me not to talk to you," I said as calmly as I could.

"I don't give a hoot what your lawyer said," he sneered. "This is between me and you. First you take my son away and now you want to take half of everything I have."

"I never took your son," I said. "He was kidnapped. I loved him as much as you did."

"How could you?" he scoffed. "If that was true you would've brought him in that day instead of leaving him in an unlocked car."

"The car was locked!" I screamed. "I don't care what you say, the car was locked."

"Like hell," he shouted. "If the car was locked, how did the kidnapper get in?"

"I don't know," I whispered. "I just know that I locked the car."

I had lived and relived that moment over in my mind a million times. I remembered very clearly pushing the lever that locked all four doors. I could still hear the click. I remember checking the door by trying to open it as had become my habit since I'd started driving.

"Well, be that as it may," he said coldly. "You lost him."

I opened my mouth to protest and knew instinctively that it would do no good. He was convinced that it was all my fault that Teddy was taken. I felt weak and sick.

"Now about this lawyer you got. I want you to call her tomorrow and tell her to get the hell off this case. We can settle this like civilized people."

I stared at him. This man who had been my husband for almost eleven years was a total stranger. My mother was right. He had no compassion. He took no responsibility for Teddy. I could have argued that if he hadn't asked me to come to his office on that awful day, we would still have Teddy. But I knew that was useless. He had decided from the start that it was my fault and he was never going to let me forget it.

"Well," he demanded. "Are you going to call her or not?"

"No," I said. "You call her, or better still, have your lawyer call her. She says I am entitled to half of whatever we've accumulated during our marriage."

His face turned red and he took a step forward as if he was going to strike me. Then, clenching his fists, he shouted, "first you take my son and now you want to take everything else. Well, we'll see about that."

He turned and stalked out of the house.

I was shaking so bad I couldn't stand. Dropping into a kitchen chair, I put my head in my hands and sobbed wildly. I called Mom when I'd calmed down and she came right over.

"We've got to stop him from coming in and out any time he feels like it," she said. "Tomorrow we'll have the locks changed. Then we'll let Joyce handle it from there."

In the end, Ted wanted a divorce from me so badly that he gave Joyce most of the things she asked for. I got the house and an allowance to maintain it. I also got a small amount of alimony, and half of the bonds he'd bought in the past two years without telling me about it.

Six months after the divorce was final, I heard from his firm that he had left town. "Your allowance will still come through this office," the senior partner told me. "He just didn't want you to know where he was living now." He looked embarrassed when he told me and I knew he hadn't approved of the way my ex-husband had handled things, but he couldn't tell me that.

The next years were predictable, I guess. If anyone should ever tell you that you get over the kidnapping of a child, tell them they are wrong. There were times when I thought I might go crazy, and without the help of my mother and friends, I might have. You never forget the feel of your child in your arms, or the feel of the warm, little arms around your neck. Everybody handles it differently, I guess. I kept loving him and wanting him back.

The job at the center went well and I was forever grateful to my mother and the director for letting me care for these children. The director, Carol Price, was a wonderful woman. I learned so much working with her and when she decided to retire, she recommended me to take over her job.

"If anybody deserves this position, you do," she told me. "I've never seen a more caring person than you. The stockholders will be here next week to talk with you, but I think they will take my recommendation."

In the end, only one board member came. His name was Mark Wallace and I liked him immediately. He was tall, with brown hair that was beginning to gray at the temples, a ready smile and warm, smiling brown eyes.

"You come highly recommended," he said, shaking hands with me. "The board members have been very pleased with Carol's work and believe she has a feel for the type of person we need for this job. As you know, we've grown steadily over the years and will probably continue to do so. We would like your recommendations as to how we can improve the center if we all agree that you are the new director."

"I am flattered, of course, for the honor, but I'm not sure I'm the right person for the job. I've never worked in such a capacity before. I know that handling employees takes a special touch, and Mrs. Price had that. She got along with her employees wonderfully."

"She assures me that you also get along with the employees." His eyes held mine and he smiled at me. "She also says she's never seen anyone who loves children as you do. She has told me of your personal loss and thinks you are one of the bravest women she's ever known. We've checked and we think you are right for the position. If you would like to think it over, that's fine. Take your time. I'll be in and out for the next few months helping with the transition."

We talked further and I called my mother after he left to ask her opinion. "Oh, darling," she said. "It sounds wonderful to me. You are a smart young lady. You just let Ted beat you down until you forgot that. This sounds like a wonderful opportunity. Think about it. Think of all the good you can do. You know how much help some of those children need."

She was right. Although the parents paid a good sum to leave their children at the center, there were always troubled children who needed our help, even though they came from well-to-do neighborhoods.

I was relieved from my duties and began to learn what Carol could teach me. Although I hadn't said definitely that I'd take the job, everyone assumed that I would. Mark stopped by periodically to see how we were doing. After two weeks, he brought a contract and asked me out to lunch.

"It'll give us a chance to discuss any questions you may have and get better acquainted."

Mrs. Price smiled and shooed us out of the office.

I learned that Mark Wallace's father had opened the center and that Mark was on the board because of that. His main job was as an architect, apparently a very successful one. He told me he had been married briefly.

"Just didn't work out," he said. "A few months after we married, she told me she was in love with someone else. She'd only married me to get even with him. Now he wanted her back and she wanted to go. I let her go, of course."

"That must have been awful," I said, remembering the hurt when I found out Ted was cheating on me with Sarah Robertson.

"It was something to get through, but I'd still like to fall in love again. I'd like a nice woman who would like to have a home and family."

"That doesn't sound like such a big task." I smiled. "There have to be a lot of women out there who would like that."

"You'd be surprised," he said. "Most women I meet want to have a career and not have babies." He laughed. "How about you? Have you found anybody since you and your husband split?"

"Actually, my husband left me. It was never a mutual decision. After Teddy was kidnapped, he never forgave me. He always blamed me and so we never had a marriage after that."

"I heard about your son," he said. "I seem to remember reading about it in the paper. Tell me about it."

At first I hesitated. I'd never discussed it with anyone in depth except my mother, but his eyes were so sympathetic and his smile was warm.

Beginning with Ted's call, I told him everything. He stopped me once in a while with a question, but mostly he just listened intently.

"I did lock the car," I repeated for the thousandth time. "I know I did. I remember it as if it was yesterday." And I was remembering. Tears rushed to my eyes and I brushed them away.

"I believe you," he said, taking my hand. "Why wouldn't you lock the door? After all, you were leaving your son in the car."

"Then how did the kidnapper get in the car?"

"Sounds like somebody else had a key. Sounds like it was a well-planned job. It couldn't have been an accident—someone coming along accidentally, and seeing the child, then taking him."

"But there were no extra keys to the car."

"Of course there were," he said seriously. "There are ways to get a set of car keys made."

"Everything was checked and nothing was found."

"I'm glad you told me," he said.

And I was glad I'd told him. He seemed to be the only one except my mother who truly believed I'd locked the car that day.

We ate lunch and chatted about the center. He assured me I wouldn't have any trouble taking over from Mrs. Price. "If anything comes up that you feel you can't handle, just call me."

I promised I would and we went back to the office.

The next few weeks were hectic as I learned the business and took over running the center. I hadn't known there was so much involved with running the big center until it became my responsibility, but I loved it. Mom said I bloomed under the challenge, but I realized it was the attention of Mark Wallace. He got into the habit of coming by around lunch and insisting I go to lunch with him. Of course I probably would've started dressing a little more professionally, but I found myself dressing with the idea that Mark might drop by that day.

I hadn't gone out with a man since Ted left. I hadn't had any interest in dating. Mom had talked about it a few times but I always brushed her off. I wasn't interested in men. I'd had my fill with Ted.

"But all men aren't like Ted," she said. "There're some great guys out there if you would only give them a chance."

"Sure." I'd laugh bitterly, the memory of my marriage fresh on my mind.

But as time passed, I realized she was right. Mark was nothing like Ted. Even when we were dating, Ted always had to do everything his way. At the time, I hadn't noticed. I was so much in love. I had to admit to myself that the way Ted treated me was my fault. I'd never stood up for myself, or demanded that he show me the respect I should've had as his wife. Well, my first love had let me down, but that was no reason to be sour on the whole male race. At least that's what I kept telling myself when I found myself thinking about Mark Wallace.

He was so kind and caring and listened to me as I talked about Teddy any time I felt like it. "I miss him so," I told him one afternoon as we sat talking in my office. "I just feel that some day I'll see him again."

I hope you do, Angela," he said kindly, and I began to cry.

I hadn't cried in a long time and I don't know why I was crying now.

Pulling me into his arms, he held me, patting me on the back.

"I'm sorry," I said, rubbing my eyes. "I don't know what made me do that."

"It's okay," he said, patting my shoulder again. "If anyone deserves to have a good cry, it's you."

How could you not love a man like that, I thought to myself as I got ready to go home that afternoon. Stopping dead in my tracks, I realized suddenly what I was thinking, and I had to admit I was in love with Mark Wallace. Oh, it wasn't anything like the love I'd had for Ted—the all-encompassing desire to make him happy. I'd always felt that was my mission in life.

With Mark I felt comfortable, able to discuss anything with him. I felt he was happy with himself and didn't need anybody to make him happy. Shrugging into my jacket, I walked through the empty center. All the children were gone and the staff had straightened up before they left in preparation for the rush on Monday morning. A rush of pleasure went through me as I thought how much I loved this place, and then a little sadness because Teddy would never know it.

Switching off the lights, I started for my car.

"Angela," I heard someone call. "Angela, it's Mark. I was coming back to see if you'd have dinner with me tonight. I guess I got here a little late."

"No, you didn't," I said tucking my hand under his arm. "I'd be pleased to have dinner with you." For the first time in a long time, I laughed.

His hand covered mine as he guided me to his car and helped me in. We chatted comfortably all the way to the restaurant and through dinner.

"I'm afraid I'm not dressed for a fancy restaurant like this," I commented as we entered.

"You look just fine to me," he said warmly, guiding me to a table. "I'd say you're the most beautiful woman here if someone asked me."

My heart beat a little faster and I felt a warm glow all over. "Thank you." I smiled up at him.

After dinner he drove me back to my car at the center. "It was a wonderful dinner," I told him, sitting in his car.

"I agree," he said, leaning across the car and kissing me on the lips. "Please say we'll do it again soon."

"Anytime you like," I replied.

And I knew there would be other times, so there was no haste to rush into anything. We still needed to do a lot of getting acquainted and assuring ourselves that this was what we both wanted.

Mark became a frequent visitor at my house and at my mom's. We were like old friends who had been away from each other for a long time. And it was such a pleasure getting to know each other. When Mark asked me to marry him, I agreed.

"There is just one thing," I told him, nestled in his arms. "I can't leave my house. If anybody should need to get in touch with me about Teddy, I need to be there."

"Of course," he said, his lips on mine.

I'd seen Mark's house and knew it was much bigger and finer than mine, but I also knew Mark. He didn't care where he lived as long as he was with me. The confidence I placed in Mark was amazing, but I never doubted it.

Teddy's birthday came and I realized with a shock that the crib in his room would no longer be appropriate for him. The little rocking chair would be too small for him now. I stared at it a long time, then stepped back and closed the door. Sadness overwhelmed me as it always did when I went into the room. I leaned against the wall and sobbed. Then the doorbell rang and there was Mark, arms opened wide. He remembered and he came.

Two weeks later on a Saturday, I was cleaning house, thinking about what I would wear on my date with Mark that night when the door bell rang. Opening the door, I saw a young woman with a worried look on her face. She kept glancing over her shoulder as if expecting someone to come after her.

"I'm Sarah Robertson," she said nervously. "Can I come in?"

"Sarah Robertson?"

"Yes, I'm Ted's wife. Used to be Sarah Robertson."

"You and Ted got married?" I asked stupidly. Nobody had told me that.

"Yes," she said pushing past me. "We got married right after he got divorced from you."

"Okay," I said, shutting the door and following her into the kitchen. "So you and Ted got married. What are you doing here?"

She stared at me with a puzzled look on her face. "You don't know, do you? You don't know that Ted is dead?"

I felt as if I'd had the breath knocked out of me. I had no feelings for Ted, but I had been married to him for a long time. I dropped down in to a chair and tried to get my feelings under control.

"Dead," I said. "He's dead."

"Yes," she said, sitting down on the couch across from me. "A disgruntled client shot him to death last week." She covered her face with her hands and began to cry.

I resisted the urge to cross to the couch and comfort her. Even though I knew she was hurting I couldn't forget that she had an affair with my husband while he was still married to me. And apparently it hadn't stopped there. I waited until she pulled herself together.

"I realize you must be upset about Ted," I told her. "I just don't see what it has to do with me."

"I have your son, Teddy," she blurted out. "Ted took him that day when you thought he was kidnapped." Her hands were still covering her face.

"Teddy?" I gasped. "You have Teddy? You've had him all this time?"

For a few minutes I couldn't breathe. I bent my head to my knees to try to stop the buzzing in my head. "Why do you have him?" I asked stupidly.

"Because he lived with us and when Ted died, I didn't know what to do with him. I started to put him in an orphanage, but realized there would be a lot of questions. I can't keep him, you see. I'm not very good with kids, but Ted thought he couldn't live without the boy, and I loved him so much I would have done anything he asked."

She sounded as if she was far away. I felt like I was in some sort of nightmare. Teddy was alive and in this woman's care. I clasped my trembling hands together and sucked in my breath. I had to make her tell me where he was.

"Where is he now?"

"He's in a safe place," she said, wiping her eyes with a tissue.

Rage surged through my body. Ted had taken my baby and pretended he was kidnapped. How could he have done such a thing?

"How could he?" I heard myself whimpering. "How could he do such a thing?"

"He wanted a son more than anything in life, and that included me or you. He planned the kidnapping and told me if I didn't help him, he'd never speak to me again."

"And you agreed?" I gasped.

"I loved him, and he told me you didn't love the boy. You just wanted to get even with him because he fell in love with me. I realized later that it wasn't true, but it was too late to do anything about it. Then when he was killed, I decided to give the boy back to you if you wanted him."

"Wanted him?" I almost screamed, rising from my chair and going toward her.

"Wait," she said, scrambling from the couch and running across the room. "If you hurt me or tell anybody about my being here, I'll take the boy and move to England. I have a job offer over there and I'm taking it. Now if you want the boy back, sit down and let's discuss this in a civilized manner."

Fear tore through me and I dropped back into my chair. "I'll do anything you ask to get my baby back," I promised, meaning every word.

"You'll have to promise not to tell anyone I was here or that I was mixed up in the kidnapping in any way. You'll have to go back with me now to get him and you can't make any phone calls. Just pack a bag and come with me."

"Yes," I said. "I'll do anything you say." It crossed my mind at that moment that this might be a big hoax initiated by Ted. I couldn't imagine the reason, but I had to be sure. "First, could you show me some proof that Ted is dead and that you really have Teddy?"

"Yes," she said, opening her purse. "Here's the death notice in the paper and the newspaper article the day it happened. And here are some pictures of Teddy and Ted together." She handed the papers and pictures across to me.

My hands shook and my heart pounded. Could it be true? Was I close to seeing my son again? I read the notices slowly and they seemed legitimate. Then I looked at the pictures of a little boy smiling into the camera. He did look like his father. He looked healthy and happy. I stared at him, holding my breath. It was him. I knew it was him. I thought for a moment I was going to have a heart attack and die right there. My second thought was, I have to tell Mark. Then I had to tell Mama, then I had to tell the whole world that my son was alive and I was looking at his picture.

I was on my feet, heading for the phone.

"No!" she said. "No. We can only do this if you don't tell anybody else. If you make a phone call you will never get Teddy back."

Her words halted me in my tracks and I returned to my chair. Nothing was going to keep me from my son. I knew I'd do anything she asked.

"Sorry," I said. "I was so excited. I wanted to tell my fiancé and my mother."

"So," she said, perhaps with a little irritation. "You're engaged to be married. How nice. How do you think he will feel about taking on a troubled boy for a son?"

"Troubled," I said quickly. "You said troubled. Is there something wrong?"

"Well, his father was shot. Of course he's upset. Wouldn't you be?"

"Yes," I said, but I still didn't like the word. "Was he okay until the shooting?"

"Okay?" she questioned. "He loved his daddy. Sometimes I thought Ted was a little hard on him but he wasn't my responsibility, so I didn't say anything."

"Does he think you're his mother?" My heart hurt but I had to know.

"Yes, I guess so," she said, turning away. "But it wasn't my idea. Ted insisted he call me Mama."

We both sat in silence for a long time, thinking our own thoughts. I don't know what she was thinking, but I thought of a little boy torn from his mother's arms and thrust into such a frightening situation. White-hot rage tore through me as I thought again about what Ted had done.

"Who took the baby out of my car?" I asked. "And how did they get in? I know I locked the doors."

"Ted really wanted his son, and wanted to make sure everything ran smoothly. He had two plans. If you brought the baby in with you, he was going to put on a ski mask and attack you from behind in the lobby. While you were caught off-guard, he'd grab the baby and run to my car so I could make my get-away.

The second plan of action was the one that actually happened. You left the baby in the car. Ted took the baby, using a key he'd had made months before. He brought the baby around the building and put him in my car. I left immediately for Maryland, where I'd set up residence earlier, telling everyone my husband and baby were coming later."

"How could Ted have done it? He was in his office."

"No, he was waiting outside to take the baby as soon as you went in the door. He got each of us cell phones, and it was up to me to call him and tell him which plan of action we were using. I had to drive, and didn't want to be under that much pressure, but I'd do anything for Ted. I loved him that much. The secretary stalled you until he could get back inside through a secret door that he'd found a long time ago."

"You mean the secretary was in on it, too?" I was horrified at the thought.

"Of course not," she said. "He just told her to keep you out front until he buzzed because he was on the phone. He took the phone off the hook so she would think he was really on the phone."

My fury made my whole body shake and I wanted to claw her eyes out, call the police, and have her put in jail for the rest of her life, but I knew I couldn't if I wanted my baby back.

"Now," she said, getting up. "If you want to get the boy, we have to leave right now. If not, I'll go back and get him and adopt him out to someone who wants him."

"I want him," I said desperately. "Let me get a jacket and my purse."

"I'll go with you," she said following me down the hall.

"Shall I follow you in my car?"

"No," she said. "We'll go in mine. I won't be needing it after today. You can bring it back with you."

I hated her for her coldness and cruelty in the kidnapping of my son, but I had to do it her way.

I followed her out to her car and we drove out of town and headed south. We drove twelve hours, stopping only for gas and food. She went to the bathroom with me and we ate our food in the car. If she got sleepy, she never acted like she was. We didn't talk much and she didn't want to answer any questions about the baby. It was as if she'd answered all the questions she was going to and just wanted to get this over as soon as possible.

We finally stopped at a small white house in Baltimore. I knew the airport was close by because I could hear the roar of planes overhead.

"He's in there," she said. She got out of the car quickly and headed toward the front door. She'd rung the bell and the door opened before I got there. My knees were weak and I couldn't get my breath. Was I really going to get to see my son after all these years?

Then I heard Sarah call his name and him answer. I stepped through the door and stared at the little boy running toward her.

"Mama," he said. "I didn't think you were coming back." He grabbed on to her hand as she held it out to him.

"Teddy," she said. "This is your aunt Angela. She's a friend of mine and I want you to go stay with her for a little while. Angela, this is Teddy." Her eyes warned me not to make a fuss.

Using all my willpower, I held out my hand. "Hello, Teddy."

He looked at her then back at me. There was a questioning look on his face. "I don't want to go with her." Two big tears rolled down his cheeks. "I want my daddy."

"Well, you know good and well you can't have your daddy. I told you that a bad man killed him." She turned to speak to the woman who apparently had been keeping Teddy. "Do you have his clothes ready?"

The woman nodded and turned back into another room.

I stared at my son. My arms ached to reach out to him, but I knew that would have to wait. He threw himself on the couch and sobbed quietly.

Sarah did have the grace to cross to the couch and sat down by him. "You know, Teddy, your daddy would want you to be a big boy. Now try to be a big boy for him. He's gone and Mama has to go on a long trip. Aunt Angela is a very nice woman and she'll take good care of you. Now stop crying and say hello to your aunt Angela."

The little boy sat up and rubbed his hand across his eyes. "Why can't I go with you?" he asked.

"Because I won't have time to look after you and there is no place for kids where I'm going."

"I promise I won't be any trouble," he said, trying hard to stop the tears.

"Stop it, Teddy," she said impatiently. "I told you, you can't go and that's that."

The other woman came in to the room carrying two suitcases and a battered teddy bear. She averted her eyes and sat the cases down by the door. She handed the bear to Teddy.

"Come on," Sarah said. "Let's get you out to the car. You can sit in the front seat with her and I'll sit in the back. You're dropping me off at the airport on your way out of town."

My heart was breaking all over again as I watched the boy follow her to the door. She pushed him through and headed him out to the car. She looked at her watch impatiently. I realized she'd timed this visit almost to the minute so she wouldn't be caught at the airport if I should decide to call the police.

I followed my son out to the car and watched as Sarah tucked the seat belt around him. She handed me the keys as she got in the back seat. "Go to the next street and turn left."

She gave directions all the way to the airport. Taking the keys from me, she opened the trunk and gave the man her suitcases. She hurried after him and quickly checked her ticket. For a moment I thought she was going to leave us without the keys to the car. But she hurried back out of the airport. Opening the door on Teddy's side, she gave him a peck on the cheek and handed me the keys. "Don't do anything you'll regret," she said under her breath, handing me an envelope. "This is in case the police should have any questions. I don't want them to blame me for what happened."

The paper crackled as I stuck it in to my purse. She stared a me a long moment, then turned away.

"Be a good boy," she told Teddy, patting him on the shoulder. He looked after her almost in terror as she walked quickly into the airport and disappeared.

Starting the engine, I pulled away from the curb. I felt as if a miracle had just taken place. I was sitting in the car beside my son.

"Teddy," I said gently. "Would you like to stop and get something to eat? Are you hungry?"

"No," he said with a catch in his voice. "I just want my daddy to come back."

"I wish he could, too, sweetheart," I told him. "I am so sorry that he had to leave you. I know you miss him terribly and I'll do everything I can to help you through it. If you feel like crying, please do so. It's only natural that someone should cry when they lost their father."

Suddenly, without warning, he began to cry. I pulled into a lighted service station area, and turned off the car. I moved to his side of the car, loosened his seat belt, and pulled him into my arms. He slumped against me and my arms held him close as he sobbed out his hurt. Tears overflowed my own eyes and I cried with him.

I don't know how long we sat there, but gradually his tears ceased and he pulled away. "I hope you don't think I'm a crybaby," he said, sounding very grown up. He fastened his seat belt and looked straight ahead.

"Of course I don't think you're a crybaby. There are times when all of us cry, even grown men. It's a healing for us to cry."

"My daddy never cried," he stated bluntly.

I eased over on my side and drove out of the parking lot. I had to stop and ask directions to get back on the highway but we were soon there. "If you need to go to the bathroom or want something to eat, just tell me," I said, looking sideways at him.

My heart pumped and my hands tightened on the steering wheel. He was such a wonderful looking boy, although his eyes were so sad. Soon his eyes drooped and his head lolled over and he was asleep. I wanted to stop and put him in the backseat, but I was afraid he wouldn't like that.

I drove for two hours and was just beginning to get very tired when Teddy woke up and rubbed his eyes. He looked startled when he saw me.

"Did you have a good rest?" I asked gently, smiling at him.

His face remained solemn and he just shook his head.

"We're going to need to stop soon and find a place to sleep," I told him. "I'm getting hungry, too. Are you?"

"Yes," he said. "And I think I need to go to the bathroom."

We stopped at a motel. He followed me into the lobby and held my hand as we crossed over to the desk. "We'll check in and use the bathroom, then see about what suitcases we need to bring in. How's that?"

He looked up at me in surprise. "Okay," he said and I knew he wasn't used to being asked his opinion about adult things. The room was nice, with two beds. He walked around looking at everything and then went to the bathroom. "Do you need any help?" I called.

He finished and came out and washed hands. "I've been going to the bathroom by myself since I started to school," he told me.

I was exhausted, but even after getting something to eat and going to bed, I could not go to sleep. I lay looking at the child asleep in the other bed. I was in awe that this little human being was all my responsibility now. Love overwhelmed me and it was all I could do to keep from crossing over and cuddling him in my arms. He looked so young and vulnerable. I finally slept toward morning and woke to feel the child beside me. His eyes were open and looking at me.

"Is it time to get up yet?" he asked.

I lay still, feeling his warm body close to mine. I didn't want to move, but I knew he needed an answer.

"I think so," I said smiling at him. "Are you hungry? You didn't eat much last night."

"A little hungry," he admitted solemnly, as if it was a question he'd thought a lot about.

"Okay," I said, throwing the covers back. "Do you shower in the morning or afternoon?"

"Morning." He said a slight grin on his face.

"Do you need my help or can you do it by yourself?"

"If you turn the shower on, I can do it."

We showered and dressed and found a pancake place. He solemnly ordered pancakes and sat back waiting for me. "Bring me the same thing," I said and he smiled.

I kept wondering when I could call Mark but I didn't want to talk in front of Teddy, so we traveled most of the day, getting in late in the afternoon. There were four messages on the answering machine. I listened to Mom, Mark, and the assistant at the center asking me to call.

"Why don't you go down the hall to the room on the right and get settled in," I told Teddy, "while I call my job and tell them I won't be in tomorrow, either."

"You don't have to stay home with me," he said. "I can stay here and watch television."

"I don't think so," I said, showing him to the guest room. "We'll have to get you registered in school soon. We don't want you to get behind."

"Will my mama be gone that long?" he asked, his head to one side.

"I imagine so," I said, trying to sound casual. For a minute I thought he was going to cry, but he straightened his shoulders and asked about the bathroom.

I grabbed the phone as soon as I heard the door close. Mark answered on the second ring.

"Mark," I said. "This is Angela. I found Teddy. I brought him home with me. He's here now."

"Angela," he said. "I was worried about you. Where did you go and what about Teddy?"

"I can't talk now."

"I'll come right over," he said.

"No," I told him. "He's scared and doesn't know what's happening. I have to spend some time with him by myself. He doesn't remember me as his mother. Please tell my mother. I have to go now. I'll talk to you later. I love you."

I heard Teddy come out of the bathroom as I hung up the phone.

"Let's get your suitcases and settle you in your room and then we'll see about something to eat."

He helped me carry in the cases and opened them. Putting his things away, I had to struggle to keep from wrapping my arms around him and telling him how much I loved him. But I knew I couldn't do anything to scare him.

He helped me in the kitchen, staying close when I asked him if he'd rather watch television. "I guess not," he said, sounding so serious.

Is he always this serious, I wondered, or is it because his father's dead.

I helped him in to his pajamas and tucked him into bed. "Would you like me to read you a story?" I asked.

"I'm almost too big to have stories read to me," he said. "My dad used to read to me, but he stopped when I got too old."

"Well, this is a special time," I said, rummaging in the bookcase in the den for a book of fairy tales. I made a mental note to get something for his age the first chance I got.

"Okay," he said, moving over to make room on the bed.

"Oh, by the way," I said as casually as I could. "My room is just down the hall. I'll leave a night light on and if you get cold, come and get in bed with me."

He opened his mouth to say something, his eyes traveling around the strange room and out into the hall.

"Okay," he said in a small voice, and my heart broke all over again.

Sometime in the night I woke to find him curled up on the foot of my bed. Gathering him in my arms, I tucked him in beside me, my heart overflowing with love.

We spent the next day getting acquainted. He told me the things he liked to eat and the things he liked to play with and that he liked school okay, but he needed somebody to help him with his homework. I told him what I did for a living and asked if he'd like to go down to the center and meet all the kids.

"Are they kids to play with?" he asked.

"Yes," I told him. "You can play with them before school and after school, and we might even invite some of them over some time."

"They'd probably make a mess," he said, his eyes looking sad again.

"Well, messes can be cleaned up," I said cheerfully. He just stared at me skeptically. Apparently, he hadn't been allowed to make messes.

It was a wonderful day for me and he seemed to enjoy it, too.

The next morning I took him to work with me and he was fascinated by all the other children. He ran around them and then backed off as if he didn't know what to do. After the other children had left for school, he played with their toys and talked to the younger children.

Mark came at ten o'clock. I rushed into his arms and told him how much I loved him and how much I'd wanted to tell him everything, but he understood when I explained everything.

"You'll have to call the police," he said. "They'll have to know he's been found."

"I know," I said, "but I don't want them questioning him. They must leave him alone."

"How about if I go down in person and tell them how it is?"

"Would you, Mark?" I said, hanging on to his hands. "The detective who handled the case was Brooks. I'm sure he'll understand."

In the end there was very little publicity and the police were very discreet when they realized the kidnapper was dead and his accomplice had skipped the country. Teddy looked for his mother to come back for him for almost six months and then it was like he gave up and accepted me as the one in his life now. He was a very curious little boy and asked many questions after he got used to Mom and Mark.

"Why don't you let me be your grandmother?" Mama asked him one day as he sat on her lap, reading her a story from one of his new books.

He thought about it for a minute and then agreed. "Don't you have any grandbabies of your own?" he asked. Sometimes he surprised us with how smart he was.

He wanted to know all about Mark and why he visited at the center so often.

"He's my boss," I explained, and then saw the doubt on his face. "And we're in love with each other. We want to get married one of these days. What would you think of Mark moving in here?"

"Where would he sleep?" I could see he was worried about Mark taking his room.

"In my bedroom, of course." I smiled reassuringly at him.

"Who is going to sleep in the room with the baby crib?" he asked.

My heart almost stopped and I panicked. Why hadn't I locked that door? I walked over to where he sat in front of the television. Dropping down in front of him, I took his hands in mine. "A long time ago I had a little baby."

"What happened to it?"

"It was a boy and somebody stole him from me."

He frowned and pursed his mouth. "Did someone want a baby, too? Is that why they took him?"

"Yes, dear," I told him. "I guess it's time to move the things out of the room and store them."

"But what if the people who stole him bring your baby back? Where would he sleep?"

"It's been a long time and I don't believe they're going to bring him back."

He looked so sad and then climbed up in my lap and hugged my neck. Tears poured down my face as I held him close and rocked us back and forth.

Soon he was looking forward to going to the center and then on to school. We had a little trouble explaining everything to the school and his teachers, but they decided to cooperate. If he wondered why my last name was the same as his, he never asked. I was his aunt Angela, becoming someone he could depend on.

Mark was at the center almost every afternoon and began dropping by the house. We often took Teddy out for pizza, which he loved. He would jump up and down on the seat and wait, wide-eyed, as the waitress brought the big pizza to our table.

Mark and I decided it was safe for us to get married now. Teddy loved him almost as much as he loved me. He was fascinated with every detail of the wedding. Mark asked him to be the ring bearer and he was so cute dressed in his tux and walking down the church aisle so solemn, so afraid he would make a mistake. I explained to him about the honeymoon and how he could stay with Mom while we went on a three-day honeymoon. His eyes grew round and scared.

"Don't worry, darling," I told him. "I'll call you every day and we'll be back Sunday night. Grandma will take good care of you, and I want you to take good care of her."

His lower lip quavered just a little, but he straightened his shoulders and took Mom by the hand. She squeezed his hand and assured him the days would pass fast and we'd be back before he knew it. I knew he was worried that he was going to lose someone else that he loved. Mark knelt down beside him and looked him in the eyes. "We'll be back, son, just like we promised."

He smiled and threw his arms around Mark's neck and my heart broke all over again.

We had a lovely time on our honeymoon. Mark was a wonderful lover. So kind and considerate, so aware of my needs and anxious to please me. I knew that this was the way it should be, not Ted's way. When Ted finished with me, he'd turn on his side and go to sleep. Mark cuddled me, telling me how much he loved and enjoyed me. I was deliriously happy. I had a man who loved me and my son was waiting for me at home.

Teddy threw himself into my arms when we returned. We immediately became a family. Mark was wonderful with Teddy and Teddy followed him around like a little puppy when he was home. I took him to the center every day and brought him home every night. Mark usually went in earlier than us and would greet us in the kitchen in a big white apron, waving a fork around which made Teddy giggle. We still left our bedroom door open in case he wanted to come see us at night. The nightmares soon stopped, and he stopped asking about his mother. He never came to our room any more except to roughhouse with Mark.

One afternoon he came into the center after school. I could tell there was something on his mind.

"Hi," he said, dropping down on the couch in my office.

"Hi, sweetie," I said. "Did you have a good day?"

"It was okay."

I realized there was something he wanted to discuss with me. I laid down my pen and closed the file I'd been working on.

"Something wrong?" I asked.

"The little baby that someone stole from you, was his name Teddy, too?"

My breath caught in my throat and I tried frantically to decide what to say. But one look at his face, I knew I couldn't lie to him. "Yes," I told him.

With a thoughtful look on his face, he got up and came around the desk. "Is it true that I'm that little boy?"

Terrified, I struggled to give just the right answer. Taking his hands in mine, I said, "yes, dear, that little boy was you."

"Then the room at our house used to be mine?"

"Yes, dear," I told him. "That room was yours."

He stared at me a long time. "Then you are really my mother?"

"Yes, dear," I said softly. "I am really your mother."

"Then it was my daddy who stole me from you. Why would he do that?"

"He loved you very much," I said, struggling to keep the bitterness out of my voice. "We were getting a divorce and he wanted you with him." His eyes grew big and I could tell that he was remembering something important to him.

"I'm a little tea pot, short and stout," he began to sing. His eyes grew wider and suddenly he was on my lap, his arms around my neck. Both of us began to cry. He'd remembered our little game from so long ago.

Mark found us that way, wrapped in each other's arms, crying our eyes out.

"What's the matter?" he asked, alarm in his voice.

"My mama got her little boy back," Teddy said solemnly. "My daddy stole me and took me away when I was real little. I remember I cried for my mama, but my daddy kept telling me Sarah was my mother. But she isn't. Aunt Angela is really my mother."

"Of course she is," Mark said, kneeling beside the chair and gathering us both in his arms, then the three of us cried again.

On the way home, Teddy kept up a running stream of conversation about what had happened at school that day, and how one of the bigger boys had told him that his aunt Angela had lost a little boy named Teddy.

At the house, he went to his room while I sat on the couch, trying to accept every thing.

"Mama," I heard Teddy say, and it was the sweetest sound I'd ever heard.

"Yes, dear?" I said.

"Do you think I could move back in my old room? I always liked it there."

"Yes, of course," I told him, my heart running over. "As soon as Mark comes home, we'll move everything in for you."

"Do you think I could keep the rocking chair?"

Unable to speak, I just nodded at him.

Three years after Teddy came home, Mark and I had a little girl. We named her Judy, after my mother. Teddy is so proud of her. He pushes her around in her stroller and lately he's been trying to teach her the little teapot song. He insisted that we move the crib back in the guest room for her. He's still not able to give up his old room, and we're more than happy to let him keep it.

THE END

EMPTY CRADLE
Will my needs destroy our love?

She walked over to me and asked, "Melanie? Are you okay? You look like you're in pain."

It was the second time that day that someone had asked me if I was in pain. I finished packaging Mrs. Durbin's box of chocolate-dipped strawberries. Another cramp hit me, and I bit my lip to keep from crying out. Summoning a smile, I said, "Just a little headache." It was a lie, but I didn't think it was appropriate to blurt out to one of my regular customers that my period cramps were about to bring me to my knees—even if it was a woman.

Somehow, I managed to take Mrs. Durbin's money, give her change, and flash her one last smile before I whispered in my employee's ear, "I'll be right back."

Somehow, I managed to take Mrs. Durbin's money, give her change, and flash her one last smile before I whispered in my employee's ear, "I'll be right back."

The stock room was my destination. It was a small, dark room, but it was cool and quiet. I sat on a stool we used to reach the top shelf and gripped my middle, moaning. Maybe I am having a miscarriage, I thought, tears pricking my eyes. David and I had been trying to get pregnant for over a year. So far, no luck.

I was over thirty, and my biological clock was ticking.

If only we hadn't waited so long to start trying, but I knew it was no use bemoaning that fact now. We had thought we had time.

Another cramp speared through my belly. I bit my lip. If I was having a miscarriage, then it wasn't the first because I'd been cramping like that for months.

I knew that I needed to go to the doctor, but I was one of those people that was terrified of finding out something was wrong. If I couldn't have children, then I wanted to put off dealing with the fact as long as I could.

The door opened slowly, slanting a bar of light where I sat. It was my employee, Rhea. She held a glass of water. In her other hand, she opened her palm to reveal two pain relief tablets. Rhea swore by them. Me, I hated taking any medicine, even the over-the-counter stuff.

But this time, I reached out without hesitation, grabbed the pills and water, and downed them in one grateful gulp.

"Pretty bad again?" Rhea asked sympathetically.

I nodded, still clutching my cramping stomach. "Just like the last three. Maybe worse."

Rhea, who methodically researched everything of interest on the web, said, "It's probably endometriosis. That's the common cause of severe cramps and bleeding. You should go to the doctor."

"I'll be all right," I said, silently willing her to leave me in peace. I'd already thought of the possibility, and it rated right up there with things I didn't want to know. I knew from my own research that if it was bad enough, it could cause infertility.

After a hesitant moment, Rhea left, pulling the door shut behind her. She was a good worker and a good friend. But I didn't want a friend at the moment.

I wanted the pain to stop.

And I wanted a baby. Then my life would be complete. I had a wonderful husband, a great career, and a modest, sweet little house in a good neighborhood. Sometimes, the near-perfection of my life scared me. Other times, I told myself that I deserved it after the childhood I'd had.

Then there were the dark times, when I wondered if God was punishing me for my past sins.

Giving into the stress-related urge to eat, I got up and used the step stool to retrieve my calorie-laden cookies I had stashed at the corner, top shelf. It was hidden with a package of containers. From the moment I started trying to get pregnant, I had mostly tried to eat more healthily.

Knowing Rhea would let me know if she got overwhelmed, I let my mind wander back to my childhood. Thinking about what I'd had to overcome to get where I was usually helped me to get back my focus.

The youngest of eight siblings, I grew up in a small, poor town in Arkansas. My daddy had been a seasonal farm worker, so the winters were always the hardest, when work was scarce. Mama, when she wasn't giving birth to yet another child, took in sewing and worked on the farm with Daddy chopping cotton, and later in the fall, picking over what the cotton-picking machines had left behind. The house we lived in belonged to the farmer. Even the old pickup Daddy drove belonged to the boss.

As the youngest, my earliest memory was of playing in the fields while my parents and older siblings worked. I'd take them water, and play in the shade until I was covered in dirt from head to toe.

I was eight when my oldest sister, Selena, got pregnant by some boy she'd been seeing at school. She'd been fourteen at the time, and I remember my daddy screaming and shouting and threatening to go after the boy responsible with his gun.

He hadn't carried out his threat, but my older brothers caught the boy out and beat him within an inch of his life. The sheriff came out to question my brothers, but Mom and Dad stood firm in their story that my brothers had been with them all evening, helping Daddy work on one of the farmer's broken cotton pickers. But I knew better. I'd seen Mama smearing grease on my brothers' clothes and face.

That night, pretending to be asleep in the bed I shared with Selena, and another sister, Harriett, I listened as Harriett consoled Selena and confessed that she thought she was pregnant, too. As I lay cocooned between them in the big bed, I heard their plans to run away together. They planned to pool their money and ride the bus all the way to Chicago. Mom's younger sister lived right outside the city with her rich husband.

I'd only met my Aunt Priscilla twice in my life, but I'd never forgotten her visits. She'd brought presents for all of us, and she told us about life in the big city and what a great job her husband, Daniel, had as plant manager in a factory. She'd taken us for a ride in her new car, laughing as we sat in the back and yelled as the wind tore through our hair.

I felt sorry for Mama, whose lips tightened every time they landed on her younger sister. Later, I realized that she'd been jealous of Priscilla for having a better life.

The next morning was a Saturday, and I had followed Mama outside to help her hang wash out on the line that stretched across our backyard. In a guilty whisper, I told her about Selena and Harriett's plans to run away and go to Chicago and live with Aunt Priscilla. It wasn't that I wanted to get them into trouble; it was that I didn't want them to leave. We were a family. We might have been poor, but I'd been taught that family stuck together.

But Mama hadn't even tried to stop them, or even tell them that she knew about their plans. She let them leave. I don't even think she told Daddy. When I realized they'd gone, I ran to my mother and demanded to know why she didn't stop them.

I'll never forget her words, or the cold look in her eyes when she told me.

"They've already messed up their lives, Melanie. If I made them stay, then I'd have two more mouths to feed, and they'd keep on having babies. Let Priscilla find out what real life's is like. She's been lazy all her life."

I'd started crying, already missing my sisters. Mama had thrown the wet sheet she'd been hanging aside and grabbed me hard by the shoulders. She squatted down to eye-level; the look in her eyes freezing me to the bone.

She gave me a little shake as she hissed at me. "You'd better learn your lesson, girl. I've got enough on my hands without raising a passel of grandchildren on top of my own. You hear me?"

"I . . . I hear you, Mama," I had stammered back. I had heard her all right, but at eight years old, I didn't exactly understand every word she meant. She'd let go of me and resumed hanging the sheets. Her mouth formed an angry line, and her movements were jerky and agitated.

"You're gonna do better than your sisters," she'd went on to say, mostly muttering as if to herself. "If I have to tie you to me and work my fingers to the bone, you're gonna have the life I never had a chance to have. I'll do it if it's the last thing I do."

More than a little frightened by her behavior, I tried to sneak away, but she reached out and snatched me back, grabbing a handful of my hair to hold me in place. I'd gotten whippings before, plenty of them, but Mama had never mistreated me in this way. I realized, then, that Mama was a whole lot more upset about my sisters leaving than she let on.

"Mind me, Melanie. Don't let no grubby boy talk you into doing it before you get a ring on your finger. You concentrate on your schoolwork so you can get a scholarship. You're going to be the first one in the family to go to college and make something of yourself."

"Yes, Mama," I had whispered, tears slipping down my cheeks. My head stung where she held me, but I didn't dare try to pull away. I think she would have ended up with a handful of my hair if I had tried.

She finally let go of my hair, and for a moment, I felt her gentle touch against my cheek. Then she was hugging me to her and crying as if her heart were broken. I realized later that it probably had been breaking. As much as she wanted to be tough and unmoved by Selena and Harriett's decisions, she was a mother, after all.

Gathering my courage, I patted her back and reminded her that I wasn't the only daughter she had left. There was Brenda, who was seventeen. She had her own bed—although all the girls shared the same room—and kept mostly to herself. I'd never been as close to her as I had been to Selena and Harriett.

But Mama had said sadly through her tears, "No, honey. I don't think we're going to have her much longer. She's head over heels for that Summerhill boy."

"But I thought you liked him?"

I felt her take a deep breath, hesitating, as if she were searching for a way to explain to me so that I would understand. "I do but he's a farmworker. She'll end up with a bunch of kids, working herself to death."

Mama had been right about Brenda. She dropped out of school halfway into her senior year and got married to Nate Summerhill. Daddy helped Ronnie get a job on the farm where he worked, and they moved into a tiny house down the road from our own house. Within the year, Brenda was pregnant with her first baby.

I don't think I'll ever forget how hard Mama cried the day Brenda got married. It was the same day I vowed to myself, then and there, that I would make Mama proud of me. I would study hard and get that scholarship, and I would resist the temptation of boys so that I wouldn't disappoint Mama.

Oh, how naive I'd been, thinking I could resist the power of first love where my sisters had failed. . . .

A glance at my watch told me I still had two hours to go before I could close shop and go home, maybe lie on a heating pad. Sometimes it helped, sometimes it didn't.

We had a rush of people during the next two hours, so time passed swiftly. When I got home, David was in the kitchen throwing a pasta salad together. He took one look at my pinched expression and pulled out a chair.

"Sit before you fall. Cramps still bad?"

I gratefully sat. The pain meds had worn off. "Yes, they're still bad."

"I want you to see a doctor," David said for about the hundredth time in the past few months. "This isn't normal. I had three sisters, and I know this isn't normal."

I looked at the man I had married seven years earlier, the man I loved with all my heart. He was a wonderful husband. A man with more heart than most women I knew. He was a born father.

The thought made me want to burst out bawling. What if I couldn't give him a baby? Would it be fair to David, who would surely make the best father in the world, to have to live and die without having a child of his own?

Swallowing a burning ball of tears, I said, "I thought we agreed we wouldn't start panicking until we'd been trying for two years."

David sat two bowls of pasta salad on the table, and then returned to the counter for flatware. "I'm not talking about having a baby. I'm talking about you being in so much pain with your periods. I think you should consider the possibility that something might be wrong."

Which was precisely why I didn't want to see a doctor. David knew how I felt, so why was he pushing me? Was he thinking of me, or was he worried that I wouldn't be able to get pregnant? I immediately felt ashamed of my thoughts. David and I had been happy—just the two of us—for the past seven years. I had no reason to believe he would stop loving me just because I couldn't have a baby.

Yet the fear remained. I couldn't shake it. I knew that part of it was because I wasn't sure I could be happy without a child in my life. Would my needs destroy our love?

I took a sip of the iced tea David set before me, trying not to grimace at the bitter taste. My husband was a whiz at cooking, but he had never grasped the art of making good iced tea. "If it happens again next month, then I'll make an appointment."

"That's what you said last month." David stabbed at his pasta salad, letting me know he was upset. "I know you don't like doctors, but your pap smear was normal last year, wasn't it? You know that you don't have cancer."

I started to remind him that pap smears didn't detect ovarian cancer, but I bit my tongue, deciding there wasn't any reason to spread my paranoia. David worried enough about me. Instead, I tried changing the subject.

"I talked to Mom, yesterday. She said that Dad shot a deer."

My ploy didn't work, although David was an avid deer hunter, and once a year he and my dad went hunting during deer season. This year, David had to cancel. One of his employees had broken his leg, and David was on deadline to get several cars restored and ready for their impatient owners.

"Don't try to change the subject, Melanie," he said, pointing his fork at me. "Rhea said—"

"She called you?" Before I could gather steam over her defection, David continued.

"She said you were hurting pretty badly today, and that you had to sit down. She thinks you should see a doctor, too."

"Rhea needs to mind her own business," I said sharply. "I wished you two wouldn't gain up on me."

"Somebody needs to." David's eyes narrowed, making me tense up. "I could always talk to your mother."

"Don't you dare worry Mom!" I said. I rarely raised my voice to anyone, but David was pushing the right buttons. "You know she has heart problems."

"It was a slight heart attack," David pointed out mildly. "And she's fine now, so don't use that excuse."

"Still, I can't believe you're thinking about worrying an old woman about a silly thing like cramps."

"It's more than that, and you know it, Melanie. You're not only in a lot of pain, you're pale as a ghost." His eyes softened. He put his big hand over mine. "I don't want anything to happen to you. I don't think I'd want to live without you, honey."

Part of me suspected that he was manipulating me, but another part—the part that loved him like crazy—melted at his words. "I don't think I'd want to live without you, either."

Thankfully, he let the subject drop. We talked about Daddy's deer and the renovations they making on the farmhouse where I'd grown up and my parents still lived. They had refused to let us help them buy another house, but after a lot of bullying, we had finally convinced them to let us help them with renovations. David and I had gotten financially comfortable over the past seven years with our businesses, so we could afford to help.

Selena and Harriett had remained in Chicago, and they only returned once or twice a year for visits. Selena now had five children and was working on her fourth marriage. Harriett had two children and was going through her second divorce. Just as Mama had predicted, Brenda and Nate had a houseful of kids—seven at last count—and Nate still worked for Daddy's old boss. They had moved to a bigger house, but otherwise nothing had changed.

Three of my brothers were married and settled in different states, and my fourth brother was doing time for drug possession.

After dinner, I helped David clear the table, trying to hide the fact that the pain medication I had taken at work had completely worn off. The cramps were back with a vengeance, sharp and, sometimes, taking my breath away with their severity. When David disappeared into the living room to watch the evening news, I took four pain relievers and started running some bath water, thinking a hot soak would help.

I was in the bedroom gathering my nightclothes and some clean underwear when the worst cramp ever, brought me to my knees before the dresser. I choked back a moan and held my stomach, trying to ride it out.

"Honey?"

It was David. I turned my head and saw him standing in the bedroom doorway, his expression panicky. I tried to reassure him, but the pain robbed me of my breath.

"That's it," he said, striding toward me to help me to my feet. "I'm taking you to the emergency room right now."

I might have protested if I had been able, but this time, the pain wasn't letting up. With David's help, we made it to the car. As he strapped me in, my mind whirled with possibilities. Maybe it is my appendix, I thought hopefully. Maybe it has nothing to do with my female organs at all.

But I knew that I was fooling myself. The pain wasn't just in my right side, it was across my entire lower stomach, as if there were tiny knives inside my uterus, cutting me to pieces.

At the hospital, David practically had to carry me inside. He argued with the woman at the front desk until she finally gave up and took us straight back to the emergency rooms.

A brisk-looking nurse came in and took my vitals. "Is there a possibility that you could be pregnant?" she asked, scribbling something on my chart as she spoke.

Through clenched teeth, I answered her. "We've been trying for more than a year, but I'm not late or anything."

"Hmm," she said, then disappeared. She returned seconds later with a cup. "Can you get me some urine? If you're having a miscarriage, it will still show positive on the test."

David helped me to the bathroom, then back to the cubicle afterward. We waited in silence for thirty minutes before a doctor came in with my chart. "Mrs. Malone? How are you feeling today?"

I never understood why doctors and nurses asked that question when it was obvious that I wouldn't be there if I felt terrific.

"Not too great," I said, wondering if my answer surprised him. He shot me a frown over the rim of his glasses and scribbled something down. "On a scale of one to ten, how would you rate your pain?"

That answer was easy, since another hard cramp was attacking me. "Nine, maybe ten," I gasped out, clutching the bed railing.

"Can you give her something for pain?" David demanded, sounding angry.

The doctor looked unperturbed. "Well, she's not pregnant, but we haven't ruled out appendicitis, so we'd better wait for the lab work. Someone will be in to draw your blood."

I wasn't pregnant. Why did the words cut through me like a knife? I had known it was unlikely. If I had been pregnant, I was definitely losing the baby.

"We're not leaving here until we find out what's causing this," David said with uncharacteristic belligerence. When the doctor looked at him, David turned a little red. "You don't know what I had to go through to get her here."

The doctor left, and a young guy came to draw my blood. After he left, I curled into a fetal position and prayed for unconsciousness. At that point, I didn't care how many doctors paraded in to look at me. I just wanted the pain to stop.

It took a half hour for the blood test results to come back. A nurse came in and told me that the doctor had ruled out appendicitis, so she was giving me a shot of something to relieve the pain.

By the time the doctor returned, I was floating blissfully in a drug-induced cloud. I could still feel the pain, but I no longer cared. David and the doctor talked over me, and I listened with a detached mind.

"I recommend we get her checked in and have a surgeon evaluate her in the morning," the doctor told David.

David didn't hesitate, and I could hear the relief in his voice. "Fine. That's what we'll do, then."

"He may want to do exploratory surgery."

"If that's what it takes."

At that point, I tried to muster a protest. In the end, I felt myself drifting off to sleep instead.

The rest of the long night the nurses kept me relatively pain free. They even changed my sanitary napkins, and I didn't muster more than a feeble protest that I could do it myself. Who was I kidding? My bones felt like mush. I couldn't block a needed sneeze.

David never left my side. Once when I opened my eyes, I saw him sitting upright in the uncomfortable looking chair beside my bed, dozing.

Early in the morning, a woman doctor came in to examine me and talk to me. Since I was a little more lucid, I figured they'd skipped the last pain medication so that I would be able to understand what was going on.

The woman doctor turned out to be a general surgeon. Her name was Dr. Clayton. She probed and poked my abdomen until I took her hands and held them still, glaring at her. "That hurts," I said, just in case she didn't know.

She arched her brow slightly and slowly removed her hands. "Well, something's going on in there, that much we do know." She looked across the bed at David, who stood hovering anxiously. "Are you her husband?"

He nodded. "She's been having really bad periods for about four months now."

"Probably endometriosis," she said. "But I can't be sure until I get in there to take a look." She looked at me again. "Is that what you want me to do, Mrs. Malone?"

I opened my mouth to tell her, "No!" but David wouldn't give me the chance.

"Yes, she is," he said firmly. He centered that firm look on me, daring me to argue.

As if on cue, a cramp hit me, doubling me up in the bed. I heard myself moan, then the doctor called for a nurse. A few moments later, the pain eased.

"I think we need to get her in as soon as possible," Dr. Clayton said in a worried tone that sent fear streaking through me. "She might have an ovarian cyst about to rupture."

I grabbed David's hand, pleading with him with my eyes. He squeezed my fingers. I could tell by the resolution on his face that he wasn't going to change his mind, nor let me change mine. Not that I had been given a choice in the first place.

During the next two hours as I was prepped for surgery, I fought old, painful memories by focusing on the good ones. Like the day I met David. I had been searching for just the right building to open my candy shop, and hadn't been keeping my eyes on the road as well as I should have. I had bumped the car in front of me with just enough force to spill the hot cappuccino I'd been holding in my hand.

The hot liquid went into my lap. I shrieked and scrambled to get my soaked sweater off my lap, unwittingly hitting the gas pedal instead of the brakes. The second time wasn't just a bump. I rammed him hard enough to deploy my air bag. The force of the air bag broke my nose and my favorite pair of sunglasses.

The angry man who jerked open my car door didn't remain angry for long. "Oh my God! Are you okay? Your nose is bleeding."

I scraped my broken glasses from my face and held my hand to my dripping nose. My eyes were watering from the pain.

"I think it's broken," I said in a nasal, Southern drawl.

He thrust a handkerchief into my hand. "Here, use this. I'll call an ambulance."

I took the handkerchief as I said, "I don't need an ambulance. There's not much they can do for a broken nose." Over the handkerchief, I saw the stranger smile, and it hit me with a jolt that he was good-looking and in his late twenties or early thirties. He looked young, but there were enough fine lines around his eyes and mouth to convince me he wasn't too young.

"You sound as if you're speaking from experience. I take it this isn't the first time you've tried to drive your car into someone's back seat?"

I shook my head, and then winced as the motion caused pain. "No. My brother broke my nose when I was five." I didn't add that he'd been fighting one of my other brothers over the last piece of fried chicken and had accidentally caught me in the nose with his elbow. Those weren't the kind of embarrassing moments you shared with a stranger. In fact, I don't think I ever shared that story with David. Those weren't the good old days for me, so I didn't reminisce like a lot of people do.

By the time a patrol car came to record the accident, I knew that David was divorced. He worked for a body shop, and he planned to open his own shop soon.

He'd had a rough marriage that had lasted ten agonizing years, so we had sort of made a silent trade; I didn't push him to talk about his life with his ex-wife, and he didn't push me to talk about my childhood. What he learned was strictly on a volunteer basis only and vice versa.

We started dating right after the accident. Our conversations were lively and broad. Since we were both contemplating opening our own business, we had plenty to talk about, and we both understood that our careers were important to us.

We weren't in a hurry to get married, but somewhere along the way his apartment became emptier and emptier as he spent more and more time at my place, which was slightly bigger. The next step seemed natural.

One weekend when we both had free time, we rented a chapel, invited a few friends, and got married. I had never been one to dream of a big wedding. It just hadn't ever appealed to me, so our sweet, quiet ceremony suited me just fine. I invited my parents, but they were homebodies, so they didn't come, and that was okay with me, too.

If David thought it was strange that I hadn't invited my whole family, he was wonderful enough to keep his curiosity to himself. I think he sensed that I was embarrassed about my upbringing, that I was proud of me for rising above and beyond it. I'd gone to college and had gotten a business degree. After that, I'd worked for a catering firm to broaden my experience. Now I was ready to strike out on my own, and my choice of business was a candy shop.

Candy was something I'd never had much of as a child. Aunt Priscilla had always brought candy when she visited, and it was like Christmas, only better.

While we were dating, David and I discussed having children. It was by mutual agreement that we decided to wait until we were financially secure and ready to commit to raising a child.

"Mrs. Malone? The anesthesiologist is going to give you something to make you fall into a deep sleep. Can you count backwards from one hundred for me?"

Is she insane? I thought, gazing at her through drug-fogged eyes. Then my vision sharpened for an instant. The nurse reminded me of someone from my past.

Panic clutched me with steely claws. Suddenly, I was fifteen again. . . .

When I awakened, I saw the face of a different nurse.

"Are you in pain?" she asked, briskly checking my pulse.

I thought about the question, then shook my head. Surely I had just closed my eyes? Maybe the surgeon had been delayed, and they'd brought me back to consciousness until he arrived.

My mouth felt like cotton. I wallowed my tongue around, searching for moisture. Anticipating my needs, the nurse put a straw to my dry lips, waiting patiently for me to take a sip.

I did and finally I could speak, although my voice was a croak. "What happened?"

"You're in recovery. The doctor will be in shortly to talk to you."

That wasn't good enough. "Where's my husband?"

"He's waiting for you in the surgery waiting room. I've called to tell him you made it through surgery just fine."

"I want to see him." Suddenly, I felt that I needed to see my husband more than I needed to breathe.

The nurse patted my arm, but she sounded distant as she said, "You'll be going up to your room in a little bit. Meanwhile, try to sleep."

Left with little choice, I closed my eyes.

When I awakened again, I lay there with my eyes closed, feeling my heart pounding like a distant drum in my ears.

David was arguing with someone.

"You don't understand. The doctor needs to be here when she wakes up."

"I do understand, Mr. Malone, but Dr. Clayton has other patients to see. She'll be here shortly."

I smiled to myself as I heard David mutter the B word beneath his breath. I didn't have to open my eyes to know the nurse had already left the room. My David would never be openly disrespectful to a woman.

"Shame on you," I whispered, but it came out more of a whispery croak. Almost instantly, I felt David's hand in mine.

"Honey? Are you okay? How do you feel? Do you need some water? They said you would be thirsty. . . ."

My eyelids fluttered open. They still felt as if something weighed them down, but I managed to keep them open long enough to view David's pinched, concerned face. "Water would be good."

He held a cup to my lips, and I took a short swallow.

"They won't tell me anything," he said, his voice thick with frustration.

Focusing everything I had, I managed to give his hand a weak squeeze. "Patience, honey. Just have a little . . . patience."

I let my eyes close again, and I think I might have dozed. The next time I came to, I heard a different voice calling me awake. It sounded authoritative and vaguely recognizable.

"Mrs. Malone? It's Dr. Clayton. Can you hear me? I need for you to wake up."

Dr. Clayton. The surgeon. Adrenaline shot into my veins. My eyes snapped open. Dr. Clayton was watching me, and I noticed what looked like a speck of dried blood on the outside corner of her glasses. Maybe it was ketchup, or salsa. I liked those possibilities a lot better.

"How do you feel?" she asked, pulling back the covers to look at my belly.

Figuring I had another scar in the making to match my old one, I tried to joke as I said, "Like a really ripe watermelon, as if the slightest touch will split me open."

She pulled the covers back over me, the corners of her thin lips lifting in a semblance of a smile. But it faded abruptly, as if she were suddenly remembering something unpleasant.

The sight of that fading smile made my heart pound harder. She had a look in her eyes that I didn't like one single bit.

I squeezed David's hand to let him know that I was scared. He squeezed back in acknowledgment. I think we both knew we were about to hear some really bad news. A part of me—the panicking part—wanted to shout at David that I had known this would happen. That if we had left well enough alone, then we wouldn't be on the verge of hearing . . . whatever it was that Dr. Clayton was about to tell us.

As irrational as that sounded, it's what I believed with all my heart.

"Mrs. Malone, you had severe endometriosis."

I swallowed dryly. "Is . . . is that why I can't get pregnant? We've been trying for over a year." Hope flared in my chest. If she had found it, couldn't she get rid of it? Maybe I could get pregnant now!

But Dr. Clayton didn't tell me what I wanted to hear. Instead, she stunned us both with the most horrible—and unbelievable—news I could imagine hearing.

Frowning slightly, she said, "Obviously you don't know." She hesitated. Frowned harder. "I don't know how this could have happened without your knowledge, but . . . I'm afraid your tubes have been cut and burned."

I couldn't believe what I was hearing. I'd just undergone emergency exploratory surgery, and now the doctor was telling me that my tubes had been cut and burned!

Not cut and tied, but cut and burned. I wasn't stupid. I knew that's what doctors did when they wanted to make absolutely certain there wouldn't be a chance a woman could get pregnant.

Sometimes cut and tied came loose and rejoined. But cut and burned didn't.

I could feel the shock humming through my husband's hand where he held mine so tightly. His grip hurt, but I knew that he wasn't aware of it. I was thirty-eight. He was thirty-nine. We had finally decided our lives were ready for a child, one we could nurture. This would be a child who wouldn't have to grow up in a dysfunctional family, as I had.

Now, the surgeon was telling me I wouldn't have that chance.

"I don't understand," I heard myself saying. I don't think I've ever seen anyone frown as hard as Dr. Clayton did at my words. She was clearly as confused as I was.

"Like I said, I don't know how this could have happened." She hesitated, consulted her chart, then said, "Your medical history states that you've had surgery twice prior to this morning?"

I swallowed hard. She can't possibly know the truth, I told myself. "Yes, I had a bowel blockage that required surgery when I was twenty-two. When I was fifteen. . . ." I swallowed again, convincing myself that the lie I was about to tell was nobody's business but my own. And David's, but I couldn't think about that now.

"When you were fifteen?" Dr. Clayton prompted.

I looked into her intelligent blue eyes and saw that she knew the truth. But I also saw that she wasn't going to give me away. Thank God for patient confidentiality, and my ability to lie convincingly. "When I was fifteen, I developed an inguinal hernia."

"I see." Clearly she didn't and knew that I was lying.

I didn't dare look at David to see if he was swallowing my lie yet again. Hot tears trekked down my cheeks. I was confused and angry. Who and why would anyone do this to me without my consent? How could I not have known?

Maybe it was a mistake. It happened on television. Maybe it had happened to me. Nurses grabbed the wrong patient. Wrong chart, wrong instructions. Suddenly, I was being condemned to motherlessness for the rest of my life.

Whoops. Sorry. Our mistake. Hey, what she doesn't know won't hurt her, so let's not tell her.

It was only one of the many possibilities that began to go through my mind. One thing was certain, however. I would have to tell David the truth. He would have to know that I had given birth to a baby girl when I was fifteen.

After the doctor left, David was furious. He stomped out of the room to call our lawyer, threatening to sue every doctor who had even looked at me in the past twenty-five years.

I let him go, needing to gather my thoughts and decide how best to tell my husband that I had been lying to him the entire time I had known him. I cringed at the thought, knowing that lying had been one of the single most problems in his first marriage.

She had lied to him about wanting kids. She had lied to him about a lot of things. And in the end, she had lied to him about having an affair with his best friend. Lied to him right up to the day he had caught them, naked and sweaty and laughing as they frolicked in the bed David and his wife had slept in. Had made love in.

These were the little tidbits he had fed me over the years I had known and loved David. Although I had never pressured him to tell me, there were painful tidbits that had seemed to be wrung out of him. They were like a recurring boil that kept festering and festering, then subsiding, only to return, until he could keep the pain to himself no longer.

The most painful confession of all had been the night David and I had celebrated our third anniversary. We'd rented a hotel downtown, the honeymoon suite. We'd had too much wine, and he'd told me about Rayshell's abortions. He just blurted it out with this God-awful look on his face.

On the day they'd split for good, she had flung the terrible truth in his face. She'd been pregnant twice; both times, she had gone behind his back and gotten rid of the babies. His children.

That was the same night I had told him about my sisters leaving, and Mama's reaction. I don't even know if he remembered my telling him, because he'd never brought it up again.

How would David react when I told him that I'd had a baby and had given it away? Although my parents hadn't given me much choice at the time, I hadn't fought them, either. The awful disappointment on my mother's face had stilled any urge in me to fight for my baby. I knew without a doubt that if I had fought to keep her, I would have been homeless. How could I have taken care of a baby by myself at fifteen? Unlike my sisters, I hadn't had the courage it took to get on a bus and head across the country.

Yet knowing these facts didn't lessen my shame and guilt. Over the years, I had grown a hard shell around that guilt so that I rarely allowed myself to think about what I'd done. The rare times I did allow it, I pictured my daughter in a beautiful home with parents who loved and spoiled her.

On the day my doctor came in to tell me I could go home, I was able to talk to her alone. David had gone home to take a shower and change into clean clothes. I motioned for her to shut the door, trying to swallow the big lump that had quickly formed in my throat. She was my doctor, and I felt she had a right to know the truth. I think a part of me wanted to explain myself, too, so she wouldn't draw her own conclusions.

"I had a baby when I was fifteen," I blurted out.

She nodded, obviously not surprised. "I suspected as much. Do you think that's when the tubal litigation happened?"

My eyes jerked to her face in shock and surprise. I hadn't thought of that possibility. "Could they have done that without my consent?"

Dr. Clayton stuck her hands in the deep pockets of her white coat. She had a way of frowning that forewarned a person of bad news. "Believe it or not, underage sterilization is still legal in some states. Where are you from?"

I told her what state I was from.

"You should check. Even if it's not legal now, it probably was when you were fifteen. Are your parents still alive?"

My parents! But no, I thought. My mother would never do that to me, not without telling me . . . would she? I couldn't dismiss the possibility, as much as I wanted. Mom had been almost fanatical about my future, about making sure I didn't follow in my sisters' footsteps.

But was she fanatical to the point of destroying my chances of ever becoming a mother again? My mother was hard. She was tough and was determined. But in my mind, it would take a monster to do something like that to a child.

Because I needed to hear the words, I said them out loud. "No, it couldn't have been my parents. They wouldn't have done that to me." But even to my own ears, I didn't sound totally convinced.

Reluctantly, I forced myself to put them on my list of suspects. If it turned out to be true . . . I shuddered to think of the fall out from such a revelation. David would never forgive them. I'm not sure I would be able to, either.

I went home with a heavy heart, dreading the moment I would have to tell David.

The moment came after David helped me settle into our bed at home. He prepared a big jug of iced tea and set it on the nightstand, along with the remote control, the phone, and a pile of new magazines he'd gotten for me.

He fluffed my pillows, then stood back. "Need anything else, hon?"

"Yes. I need to talk to you." I indicated an overstuffed chair in the corner. "Can you pull up a chair? You probably need to be sitting down for this one."

His face shadowed with growing concern, David pulled the chair up and sat. He folded his hands in his lap and regarded me tensely.

I knew that he was thinking all sorts of horrible things, so I jumped right in. "I never told you what happened to me when I was fifteen. I should have, but there never seemed to be the right time." I looked at my hands. "Still, that's no excuse. I guess the only excuse I do have is that I just wanted to forget it ever happened." Glancing at him, I saw the stark pain in his eyes and guessed what he was thinking. I shook my head. "No, I didn't have an abortion." When he relaxed a fraction, I continued. "But I did get pregnant. My parents made me give the baby up for adoption."

"Oh, hon." He grabbed my hand and held it tightly. His face was twisted in sorrow for me.

For me! He wasn't furious. He wasn't mad at me.

Perversely, I said, "How can you feel sorry for me? I gave my baby away to strangers!"

"You didn't have a choice, hon. You said that your parents forced you to."

"I didn't fight them," I admitted shamefully.

"You were fifteen. I doubt that it would have done any good. What were your options? Take the baby and go . . . where? Live . . . where? How?"

"I could have gone to Aunt Priscilla, like my sisters did."

"Alone? With an infant?" David sounded incredulous. "Come on! Why are you beating yourself up over something you had no control over?" Suddenly, his eyes widened in shock. His jaw went slack, then hardened to rock. "Did they . . . do you think your parents are the ones that made sure you couldn't get pregnant again?"

To be absolutely fair, I hesitated before I shook my head. "I can't believe they would do that to me. Mom was obsessed, but . . ." I shook my head again, more emphatically. "She knows we've been trying to have a baby. She even told me she would start on a baby quilt."

"Maybe she's blocked it from her mind," David suggested, still frowning fiercely.

He wanted someone to blame, and I knew that I was damned lucky he hadn't picked me.

"Or maybe the doctor did it on his own. He knew our family history, knew that my sisters had already gotten into trouble, and how badly Mama had felt about it."

"I don't think he would risk his license, hon." David considered for a moment, then shook his head. "No. I can't imagine a doctor making a decision like that on his own."

"Then maybe it was a mistake. I had surgery when I was twenty-two. Maybe they had the charts mixed up and—"

"Honey," David broke in gently. "You're grasping at straws, and I understand why. You need to face the very real possibility that your parents are responsible for this."

I knew that David was right, but I wasn't ready to believe it, or even consider it for any length of time. "It all sounds so bizarre. I can't believe those kind of barbaric things happened such a short time ago, and that it happened to me. If that law hasn't been changed, then we need to do something about it so this doesn't happen to someone else."

"I agree, but, first, we've got to get you well. I'm going to go make dinner. Why don't you take a nap?" His lips lingered on my forehead, assuring me that he didn't blame me for what had happened.

He made it to the door before I stopped him. "David? Don't you want to know the how and why?"

He smiled faintly. "I think I know the how, and you can tell me the why whenever you're ready. No pressure, okay?"

When he'd gone, I lay there, wondering how on earth I'd gotten so lucky to find a wonderful, unique man like David. His calm demeanor didn't fool me. I knew that he wouldn't stop until he found out who was responsible for sterilizing me. They had not only hurt me, they had hurt David. It was every bit as much about him as it was about me.

It was about our future.

I tried to sleep, but I just couldn't. My mind kept trying to wander back to places I'd done my best to forget about . . . .

The boy who had managed to make me forget my mother's constant reminders and my sisters' plight had been in the same grade with me, but he'd been two years older, having been held back twice. We'd been paired to do a science project together, and since I had a reputation for being a little nerdy, I could tell that he was pleased he'd gotten me; it meant that he wouldn't have to do much of the work.

I was nervous around boys, and even more nervous around Arthur. He was practically a man; I was a studious, shy fifteen-year-old.

But Arthur was experienced in putting a girl at ease, as I soon discovered. He joked with me, teased me, and flattered me. I'd never had that kind of attention from anyone, especially a man. Daddy had always been too tired after working on the farm all day to do much more than ask us how our day had gone.

So Arthur's attention went straight to my heart, instead of my head. I realize now that I hadn't had a chance against someone like Arthur. Before I knew it, he had talked me into lying to Mom about where I was going so that we could work on our science project at his house after school.

We had done the science project, and then we'd had sex. Nobody had ever told me that a girl could get pregnant the first time she had sex. I had to find out the hard way. Frightened out of my head, I had refused to tell my parents who was responsible. I knew that my brothers probably would kill Arthur if they knew, and I wasn't entirely certain Daddy wouldn't take his gun and shoot him, too.

Telling Mama was one of the hardest things I ever remember doing in my life, and I will never, ever forget the look of stark pain in her eyes the day I told her I was pregnant.

She didn't speak to me for two solid months. If she needed to tell me something, she would have one of my brothers or Daddy tell me. Daddy, on the other hand, looked more resigned than angry. It seemed as if he'd known or suspected all along that I would follow in my sister's footsteps.

The day Mama finally spoke to me again was the day she told me exactly how it would be. I was mopping the kitchen floor one night after supper. She came in, tracking her prints on the floor that I had scrubbed hard and sat down at the kitchen table.

I could feel the hard stare of her eyes on the back of my neck for a long time before she startled me by speaking. By the time she did, my stomach was tied in knots.

"You're gonna give up this baby for adoption, you hear? After that, we're going to get on with our lives as planned. If it happens again, I'll kick you out. Do you understand?"

"Yes, Mama," I had whispered without hesitation. I think that I was so tickled that she was speaking to me again, I didn't think to argue. Besides, I agreed with Mama. I wanted things to get back the way they were, and having a baby would ruin everything. I still wanted to make Mama proud of me, and she was giving me a second chance.

My sisters hadn't been given that second chance.

I hadn't counted on the instant, overpowering love I would feel for my baby the moment she was born. Ten minutes later, a nurse had taken her from me, leaving an empty hole in my heart.

They had called it postpartum depression, but I knew better. I was grieving for my baby, a daughter that I would never see again. During those nine months, she had been slowly but surely stealing my heart with each kick, every roll. Even the hiccups had made me smile.

Daddy took me home from the hospital. When we pulled into the driveway, he stared through the windshield, making no move to get out. "Your Mama's gone to stay with your great Aunt Sharon awhile. She had a mild stroke, so your Mama's helping out until she can get back on her feet. She told me to tell you that you're in charge of the house until she gets back."

Mama came home two months later, and the baby was never mentioned again. I finished school, got a scholarship, and went on to college to get my business degree. Mama sent me money every month. Money I knew she had worked and sweated to make so that I could have a better life than she was having. How could I hate or resent a mother who loved me that much?

Maybe I could understand and forgive her for pushing me to give up my baby, but if she'd done the unimaginable, if she had ordered the doctor to cut and burn my tubes . . . then I didn't know if I could ever forgive her for that. I could understand her obsessive reasoning, yes, but forgive?

I must have dozed because it was dark when I awakened next, and David was standing beside the bed with a tray. He'd turned the lamp on.

"Your mother called to see how you were doing," he said, waiting for me to sit up so that he could position the tray.

I gave him a sharp glance. "You didn't tell her, did you?"

"No." He looked grim as he tucked a napkin beneath my chin. "I didn't."

"Good, because I want to tell her in person. I want to watch her reaction."

David sat down as I began to eat. "You've been doing some thinking," he guessed shrewdly.

"I have." I speared a carrot and put it in my mouth, not really tasting it, but knowing I needed the nutrition. "I think there's still a possibility—however slight—that there was a mix-up when I had surgery last, and I still think there's a slight possibility that Dr. Reynolds decided to play God without my parents' knowledge." I looked at David. "But I've come to the conclusion that my mother is most likely the one behind this atrocity."

David's voice was dangerously soft as he said, "I agree. She had the motive, and she had the power."

"But she didn't have the right." Suddenly, I couldn't eat another bite. My mother had betrayed me in a way that was nearly beyond my comprehension.

"Do you think your Dad knew about it?" David asked.

"It doesn't matter. He would have gone along with Mom, so it doesn't matter. Daddy worked hard, but he left Mom in charge of us kids."

"When you're well enough, we'll take a trip down there and confront them together, face to face."

"Yes, we will." My gaze met his. The look of overwhelming love, mixed with sorrow and sympathy, warmed my heart and made me feel stronger. A terrible thing had happened to us, but instead of tearing us apart, it had made our marriage stronger.

It was a huge relief to know that David wouldn't stop loving me just because I couldn't have a baby.

"Do you want to call and let them know we're coming?"

I dumped a couple of trays of ice into a small cooler containing diet sodas before I answered David. The doctor had released me, proclaiming me well enough to travel.

"No. I want to surprise them." I didn't want to give Mama any time to come up with a convincing lie or an excuse when I confronted her.

"You know she hates it when people just drop in," David said.

My smile was tight. "Yeah, I know."

On the way, I told David about Arthur. From the corner of my eye, I watched as his jaw became tighter and tighter.

"He could have at least used a condom?" he all but growled when I fell silent. "If he was going to go around molesting children—"

"I was fifteen, David," I reminded him quietly. "I wasn't a child, and I knew better." My laugh held little humor. "If anyone knew better, it was me. After all, Mama had drilled it into my head from the time I was eight years old."

"Too bad she didn't educate you on birth control."

"To her, that would have been like giving me permission, and she would never do that." I hesitated, not fully understanding why I felt the urge to defend my mother after what I believed she had done. "If you had a daughter and she came to you and told you that she wanted to have sex and wanted to get on birth control, what would you do?"

David's jaw clenched so hard I thought I heard something crack.

"Well, I guess I'll never have to worry about crossing that bridge, will I?"

Although I knew his bitterness wasn't directed at me, I flinched nonetheless. "No, you won't."

"Honey, you know I didn't mean—"

"Yes, I know. I know, David."

Our hands found one another across the seat. We held hands tightly for a moment, then released them. The rest of the drive passed in relative silence.

The sun was setting as we pulled into the driveway of my parents' home. I wasn't surprised to find them sitting in the screened front porch.

But they were definitely surprised to see us.

Mama rose from her chair and burst through the screen door, wearing an apron and a flowered dress that was a bit too big for her. "What in the world?" she exclaimed as we got out of the car. "Melanie Ann, I can't believe you didn't call and let me know you were coming! I could have made fresh lemonade, or a batch of that ranch dressing bread that David likes so well."

She didn't seem to notice that I wasn't answering. Enveloping me in a cautious hug, she pulled back and looked me up and down.

"Are you okay? I mean, should you be traveling this early after your surgery?"

"I'm fine, Mama." I felt too sick inside to wonder how I could sound so calm. "Iced tea will be fine, and David's on a diet. He's trying to cut down on his carbs."

Mama waved a disgusted hand at me. "Diets! Everybody's dieting these days! Why don't they just be happy with the body God gave them?"

We followed her onto the front porch where Daddy gave me a quick hug and David a hearty handshake.

"Let's go inside and get that tea," Mama said, leading the way again. The kitchen was warm and smelled like apple pie and floor wax. "Sit yourself down at the table while I fix the glasses," Mama instructed. She began to open cabinets and gather glasses while she talked, her ample hips swiveling to and fro.

"Did I tell you that your baby brother is gonna be a daddy again? And that Brenda, she thinks she's pregnant again." She sighed and shook her head. "I guess somebody needs to tell her what's causing it."

Daddy had taken a seat at the head of the table and was staring at Mama, so he didn't see my sick expression, or David's stony jaw.

But they all heard my harshly spoken words. "Too bad you didn't 'fix' her like you fixed me, huh Mama?"

Mama swung around at my outburst. I leaned forward, breathing hard, watching her face intently. I was so tense, my bones felt brittle, as if they would snap if I moved.

"What's the matter, Mama? Cat got your tongue?" When Mama continued to stare blankly at me, I got up and moved slowly to her until we were standing eye to eye. "Don't play dumb, Mama. It's too late for that."

I heard a chair squeak behind me, then Daddy's stern voice said, "That's enough, Melanie. You've no call to speak to your Mama like that."

My burning gaze shot to his. "Don't I, Daddy? I think if anyone has that right, it would be me."

I turned back to Mama just in time to see her chin go up. "Melanie, if you're talking about the baby I made you give up—"

"No, Mama," I cut in coldly. "I'm talking about the babies you made sure I would never have."

"I don't know what you're talking about," Mama said convincingly. She still stared at me with what appeared to be genuine puzzlement.

But then, I knew Mama could lie. She had convinced the sheriff that my brothers were innocent when Selena's boyfriend was found beaten nearly to death.

"Did you think I wouldn't ever find out?" I demanded. Although I didn't think I could actually bring myself to hit my mother, I wanted to. Oh, how I wanted to. "After the surgery, my doctor told me I'd been sterilized. At first, I didn't want to believe you'd do such a terrible thing, but eventually I realized it had to be you."

Mama stared at me, then looked at David, her face white with shock. "Is she okay? Is . . . did something happen that I don't know about?"

David rose and joined me, slipping a comforting arm around my waist. "Something happened, but we believe you knew about it. It's true. Her tubes have been cut and burned without her knowledge or permission. Are you saying you didn't have anything to do with it?"

I could tell by the derision in David's voice that he didn't believe it anymore than I did.

But Mama stuck to her guns and even managed to sound outraged that we would believe her capable of such an atrocity. "That's exactly what I'm saying!" she said. "Is that why you. . . ." Her incredulous gaze darted back and forth between us. "Is that why you drove down here? Because you thought I—you believe that I—" She choked up and couldn't continue. Big tears welled in her eyes, and the sight of them stunned me.

It had been a long time since I'd seen my mother cry.

"Oh, baby," she said, lifting a hand to her chest. "As horrible as I was to you, I would never, ever do something like that."

She reached for me, and I jerked out of her reach. My nails bit into David's arm. "Let's get out of here," I said, my voice strangely hoarse. "She's never going to own up to it, and I can't stand the sight of her any longer."

We moved as one to the door, but Daddy spoke before my hand landed on the screen.

"I did it."

His words fell into the shocked silence. Behind me, I heard my mother gasp. I could feel David draw in a long, hard breath. Then I felt him tense against me. His anger was almost palpable.

My first thought was that Daddy was covering for Mama. But he took care of that theory very quickly.

"I told Doc Reynolds to do it," Daddy said in a voice barely above a whisper. "He didn't want to, but I kept on at him until I convinced him it was for the best."

Slowly, I turned. David turned with me, gripping my shoulders so hard I went numb. I stared at Daddy, at his twisted, anguished expression, and felt nothing. Not anger. Not love. Just . . . nothing. "Why?" I asked. My eyes were burning. I sensed Mama looking at me, but I couldn't take my eyes off my father.

His gaze dropped from mine. He stared at the floor. "Your mother didn't go to St. Louis to take care of your great Aunt Sharon."

"Wade, don't," I heard my Mama plead in a strangled whisper.

"Be still," Daddy told her. "Melanie's a grown woman, now. She has a right to know the truth." To me, he said, "She had a breakdown the day you had your baby. I had to take her . . . I had to take her over to Rockford, to the mental institution." His voice pitched low, turned shaky as if he were experiencing it all over again. He wiped a hand over his mouth.

"I came home and found her unconscious. She'd taken a whole bottle of those nerve pills Doc Reynolds had given her."

He looked up at me then, his eyes red-rimmed and glimmering with tears. "I nearly lost her. We nearly lost her. She wanted you to have a good life, different from her own. Different from what she knew your sisters were going to have. She had to work too darn hard, and maybe that's my fault. But I couldn't take the chance that you would get in trouble again."

"Damn you, Wade," David ground out. His grip on my shoulders tightened so hard I gasped. He heard me and eased up, but the tension in his body didn't lessen. "What you did was criminal. I don't care if it was within your rights at the time."

Daddy looked at me, and I couldn't look away from the raw anguish in his eyes. "I'm sorry, darling," he said to me. "At the time, I thought I was doing the right thing for you and your mama."

The numbness in me began to slowly give way to the pain of reality. My father had done this to me. He had ordered the doctor to sterilize me, make me barren so that I could never hurt Mama again.

Because of what my sisters had done, because of what I had done, Mama had tried to take her own life.

The sound of Mama crying softly finally filtered through my pain and shock. I looked at her, my neck creaking as if I were a thousand years old. She stood in the middle of her remodeled kitchen, the bright yellow linoleum gleaming from a fresh waxing beneath her slippered feet. She hadn't gone to Daddy. Hadn't taken his side, as a wife of nearly fifty years should or would have.

She had taken a stand, however unconsciously, torn between her husband and her daughter. What he'd done had been terribly wrong, but he'd done it for her.

I took a step in her direction, but the hard grip on my shoulders held me back.

"Are you sure?" David asked, not sounding sure at all.

Taking a deep breath, I stepped out from beneath my husband's loving hands and went to my distraught mother. I held her in my arms as she sobbed, and I found myself sobbing with her.

While I haven't exactly forgiven Daddy for what he did, I've come to understand why he did it, and in understanding, we've formed a silent truce of sorts.

With the help of an excellent fertility doctor and a second mortgage on our house, David and I are expecting a baby in the spring, thanks to science and in vitro.

THE END

A Sister's Tragedy
THE BABY WAS RIPPED FROM HER BODY

Katherine and I stood nervously on the porch. I hadn't wanted to ring that doorbell, and I'd suspected that my sister hadn't wanted to be the one to do it, either.

I'd bitten my lip, feeling ridiculously guilty. This is going to be tougher than I thought, I said, twisting the strap of my purse between my fingers. For a moment, I'd thought that I was going to be sick.

"Yeah," Katherine agreed. It might not have been so bad if only one of us had good news. "But for both of us to walk in there and tell them that we're pregnant seems," She shrugged. "Well, it seems almost cruel."

Katherine and I stood nervously on the porch. I hadn't wanted to ring that doorbell, and I'd suspected that my sister hadn't wanted to be the one to do it, either.

I'd bitten my lip, feeling ridiculously guilty. "This is going to be tougher than I thought," I said, twisting the strap of my purse between my fingers. For a moment, I'd thought that I was going to be sick.

"Yeah," Katherine agreed. "It might not have been so bad if only one of us had good news. But for both of us to walk in there and tell them that we're pregnant seems—" She shrugged. "Well, it seems almost cruel."

"But it's one of the rules," I reminded her, as well as myself. "I thought that everyone did really well when Noreen told us that she'd finally conceived."

"Maybe you didn't notice Maggie sneaking off to the bathroom and coming back with red eyes," Katherine pointed out. "Or maybe you weren't watching Amanda's face. She looked positively stricken."

I'd touched my younger sister's arm, and I'd noticed that she was trembling. "Katherine, I never told you this, but for the rest of the night, I hated Noreen." My face burned with shame at my confession. "All of us have tried for so long, and have had so many disappointments. Cherie, most of all, I think. She's had five miscarriages."

"Cassie lost two babies to SIDS," Katherine said. "We've all suffered. But, when we started this group, we agreed that we'd share the good news, as well as the bad. If we don't tell them, it'll look like we're ashamed. And I'm not ashamed." Katherine's voice was firm. "I deserve this baby—and so do you."

I'd realized that some women in the group hadn't approved of Katherine's methods of conceiving a child. She wasn't married, and had turned to a sperm bank. After nearly a half-dozen failures, it had finally happened—she was pregnant. I was happy for her. And, of course, I knew how responsible my sister was. Marriage just wasn't in her plans, and her biological clock was ticking. At thirty-six, she was two years younger than I.

"Okay, let's get this over with." I'd taken a deep breath and pressed the doorbell. The tension inside of me had begun building slowly as we'd waited. What was taking so long? Had the others found out? Didn't they want us to join them? I'd known that my thoughts were ridiculous, but, even still, I hadn't been able to stop worrying.

"Maybe we've got the date wrong," Katherine ventured. She was clearly ready to give up and flee down the sidewalk to her car.

"Don't be silly. You know that we always meet on the first Monday of the month, and that it's Patricia's turn to host the meeting."

I'd winced inside as I'd thought about Patricia, and how desperately she'd longed for a baby. She'd been married for fifteen years, and was still childless. The doctors were baffled, which, in my opinion, was worse than if they'd been able to identify the cause of her infertility. To compensate for her childless life, she'd started a top-notch daycare facility, which she operated from her home. It might have helped, at first, but she had recently confided in the group that it was becoming painful to watch the children leave every day, and go home to their parents.

Finally, the door had opened. Katherine had stifled a guilty cry, and I'd jumped.

Patricia answered the door, and it was obvious that she'd been crying. "Stephanie got her period," she announced immediately, her eyes filling with more tears. "She was ten days late this time. She really thought that she might be pregnant."

Hesitantly, we'd followed Patricia into her living room. I hadn't dared to glance at Katherine. I'd known that I would probably find the same guilty look on her face that I'd had on mine. Not for the first time, I'd found myself wishing that I hadn't come to the meeting. I could have gone to the group's website and made the announcement there. It would have been the coward's way out—I'd realized that—but, at that moment, I'd felt like a big coward.

Before we could step into the living room, Katherine had grabbed my arm and held me back. "Maybe we should wait, and tell them another time," she whispered.

I'd realized that she was thinking about Stephanie, but I shook my head. Not because I was cruel, but because I knew that I had to get it over with. It was now or never.

"Let's just tell them, Katherine. They have to know," I insisted.

"No, they don't," she protested.

"Yes, they do." I was determined to be brave.

The group was gathered around a sobbing Stephanie, offering tissues, hugs, and heartfelt consolations. I'd waited my turn, aware of a nervous Katherine behind me. At that moment, it was hard to believe that she was a public defender, with a pretty fierce reputation.

When the group had finally thinned, I'd approached Stephanie. I'd flinched at the blatant despair on her face. She was only thirty, but she'd been married for ten years, and she and her husband had wanted a child badly for so long. In fact, Stephanie had told us that she'd suspected her husband was looking around for more fertile pastures. Her misery had made me want to hunt down her husband and castrate him. I'd wanted to let him see what if felt like to be the one who was incapable of creating a child. I'd always thought that couples were supposed to love one another enough to be happy without children—if that was to be their lot in life.

But, unfortunately, since joining the group five years ago, I'd discovered that, all too often, that wasn't the case. Faced with infertility, marriages often fell apart. Couples blamed one another. Resentment brewed. Husbands left, and at least one woman from our group had filed for divorce after learning that her husband was incapable of ever fathering a child.

I was so thankful that Gordon and I had a good, solid marriage. Sure, he'd wanted kids as much as I had, but never, for a moment, had he ever made me feel as though I'd let him down.

"Stephanie?" I'd waited for Stephanie to focus her red, swollen eyes on me. My gut had clenched at the thought of telling her that I was pregnant, but I'd steeled myself. "Don't give up." I'd forced a smile that had felt stiff and phony. Maybe, deep down, I'd realized that nothing I could have said that would have made her feel better. But I knew that I had to try. "It will happen. You just have to have faith."

She'd nodded, looking so miserable that I'd wanted to cry with her. Blowing her nose loudly, she'd peered at me with a trickle of hope in her eyes. "You sound as if you really believe that."

"I do." Then I'd straightened, glancing around me at the weeping women, all of whom were sharing Stephanie's disappointment as if it were their own. Would they be able to share my happiness as graciously? I knew that I was about to find out.

Ignoring Katherine's horrified, expectant face, I'd taken a deep breath and begun. "Katherine and I have some wonderful news to share—something that should lift everyone's spirits, and give you all hope." I'd realized that there wasn't any other way to do it other than just blurting out the news. "We're pregnant."

The room was completely silent. The group of women had just stared blankly at me. I didn't think that anyone had even blinked for a solid thirty seconds. Then, finally, Patricia had moved forward to congratulate me. But her smile was stiff, and I didn't think that the tears in her eyes were tears of joy.

"I thought that it went fairly well," my sister said later.

Katherine was so obviously trying to put a positive spin on things that I couldn't help but laugh.

"We're lucky that we got out of there alive," I said bluntly. "I don't think that we'll be welcome back."

"There's no reason to go back," she said as she followed me into my kitchen.

The house was dark. I knew that Gordon had gone to bed early. He owned his own construction company, and he was currently on deadline to finish a community building. I'd begun to make hot tea. Normally, I drank coffee, but since becoming pregnant, I couldn't stand the smell, or taste, of coffee.

"I have to admit, I'll miss the group meetings," I told her.

"Me, too." Katherine had taken a seat at the breakfast bar and propped a forlorn face in her hand. "I feel so bad for the others. And, I feel so guilty that I'm almost sick."

I'd managed a wan smile in her direction as I'd put the tea bags in the cups and waited for the kettle to start whistling. "It's silly, isn't it? We should be celebrating, but all we can think about is how sorry we feel for the others."

"Well, you have to admit that it's kind of amazing how we both got pregnant at the same time," she said. "Me, through invitro, and you, with the help of fertility drugs."

"Yeah," I agreed. "I guess the doctors finally got the dosage just right." I'd patted my still-flat stomach, feeling awed at the thought of a baby growing inside of me.

She'd drummed her fingers on the counter. Her nails were sensibly short and buffed to a high, glossy shine. "In a way, I can understand some of the women thinking that I shouldn't have a baby. I mean, we might be living in the new millennium, but people still have a lot of old-fashioned ideas about a child needing two parents."

I'd poured steaming water over the tea bags. "They have no right to judge you. Our mother never married after Dad died, and we turned out okay."

"Speaking of Mom," my sister said. "I'm still in shock over her reaction to my decision to have a baby without a husband." Katherine had tried to make light of it, but I'd sensed her hurt. "Then you tell her that you're pregnant, too. I have to tell you—that kind of made me look foolish. I mean, you've been married forever, and you're a homemaker. You have the strength of your husband to depend upon. That makes you more responsible—you know?"

Putting her tea in front of her, I'd sat down across from my sister. "Look, Katherine. It's your life, and your decision. Don't ever let anyone stop you from doing what you want to do with your life. I chose to be a wife and a homemaker. You chose a career, and now, you want a child. There's nothing wrong with that, and you know it. You're strong enough to raise a child on your own. I can't believe that Mom would doubt that fact. She's always said you that should have been a man, because you think like one—and, you make decisions like one."

Katherine grinned. "I love you. You're not just my sister—you're my best friend. I want you to be my baby's godmother," she told me.

Her announcement brought emotional tears to my eyes. "I would love to be your baby's godmother. I want you to be my baby's godmother, too. If something were to happen to me and Gordon, at the same time—" I began.

"Don't say that! Don't even think it. Nothing's going to happen, to either of us. We're going to have beautiful, healthy babies, and we're going to grow old together. We'll have lots of grandbabies and great-grandbabies. I, for one, don't plan on dying anytime soon."

Months later, my sister's words would come back to haunt me. They would invade my nightmares, and echo painfully in my ears.

Katherine and I spent a lot of time together over the next few months. She'd had a heavy caseload, but she'd handled it with the ease of someone who'd learned to thrive on pressure. I'd gained weight at an alarming rate, while Katherine had worked out at the gym and eaten healthfully. We were as different as night and day, but we were closer than ever.

Despite Mom's misgivings about Katherine having a baby on her own, she'd soon come around and begun to share our anticipation. She'd planned a huge baby shower for my sister and me. After the shower, while we were helping her to clean up the mess, she'd confessed that she'd met someone special.

I didn't know who'd been the most shocked by her announcement—Katherine, or me. Dad had died of a heart attack when I was ten, and Katherine was eight. During all those years since, Mom hadn't had a single date—at least, not one that I'd known about. We'd came to the romantic conclusion that she'd decided that she could never find anyone to replace Dad.

Holding a pile of discarded wrapping paper against my chest, I'd finally managed to speak. "Someone special? A man? Are you talking about a man?" I asked.

Mom pursed her lips. She'd looked at me as if I were the silliest woman on earth. "Yes, Shelby, I'm talking about a man." She'd lifted one perfectly arched brow, proving that she had a sense of humor. "You didn't think I was talking about a woman, did you?"

My face had flushed with embarrassment. I'd stuffed the wrapping paper in the trash before replying. "No, I didn't think that," I insisted hurriedly. "But if you were talking about a woman, I wouldn't disown you."

"Me, either," Katherine said, trying to keep a straight face. She was busy separating our presents into two piles. We had basically gotten the same things. We were both due for an ultrasound the following month, but Mom had wanted to have the shower before she'd left on her cruise. She'd been planning it for months, long before we'd learned that we were pregnant. She had offered to cancel, but Katherine and I had refused to let her change her plans.

Suddenly, I couldn't help but wonder if she'd be going alone, as she'd planned, or if she'd be traveling with some distinguished gentleman who might, or might not, have been after Mom's money. Dad had left behind a substantial life insurance policy, and Mom had always had a head for business. With the right investments, she'd managed to make the money grow into a comfortable nest egg, even after she put Katherine through law school and helped Gordon and me with a down payment on our first starter home.

Mom had shot us both an exasperated look. "You two are just unbelievable—do you know that? His name is James Hendricksen, and he's a retired fire chief." Before we'd been able to ask more questions, Mom had changed the subject. "So, are you both going to want to know the sex of your babies?"

"I do," I told her. "It's just easier to plan that way. And, besides, I couldn't stand the doctor and nurse knowing, if I didn't."

"Same here," Katherine agreed. "I'll take either, but I really want a boy. Shelby's hoping for a girl. I guess we could always trade, if we had to."

We'd all laughed at that, and the tension had eased. So what if Mom had a boyfriend? She was certainly capable of handling her own life. After all, she'd raised us on her own.

Suddenly, I'd seen Katherine frown as she'd folded a beautiful baby quilt. "What's wrong?" I asked.

She'd shrugged, but her frown had remained. "I was just thinking about the fact that not a single person from our group came to the shower."

Mom had swiftly jumped to our defense. "I don't mean to be cruel, but their long faces would have put a damper on things, anyway." She'd sniffed indignantly. "You can bet that they'd expect you to be happy about it, if they became pregnant."

I'd stifled the urge to defend the group of women that I'd come to rely on over the barren, frustrating years before my pregnancy. Sadly, I'd understood all too well why they hadn't come. I hadn't forgotten how painful it was to watch a woman grow large with child, while I'd remained aching and empty.

As my gaze had met Katherine's, I'd seen that she was perfectly in tune with my thoughts. She'd understood, as well. She'd smiled, but the expression on her face was bittersweet.

"At least most of them sent gifts," she said quietly.

After I'd gotten home that evening, I'd gone online to the group's website to email my thanks to those who had sent baby gifts. There was a letter in my mailbox, but I hadn't recognized the user name. I'd clicked to open it, my horror slowly mounting as I'd read the hateful letter. The recipient had basically told me that I was too old to have a baby, and that I was selfish to risk having a baby with Down's syndrome. The tone had been unmistakably vicious.

As I'd sat there, feeling sick to my stomach, the phone had rung. I'd picked it up, my voice trembling. "Hello?" I said.

It was Katherine, and she'd sounded upset, too. "Hi, it's me," she began. "I just got a horrible email."

"Me, too." I'd read her mine, and then, she'd read me hers. The email she had received was longer and more vicious than the one I'd gotten, but I'd strongly suspected that it was from the same person.

"Do you think they could be right?" Katherine asked, sounding doubtful. "Am I wrong and selfish in wanting to have a baby without getting married and giving it a father?"

I'd been filled with anger toward the vicious person who had made my sister doubt her own capability. "Katherine, you're financially secure," I reminded her. "You're a solid, dependable person. You love kids, and you have deep moral standards. Don't let this sick person get to you."

"Whoever wrote this thinks that I'm a lesbian, just because I'm not married," she mumbled.

"So what if you are?" I cried, furious at the sender. "It's nobody's business but your own."

"Shelby, I'm not a lesbian," she insisted.

"You don't have to explain to me," I told her. "I know that you're not a lesbian, but if you were, I wouldn't love you any less." I'd heard Katherine sigh.

It must be the hormones getting to her, I thought, because my sister was nothing if not fearless. She didn't normally care about the opinions of others, or feel the need to justify herself. "Just because you haven't found a man who can sweep you off your feet, it doesn't make you a lesbian," I reassured her.

Katherine was silent for a long moment. "What if I find that man later—after I've already got a child?" she asked.

"If he's the right man, the fact that you have a child won't matter," I said soothingly. I couldn't believe that I'd had to reassure Katherine. Pregnancy had definitely messed with her hormones. The nasty email hadn't helped, of course. "Listen, don't give this person another thought. I'm certainly not. She—or he—thinks that I'm too old to have a baby. I'm only thirty-eight. Lots of women have babies at my age. Besides, my amnio test came out fine, so I know the baby's okay," I told her.

"I'm surprised that she didn't mention my age," Katherine said, sounding stronger. "I had to have the test done, too."

"Let's make a pact," I suggested impulsively.

"Oh, wow! We haven't done that since we 'borrowed' that money from Mom and made a pact to never, ever tell her." She giggled.

"Well, we didn't, did we? Let's agree to not let anyone, or anything, spoil our happiness over having these babies."

"Okay—agreed," she said.

"Swear," I insisted.

"I swear—okay?"

And then, she'd laughed, and I'd laughed, and everything was great again.

Katherine and I had managed to schedule our ultrasounds together. Gordon had seemed relieved that he wouldn't have to take off from his busy job to be with me. I was a little disappointed when he hadn't protested that Katherine was taking his place. But then, I'd reminded myself that I was lucky to have a sister like Katherine, and to be sharing such a wonderful event with her. Besides, I'd realized that Gordon was out of his element. He'd never been all that comfortable around kids. I was convinced, however, that everything would change once he'd held his own baby.

Dr. Granger, our OB-GYN, was a wonderful man. Katherine had been going to him for yearly Pap smears for the past few years, at the recommendation from a colleague of hers, so I'd agreed to give him a try.

I'd fallen instantly in love with his gentle bedside manner. From the beginning, it was clear that he knew and loved what he was doing. His nurse, however, was another story. From the moment that I'd met her, I'd disliked her, and I didn't normally judge people so quickly.

I really couldn't say exactly what it was about Geraldine Sweeney that had rubbed me the wrong way. Actually, I supposed it was a combination of things. She'd looked sullen, for one thing—like a sulky teenager who wasn't getting her own way. It was ridiculous, really, since she'd seemed to be around my age, or older.

The moment she'd left the room, I'd leaned over to whisper to Katherine, who was lying on the examining table next to mine as we'd waited for Dr. Granger to do our ultrasounds. "Is she always this cold?" I asked.

Katherine shrugged. "She's new. I think she's been here about six months. Maybe she's having a bad day," she said.

Determined to give her the benefit of the doubt, I'd plastered a smile on my face when she'd returned to rub gel onto both of our protruding tummies. I'd tried to catch her eye. "Do you have kids?" I asked.

I'd known instantly that I'd blundered. Her eyes were icy as she'd looked at me. "No, I don't," she muttered in a clipped, tight-mouthed way.

I'd exchanged a wry glance with my sister, who'd shrugged. I'd known that if I'd kept my mouth shut, things probably would have been okay. But I hadn't, and they weren't.

"I'm sorry," I murmured apologetically. Usually when someone said those two words, it got them off the hook. Not that time, though—and not me.

She'd pinned another cold look on me as she'd answered. "Not as sorry as I am. My first husband stabbed me in the stomach with a knife when I was four months pregnant. He killed my baby, and any chance I had of ever having another one," she said grimly.

Shame and embarrassment had flooded my body from head to toe. I'd never been so mortified in my life. And I could tell, by the mean, smug look in the nurse's eyes, that she knew it, too. She had meant to horrify and shame me with that horrendous story.

Katherine, being the lawyer that she was, had come quickly to my defense. "That's a horrible story, Geraldine," she said quietly. "I hope that he got what he deserved."

For a moment, the nurse's eyes had turned as dark as storm clouds. "He did," she muttered. Then, she'd become suddenly brisk and businesslike. "You're ready. Dr. Granger will be in directly." At the door, she'd paused. "He wouldn't be happy to know that I've told you about my personal life."

Simultaneously, Katherine and I had murmured our reassurances that we wouldn't say a word. We were silent after she'd left. Each of us was feeling foolish and guilty for resurrecting the woman's painful past.

But, we'd soon forgotten all about our guilt as Dr. Granger had come in to do our ultrasounds. Katherine went first. With our gazes glued to the monitor, we'd watched in awe and anticipation as he'd brought the image of Katherine's baby onto the monitor.

I'd seen a tiny hand, and I was able to make out the round curve of a buttock.

Dr. Granger had grinned at our excited squeals. "Do you want to know what it is?" he asked Katherine.

"Yes!" she cried. "Tell me it's a boy—tell me it's boy!" she urged.

He'd laughed as he shook his head. "Sorry, I can't do that. It's a girl."

I was afraid that Katherine would be disappointed, but she wasn't. To our surprise, she'd started laughing. Tears were streaming from the corners of her eyes. When she could talk again, she'd explained. "I knew it! I said that I wanted a boy, hoping that it would be a girl. And it is!"

"You sneak," I teased. "You wanted a girl all along?"

She'd nodded happily. "Yes. But I wasn't about to tempt fate."

I was next. You could have heard a pin drop in the office as Dr. Granger had rubbed the wand over my gel-slick stomach. Finally, we could see the outline of the baby's head, then a knee. The baby had kicked, bumping against the wand as if it were protesting the intrusion.

Dr. Granger had paused, peering at the screen. I'd held my breath. He'd shot me a grin. "Looks like you'll be sharing baby clothes, ladies."

"It's a girl?" I asked.

"It's a girl, unless—well, you know. When it's a boy, it's a boy, but when it's a girl, there's always a chance that we might be mistaken."

"How often does that happen?" I truly didn't care about the sex, as long as it was healthy, but I couldn't deny that I'd wanted my baby to be a girl.

Dr. Granger had wiped down the wand, and then, he'd wiped the gel from my stomach. "Usually, our guesses are pretty accurate, at least eighty-five percent." He'd grinned. "But I have to tell you that there's always a chance that it could be a boy. Believe it or not, doctors have been sued for being wrong."

"You're kidding." Katherine had sounded shocked. "Patients should just be glad that they have a healthy baby!"

Geraldine had come in to help us get dressed. She didn't ask about our findings, and we didn't volunteer the information. With our ultrasound pictures clutched to our breasts, we'd beaten a hasty retreat out of the doctor's office.

After Geraldine's terrible confession, I'd reminded myself of her story each and every time when she was rude or snide, or when she'd frozen me with a cold look over a question that I'd asked. I'd felt sorry for her. But, even still, she'd continued to give me the creeps. Katherine, however, wasn't so forgiving.

"I don't know why Dr. Granger keeps her on," she grumbled as we were leaving the office after a visit. She'd asked the nurse for an early appointment and Geraldine had told her in frosty tones that Dr. Granger had to make his rounds at the hospital from eight to ten. She'd said that she didn't think he'd rearrange his entire schedule just for Katherine. "She could have explained things in a nicer way," she continued as we got into my car. "She could have just said that he doesn't come in until ten, instead of making me feel like a selfish brat."

I'd made an attempt to soothe her ruffled feathers. "I don't think that she realizes how rude she is sometimes. Actually, she reminds me of my fifth-grade teacher, Mrs. Roddolico. That woman could make you feel about two inches tall, just by looking at you."

"I had that witch, too, remember? She actually told me one day that I looked like a clown, just because I had on blue eye shadow."

I'd giggled, slanting a mischievous glance at my sister. "Katherine, you did look like a clown. Mom made you throw that eye shadow away."

Katherine had pretended to pout. "Well, that's not the point. It wasn't Mrs. Roddolico's place to tell me—it was Mom's."

"That's true." I'd backed out of the parking lot, heading for the grocery store. Katherine and I had always done most everything together—most of the time without thinking. We truly were best friends. "Hey, have you gotten any more emails from our well-wisher?" I asked.

"You mean from the psycho who thinks that I shouldn't have a baby because I'm single? The one who thinks that you shouldn't be having a baby because you're ancient?"

"Hey, watch it!" I protested, laughing. "I'm only two years older than you!"

"You know, that psycho could very well be the nurse, Geraldine," Katherine mused thoughtfully. "We did give our email addresses so that we could get updates on women's health care."

I'd flipped on my blinker and turned into the supermarket parking lot. It wasn't until I'd parked the car and cut the engine that I'd replied. "Yeah, it could have been Geraldine. Or Patricia, or Stephanie, or Amanda, or Maggie, or Cherie. Should I go on?"

Katherine shook her head. "I just can't believe that any of those women could be that mean."

"You know that saying: 'Hell hath no fury like a woman scorned?'"

Katherine nodded.

"Well, I think the same goes for: 'Hell hath no fury like a barren woman,'" I told her.

My sister had sighed and placed a protective hand over her stomach. "I wish that everyone could be as lucky and as happy as we are," she murmured.

"Me, too," I agreed.

That same weekend, we'd held a barbecue at my house to celebrate our pregnancies. Framed proudly, the ultrasound photos of our little girls had held center court on the long picnic table in the backyard. Gordon and I had decided on the name Kelly Lynn, and my sister had decided on Emma Grace.

As I'd made the rounds with a tray of appetizers, I'd overheard Gordon confessing to one of his friends that he couldn't make heads or tails of the babies' sonograms. It had seemed that the general consensus among the men was that only women could "see" the babies.

How can they miss seeing the tiny hand that's waving at them in Katherine's baby's picture? I thought. And how can they not see the clear image of a knee, and the outline of a head, in my baby's picture?

I shook my head as I reached Mom. She was standing with her boyfriend, James, and James's grown daughter, Michele. It was the first time that I'd been introduced to her, so I'd put on my best smile and handed the tray of appetizers to Mom so that I could give her a welcoming hug. James had turned out to be a gem. He'd really seemed to be infatuated with Mom. She literally glowed when she was around him. I was happy for her.

"Michele, welcome to the family," I said sincerely. If his daughter was anything like her father, then she already had my vote. "Mom said that you live in Miami?" When Michele had nodded, I'd continued. "Well, you're a long way from home then, aren't you?" I asked.

Her eyes had clouded, and her smile had faded slightly. "I'm on an extended leave," she mumbled.

My gaze had collided with Mom's warning one. Before I'd been able to open my mouth again, she'd grabbed my arm and hustled me away.

"Come on, darling. I'll help you to refresh that tray," she said briskly.

The moment we were out of earshot, I'd jerked my arm free. "Mom! Why are you manhandling me? What did I say? For heaven's sake—I just said that she was a long way from home. I didn't ask her if she'd ever been to prison."

Mom didn't speak until we'd reached the kitchen, and were relatively alone. Then, she'd kept her voice low as she'd explained. "Michele is in the middle of an ugly divorce. Her husband left her for some young bimbo."

"Oh, I didn't know. Why didn't you tell me?" I asked.

"Because James just told me yesterday. I haven't had the time." She'd begun loading the tray with stuffed mushrooms. "That's not the worst of it," she went on, her voice thick with sympathy for Michele, and disgust for Michele's husband. "She just found out that the homewrecker is going to have the baby that she could never have."

I couldn't help it—I just couldn't. I'd let out a heavy sigh of exasperation. "Why is it that, when I wasn't pregnant, I was constantly running into pregnant women, or women with babies? And, now that I'm pregnant, the only women that I seem to meet—other than Katherine—are women who can't have children?"

I'd begun to slap appetizers onto a tray, not caring if I caused the cheese to topple from the crackers. "Instead of being deliriously happy, which I deserve to be, I'm spending most of my time feeling guilty!"

Mom had clucked her tongue and given me a shame-on-you look. "Honestly—I can't believe you," she chided me. "I've never known you to be a selfish, insensitive person."

"I'm not," I insisted. "I'm just sick and tired of feeling guilty for something that's beyond my power to change."

Suddenly, Mom had grabbed my arm again. "Oh, no," she said. "Katherine is talking to Michele! I've got to get out there before she puts her foot in her mouth—the way you did."

She'd left me standing there, seething. Had I been that sensitive in the past? I didn't think that I had, but I supposed that some women just couldn't help themselves. Although, I had to admit that I would most certainly have been sensitive if Gordon had run off with another woman and gotten her pregnant.

Not just sensitive, I'd admitted honestly, but devastated, and probably not prone to discuss it—just as Michele probably didn't want to be reminded of her pain.

Am I destined to feel guilty throughout my entire pregnancy? I wondered.

After Mom had chastised me over my inadvertent blunder, I'd felt rather smug when Michele had poured out her heart to Katherine and me after the party. She and James had stayed, along with Katherine, to help clean up. She'd told me the whole, awful, sordid story about catching her husband with his mistress. She'd also explained how she'd felt when she'd confronted him with the knowledge that his new lover was also expecting his baby.

I'd thought that Michele was a brave woman for holding up so well. She'd never shed a tear throughout the entire story. Katherine and I, on the other hand—no doubt due to an influx of hormones—had wept openly. We'd learned that she was a nurse, and that she was thinking of relocating to our city.

Katherine and I had exchanged knowing looks. "Well, we could certainly use more nurses with your bedside manner and kindness," I told her.

"Amen to that," Katherine murmured.

Michele had raised a brow and looked from me to Katherine, then back again. "I sense a story here," she said.

"You tell it, Shelby," my sister prompted.

"No, you tell it," I insisted. "It's nothing, anyway. It's just a nurse who needs to be on major antidepressants."

"I think she disapproves of me because I'm having this baby alone," Katherine admitted.

Mom had suddenly jumped up and begun to clear the table where we'd sat. My suspicion was immediately aroused, and so was Katherine's—especially when she'd refused to look at us.

Katherine had groaned and glared after Mom as she'd disappeared into the kitchen, with more haste than grace. "Why do I get the feeling that she never told you I was single?" she asked.

"You're having this baby alone?" Michele asked sharply.

Well, I'd really started to like Michele, but I sure didn't like her tone at that moment. I'd jumped to Katherine's defense before she was able to answer.

"Is there something wrong with that?" I challenged. I'd immediately felt like an immature teenager, and I'd realized right away that I'd sounded like one, too. "Katherine isn't alone," I went on, trying to remain civil. "She has Mom and me, and Gordon, and about a half-dozen friends who would die for her."

Okay, so that wasn't exactly the truth. Katherine had plenty of friends, but not close ones. She and I had always been best friends.

Katherine, as usual, had sounded a hundred times more diplomatic when she'd finally spoken. "It's the new millennium, Michele," she told her, without a trace of irritation. "Women make the decision to have babies without men all the time. I can afford it, so why shouldn't I?"

Michele hadn't seemed to have an argument for Katherine's logic, but I'd sensed that she didn't approve. I'd kept up my guard for the rest of the night. Silently, I was fuming. Why couldn't people just mind their own business? Why did they judge someone, as if they'd walked a mile in their shoes? And why in hell couldn't they see that Katherine was a strong, smart woman, and fully capable of giving a child everything?

Maybe Michele was just old-fashioned, I told myself, trying to be more diplomatic, like Katherine. Michele had been raised by two parents, so maybe she just couldn't imagine a child not having a father by choice.

Or, maybe she was like the others. Maybe she was jealous because we were pregnant, and she wasn't. A part of me felt mean-spirited for having those kinds of thoughts, but I couldn't seem to get around them. I'd felt as if people were attacking Katherine, so my instincts were to fight back. What hurt Katherine, hurt me.

Later, before James and Michele left, Michele had apologized to Katherine. "I was just surprised, that's all. I admire you immensely for having a baby on your own."

She had sounded sincere, but that hadn't kept me from eventually putting her on my list of suspects after Katherine's death. But then, she was one of many on my list. Nearly prostrate with grief, I'd blamed everyone.

The months following our ultrasounds had seemed to fly past. Gordon and I had turned my sewing room into a beautiful nursery, using bright, primary colors. After that, we'd helped Katherine with her nursery. After a long, exasperating debate, she'd settled on a rainbow of pastels.

Katherine had remained within the accepted weight-gain range, while I had gained nearly seventy pounds by the end of the eighth month. While Katherine had whistled the happy tune of glowing motherhood, I'd tossed back antacid tablets like candy, to stem the constant heartburn.

We'd spent our days lumbering through shops and dreaming about our babies—when we weren't talking about them, which was most of the time. Both of us had begun to anticipate the births of our children, almost to the point of delirium. Sometimes I'd literally had to pinch myself to make certain that I wasn't dreaming.

Occasionally, we'd run into one of the women from our old group. It was always awkward, but, somehow, we'd managed to stumble through the encounter. Despite my attempts not to experience those emotions, I'd almost always walked away feeling guilty for the precious baby that was growing inside me.

Mom and James had announced their engagement, and Michele had gone back to Miami, deciding that she wasn't ready to relocate. She'd made us promise to call her whenever either of us went into labor. She'd told us that she was going to try her best to take a short leave so that she could share the joyful events. Being an aunt, she said, was the next best thing to being a mother.

And then, the final countdown had begun. Katherine and I were about to see our daughters for the first time and, if our calculations were right, Katherine would be first. During the last four weeks—two for Katherine—I'd made her promise to carry her cell phone with her at all times. She lived alone, so I was understandably concerned about her going into labor with no one there to help her. I was worried about something going wrong.

She'd laughed at my concerns, but I could tell that she was getting anxious about the delivery. We'd spent a lot of time on the phone when we weren't together. Gordon had laughingly teased me about moving Katherine in with us until after the birth. But, of course, Katherine wouldn't even discuss the possibility.

"Women used to squat in the fields to have a baby, then go right back to work," she reminded me. But all her reminder had done was to induce a gruesome image of Katherine squatting in her bathroom, delivering a baby, then bleeding to death before anyone could find her.

Since we were so close, and kept in almost constant contact, I'd known, almost to the hour, how long Katherine had been missing when I'd called the police. We'd both had an appointment to see the doctor at ten o'clock. Since Dr. Granger had told her the week before that she was dilated two centimeters and could go into labor anytime, I'd been aware of the fact that Katherine was anxious to see him.

I'd called her at eight-fifteen that morning, right after I'd lumbered out of the shower. When she didn't answer, I hadn't panicked immediately. I'd called her cell phone instead, thinking that she might have gone to the market down the street for a whole-wheat bagel or something just as annoyingly healthy.

I'd started to panic when her voice mail had picked up. Trying to calm myself, I'd sat on the edge of the bed, stark naked, with water streaming from my hair. "She's probably in the bathroom and can't hear the phone," I murmured to myself. "Or she forgot her cell phone when she went to the market." Somehow, I'd managed to get dressed, dry my hair, and put on a little makeup before I'd called her home phone again. And then, I'd called her cell phone again.

There was no answer.

Giving into panic and imagining all sorts of horrors, I'd grabbed my car keys, my purse, and my cell phone and raced to the car as fast as my fat, pregnant body would allow. I'd squeezed behind the wheel and used one hand to dial her number while I'd started the car.

I'd called her seven times on the way to her apartment. When I'd pulled into the parking lot in front of the building, I'd run over the curb and given myself a painful jolt. Ignoring the sudden, sharp cramp in my lower abdomen, I'd raced into the building and lumbered up the stairs, breathing hard. Where was she? Why wasn't she answering the phone? Was she unconscious? Bleeding to death?

I'd pounded on her door, wheezing and trembling from fear and fatigue. Something was wrong. I'd felt it deep in my bones. Getting out my car keys, I'd used my spare key and let myself in, calling out to Katherine, my voice shrill and scared.

My voice had echoed in the apartment. It was silent and empty. I'd gone into each room and peeked in every nook and cranny, but Katherine wasn't there.

What I'd found in the bedroom, however, had made me lock a scream inside my throat. Her clothes were spread out on the bed. The granny panties we'd both hated, but had been forced to wear for comfort and logic. The nursing bra she'd bought in anticipation of breastfeeding the baby. And, beside those garments, was the maternity outfit she'd bought just yesterday, to wear to the office visit that morning.

Flat, comfortable shoes were sitting in front of the bed. The shower doors were still fogged, as if she hadn't been out of the shower for long, and in the kitchen, the teapot was still hot.

Her purse and car keys were on the hall table, and those items, perhaps, were the most damning evidence of all that something wasn't right. If she had gone to the market, she wouldn't have forgotten her keys or her purse. I also couldn't imagine Katherine struggling into clothes that she would just have to change out of when she returned, just to go to the market, unless she'd changed her mind about wearing the new outfit.

But even if she had decided to slip into some sweats or something, there was still the matter of her keys and purse on the hall table.

"Calm down," I said out loud to the empty apartment. Every nerve cell in my body was screaming with burgeoning panic. Where was my sister?

I'd locked the apartment door and headed back to my car. The market wasn't far, but I wasn't in the shape that Katherine was, so I'd preferred to drive. Besides, my legs had gotten so wobbly that I didn't think I could have walked, anyway.

Nobody at the market had seen her that morning.

After I'd heard that, I'd gone back to my car and called the police. They'd agreed to meet me back at Katherine's apartment. Next, I'd called Gordon and told him that something had happened to Katherine. By that time, I was completely convinced. He'd told me to stay calm and assured me that he'd be there in fifteen minutes.

The next two hours were a living nightmare. The police had refused to report Katherine missing until she'd been gone forty-eight hours, despite my insistence that something terrible had happened. I'd told them about our anticipated doctor's appointment, and I'd shown them her clothes lying on the bed. I just couldn't convince them that Katherine would have never just disappeared without telling me where she was going. She would never, ever have done that to me, knowing how worried I was about her going into labor without anyone around.

Gordon was worried about my health, and our baby. I was having cramps, but I hadn't told him. I supposed he'd caught a flash of pain on my face or something, because he'd started insisting that we go home and wait for the police to call.

"Wait for them to call?" I almost yelled. "They aren't doing anything, Gordon! They won't even consider that she's missing." The officers had checked with everyone in the building, but nobody had seen my sister since the evening before. I had spoken with her around eleven the night before, and, at the time, she had been ready for bed.

And I knew that she had gone to bed and gotten up again, because there had been steam on the shower doors, hot water in the teakettle, and her clothes had been laid out on the bed. She had been ready to get dressed when whatever it was had happened to her.

I'd clutched Gordon's shoulders. "She's been abducted, Gordon!" I insisted in a shrill voice. "Somebody came in here and took Katherine in her bathrobe. She keeps it hanging on a hook on the bathroom door, and it's gone."

Gordon had looked at me helplessly. I could tell that he was scared, too. "Maybe she put her robe in the hamper."

I shook my head violently. "No, she didn't. I checked. And she doesn't have another robe. She likes this one because it's soft from being washed so much, and it's big enough to fit around her belly." My legs had folded. Gordon had held me against his chest as I'd begun to sob. "Oh, Gordon! What happened to my sister?"

"Let's go home, honey. You're making yourself sick, and there's nothing that we can do here."

"No! No! I'm not going home," I told him. "What if she calls, and we're not here to answer the phone? No, I'm not leaving. Call Mom and have her go to our house in case Katherine calls there. I'm staying here."

I'd pushed away from him, taken two steps in the direction of the couch, and then, everything had begun to turn black. I remembered waving my arms, instinctively trying to catch myself to keep from hurting the baby, and I remembered Gordon cursing loudly as he'd caught me around the waist. Something warm had gushed between my legs. Then I'd fainted.

I'd woken up in the hospital in hard labor. The glaring overhead lights had hurt my eyes, and there had seemed to be a thousand people milling around me. The voices were clipped and professional.

"Get someone in here to do a spinal block."

"He's on his way."

"How's her blood pressure?"

"Not great."

I'd felt hands invading my body, hurting me, plunging into me as if the doctor were trying to shove his arm into my belly and drag out the baby.

"She's fully effaced and the baby's in place. Where's my kit?"

"Right here, Doctor."

"Okay. Let's see if we can get her to push. We don't have time for that spinal."

The pain was intense, but it wasn't enough to block out my worries over my sister. Through gasps and screams, I'd questioned the nurses, the doctors, and Gordon, who'd held my hand and tried to get me to breathe in between pushes. Nobody would tell me anything.

"Blood pressure's rising, Dr. Granger."

"Put her out. I think I can get the baby from here."

When I'd woken up again, Gordon was there, looking pale and worried. He was still holding my hand. He summoned a smile, but it didn't reach his eyes.

"She's beautiful, honey," he whispered.

I couldn't even think about my baby. "Have they found Katherine?" I demanded.

He shook his head. "Don't you want to see her?"

"No. I want to see Katherine." I'd started to sob. "I want to see my sister. She's supposed to have her baby first. She's supposed to be here."

"Shh, honey. We'll find her," he said soothingly.

I'd turned my face away and cried into my pillow. Gordon said something to one of the hovering nurses, and then, I'd felt a needle prick my arm. Slowly, sounds became muffled. I was drifting, floating, feeling no pain, no worries.

The next time I'd opened my eyes, it was morning. I'd turned my head and found Gordon slumped in a chair beside the bed, snoring with his mouth open. I'd tried to speak and found my voice nothing more than a husky croak.

"Gordon," I said.

He'd jerked awake, then shot out of the chair. "Honey? Are you okay?"

I'd searched his haggard face, looking for hope. I'd found none. I'd swallowed hard, dreading the question, but dreading the answer even more. "Katherine?"

He'd hesitated. My hand had found his arm. I'd dug my fingers into his skin, silently commanding him to tell me. He shook his head, his eyes gleaming suspiciously. "Honey, they've found Katherine. A maid found her in a hotel room downtown."

My throat had closed so tightly that I couldn't speak for a long moment. I'd forced the words past my constricted throat. "She's dead?"

He nodded.

I'd suppressed a sob. "The baby?"

He shook his head. My nails dug into his arm. "She wasn't pregnant when they found her. We don't know where the baby is."

My little sister was dead. She had been abducted and murdered in a hotel room. Her baby had been stolen from her womb.

I almost didn't believe it, but it was hard to ignore the truth when I'd looked into Gordon's stricken eyes. When Mom arrived, the last shred of denial that I'd been hanging on to, the last prayer that I'd been living through some kind of nightmare that I'd awaken from, had crumbled at the sight of her shocked, weeping face.

We'd clung to each other, sobbing uncontrollably. I was sore, but I'd hardly noticed the pain. I'd wanted to scream and hit something. How could something so terrible have happened to such a wonderful person? Katherine had been kind and honest, always eager to help those less fortunate. She could have been a corporate lawyer, but she had chosen to work for the people, instead.

When our sobs had quieted and I'd felt empty, yet aching, Mom had stepped aside, indicating a man standing in the shadows of my hospital room.

"Honey, this is Homicide Detective Wallace. He needs to ask you a few questions, since you were closest to Katherine, especially during her last hours. . . ." Her voice had trailed off into a whisper, and more tears had fallen as the man had come forward.

I couldn't stop crying, either. Gordon had gripped my hand, and Mom had laid a comforting hand on my leg. Some people may have thought it was strange that I didn't ask for my own baby, but I knew my baby was safe. All my thoughts were centered on what had happened to Katherine, and the whereabouts of her baby.

My voice was a hoarse croak as I'd questioned the detective. "Have you found my sister's killer? And the baby? Have you found her baby?" I demanded.

His eyes were warm with sympathy as he shook his head. "I'm afraid that we aren't making any headway. Your sister was checked into the hotel under her own name, and nobody remembers seeing her with anyone. We've combed the area, alleyways, dumpsters—all the usual places where babies are abandoned—but we haven't found anything, or any trace that a baby might have been there."

My heart had seemed to stop. I was appalled by the casual reference that he'd made to finding abandoned babies. "You mean, you actually find babies in those kinds of places?" I asked, horrified.

His mouth had tightened grimly. "You'd be surprised at how many mothers dump their newborns in dumpsters or leave them in alleys."

"That's not what my sister did!" My voice was shaking with rage. I was outraged at the thought of him thinking along those horrible lines. "My sister wanted this baby! She planned this baby. She would never abandon her!"

"He knows that, honey," Gordon said softly.

Mom's voice cracked. "We've told him how much Katherine wanted her baby."

"How did she die?" I asked bluntly. I didn't want to know, but I had to know.

Detective Wallace hesitated. "We won't know for certain until we get the results of the autopsy, but it appears that she was given a lethal dose of potassium. It stopped her heart. The needle and the vial were lying next to her on the bed. Whoever killed her used surgical gloves, and that person knew what they were doing."

I'd closed my eyes and swallowed hard, forcing myself to listen—to ask questions. "Why? Why would anyone want to hurt Katherine and her baby?"

"I don't know the answer to that, ma'am. At least, not yet. I was hoping that you could help us. Did your sister have any enemies?"

Despite myself, I'd laughed harshly. "She was a lawyer—what do you think?" I'd hesitated, remembering the nasty email and the reactions of the women in our group. "She and I did get an email from someone. Hers was a bit more vicious. They didn't think that she should be having a baby alone."

The detective had flipped open a notebook and scribbled something. "Any chance that you kept the email in your file?"

"No, I didn't. I deleted it immediately." I'd bitten my lip until I'd tasted blood. "I never thought that I'd need to see it again."

"Anything else? Your mother told me that you and Katherine belonged to a group for infertile women. I would imagine that your pregnancies aroused a lot of envy in some of those women."

"Yes," I admitted. "But Katherine and I talked about it, and we decided that we'd probably have been just as envious."

Detective Wallace had stared hard at me for a long moment. "Was there anyone who seemed particularly upset about your sister planning single motherhood?"

"I think some of them disapproved," I mused, assuming that he was still talking about the group. My gaze had flickered to Mom's. "Even Michele voiced her shock over Katherine deciding to have a baby without a father."

"Michele?" the detective asked.

Mom spoke up. "She's my fiancé's daughter. She lives in Miami."

"Did she say why she disapproved?" he asked.

"She apologized later, saying it was just a shock," I told him. My dry lips twisted. "It was like I was telling Mom—it seemed that when we became pregnant, candidates for that support group we belonged to seemed to come out of the woodwork."

"I don't understand," Detective Wallace said sharply.

Quickly, I'd explained. "Michele's husband left her for another woman, and now, he's having a baby with the other woman. Michele couldn't get pregnant."

He wrote down something again. "I know you're probably tired. When you feel better, do you think you could give me a list of names of the women in the group, and anyone else you can think of who might be capable of doing something like this?"

I'd nodded, tears streaming down my face again. I just couldn't believe that Katherine was gone. "Do you think you'll find her baby? I'm her godmother, and I want her back."

"If she's still alive, and we do find her," Detective Wallace told me, "then chances are, we'll find your sister's killer. Our theory right now is that someone wanted your sister's baby so badly that they'd kill to get it."

"Her," I corrected him in a strangled whisper. "My sister's baby is a little girl." I broke down and began sobbing again.

Gordon held me tightly, and Mom pushed the detective aside and pressed close to me, crying quietly with me.

Suddenly, all I could think about was my own baby. I'd felt ashamed for neglecting her, and I was irrationally terrified that she was in danger, too. I'd clutched Gordon's shoulders, my eyes burning and raw.

"Get our baby in here. I want to keep her in the room with me."

Gordon had nodded and left the room. He'd understood my paranoia without explanation. Mom had continued to hold me, murmuring that everything was going to be all right.

But she'd lied. Nothing would be all right again, because they couldn't bring my sister back. The only thing left to do was to find the baby, and get her out of the clutches of a madwoman, or madman.

That she might already be dead, like Katherine, was something that I'd refused to consider.

I'd heard a noise at the hospital door and glanced up to see Gordon standing there, holding a bundle in his arms. I'd seen a pink hand waving madly over the folds of the pink-and-blue striped receiving blanket, and my heart had filled with a fierce, hungry love. He'd brought her to me and settled her into my arms.

I'd stared down at my daughter through a blur of tears. She was beautiful. Perfect. Yet, a cloud had hung over what should have been one of the happiest days of my life. Katherine should have been there with me, holding her own precious bundle as we'd shared the joy of finally becoming mothers. We should have been comparing the length of fingers and toes, the shape of ears and eyes, and speculating on what eye color our girls would ultimately have.

We had planned to take walks together with our babies. We'd pick out matching outfits, and we'd promised to make sure that the girls became as close as Katherine and I had been. We had looked forward to the first tooth, the first step, the first day of school. But there wasn't going to be a "we." Just me, and Gordon and my baby, whom I'd now decided to name Katherine, after my sister. We'd call her Katie. I know that I was lucky to have Gordon and Mom, but they couldn't replace Katherine. Katherine and I would have been able to discuss even the smallest detail about our daughters' lives and find the conversation interesting.

But Katherine was gone, and I was determined to find her baby. I wanted to give her baby the love and care that Katherine would have given her. I wanted to keep my promise to Katherine. A sob had escaped me as I'd studied my beautiful little girl.

Oh, God, Katherine, I thought, my heart breaking all over again. I can't believe you're gone!

Later, as Katie had slept peacefully in a crib by my bed, I'd begun making the list that Detective Wallace had requested. The hospital door had opened. I'd looked up from my list to find Michele breezing into the room.

Her face had lit up at the sight of my sleeping baby. She'd kept her voice a whisper as she'd stared down at Katie. "God, she's gorgeous, Shelby. You're so lucky."

Then her gaze had met mine, and I'd read the sadness and sympathy there. Mentally, I'd crossed her from my list. How could I consider her a suspect when she was standing right in front of me, admiring my baby? I didn't see madness in her eyes—just a great empathy for my loss, and, yes, just a tad bit of understandable envy over the baby.

"I'm so sorry about Katherine, Shelby. It's a horrible tragedy."

"Yes." Because I was tired of tears, I'd concentrated on my sleeping baby and tried to swallow the knot in my throat. "I don't know how anyone could do something like that."

Michele slipped a finger into the tiny hand, and Katie had automatically curled her fingers around it. "It's awful, but you have this little miracle here, right?"

I was proud of my baby. I loved my baby immensely, but it seemed disloyal and selfish to wallow in happiness while my sister lay on a cold, steel table somewhere, getting cut open in the hopes of finding a clue that would lead us to her killer. And her child—who knew if she was being tortured, or abandoned? Detective Wallace had said that he believed someone had taken the baby, someone who wanted a baby so badly that they'd lost touch with reality. But what if he was wrong? What if something else had happened to my sister's baby? What if the person who had taken her had panicked, and left her somewhere to die?

"I got here as soon as I could," Michele said softly, stroking Katie's cheek. "Daddy called me. Is there anything that I can do to help?"

"Be there for Mom," I said, choking up. "Because I can't be right now. I know that she's having a terrible time."

"I'll go right over," she promised. "But I have to go back to Miami tomorrow. There's a nasty flu going around and I had a terrible time getting someone to cover my shift just for two days."

"I understand. Thanks, Michele."

"Daddy's with her now, Shelby. We'll take care of her until you're stronger. Meanwhile, you take care of yourself and this little angel. You and Gordon deserve a baby."

"Katherine deserved one, too," I said, a bit more sharply than I'd intended.

Michele had looked startled, then her eyes grew moist. "Of course she did. I can't tell you how sorry I am that this has happened."

But sorry wouldn't bring Katherine back, and it wouldn't help me to find her baby.

That night, I'd slept fitfully, my dreams full of shadowed faces reaching for my baby. I'd kept a hand on my baby's back as she'd slept beside me in her crib. Once, a nurse had come in and seen that I was awake.

"Can't sleep?" she asked, her face and voice gentle.

I didn't have to ask to know that rumors of my sister's horrible death had already made the rounds among the hospital staff. "No, I can't sleep. I'm having bad dreams."

"The doctor left orders to give you something to help you relax if you needed it."

The thought of being drugged frightened me more than the nightmares. "No," I said firmly.

Early the next morning as I was breast-feeding Katie, Detective Wallace came in. He saw what I was doing, then kept his gaze carefully averted. If I hadn't been so grief-stricken and exhausted, I might have found his reaction amusing. Breast-feeding was a natural occurrence, and I supposed I'd never understand why it made some people uncomfortable.

"Any news?" I asked.

"The autopsy confirmed what we suspected about how your sister died," he answered in a low, apologetic voice. "Someone knew exactly how much potassium to administer to stop a person's heart."

I'd kept my head lowered, watching as my daughter ate hungrily. I knew it was difficult enough for the detective to tell me the sickening details, without having to see the anguish that I knew was reflected on my face.

"Did you make the list?" he asked.

I'd pointed to the nightstand beside my bed. He'd picked up the list and skimmed it.

"Michele Richardson isn't on here. Any particular reason why you think she couldn't be a suspect?"

Shifting the baby to the other side, I'd helped her to find my nipple before I'd answered. "She was here last night. She flew in from Miami.

I just don't think she could have done it. She seemed so—" I hesitated.

"Innocent?" Detective Wallace's smile was cynical. "Ma'am, when you're in my business, looking innocent is a clue." He shrugged. "But, I'll leave her off the list, unless something comes up that puts her in the spotlight. With her living in Miami, it's probably a long-shot, anyway."

He'd tapped his pen against the list, and something in his expression had made me instinctively tense up.

"What is it?" I demanded. I didn't want anyone keeping information from me, no matter how painful.

"Well, it's about your sister's life insurance." He'd stared at me as if he could see right through me.

I'd flushed without knowing why. "My sister wanted to make sure that her baby would have everything she needed, if something happened to her. I don't think there's anything wrong with that, do you? I have life insurance, and so does my husband."

"So you knew you were the beneficiary?" he asked.

"Yes, I knew. I was—I am—the baby's godmother, too. Katherine wanted me to take care of her child, should anything ever happen to her." My throat ached with tears. "She was a cautious person, but I don't think she ever thought something like this could happen." Not in a million years, I thought sadly.

"Who does?"

My arms had tightened involuntarily around my baby. "You don't think that I had something to do with her death?" I asked in shocked disbelief.

"You have to understand that I'm just doing my job," he explained. "I'm exploring every possibility. You do want me to be thorough, don't you, Mrs. Wiest?"

"Of course. Besides, I had the perfect alibi, didn't I? I was giving birth to my baby." Suddenly, the entire conversation had begun to feel surreal. But then, so did the idea of my sister getting murdered, and someone stealing her baby.

Detective Wallace had glanced briefly at the now-sleeping baby in my arms. He'd stuffed the list in his pocket. "I'll get started on these interviews right away, and I'll let you know if I come up with anything."

I was relieved when he was gone. I knew that I had nothing to feel guilty about, but just being alive while my sister was dead had made me feel a certain amount of guilt, and a shameful sort of fear. What if the psycho who had killed Katherine and taken her baby had decided to pick me, instead? Katherine would have been the one grieving.

Mom, Michele, and Gordon came in an hour later. Michele came to say good-bye. Gordon and Mom were going to take us home. I'd wept on the way downstairs to the car as a nurse had pushed me in a wheelchair. In my purse, I'd had a prescription for an antidepressant, which the doctor had strongly recommended that I take. Grief, on top of postpartum depression, wasn't anything to fool around with, he'd cautioned. He'd insisted that I'd need all the help I could get.

Since I had, indeed, felt as though I were sinking into a big, black hole, I wasn't about to argue with him. Not only did my baby need me, but Katherine's baby would need me, as well—when we'd found her.

I'd refused to consider the possibility that we wouldn't find her. I vowed that I would make it my life's goal, if I needed.

Gordon had helped me into the passenger seat and buckled the baby into the infant seat in the back. Mom rode in back with Katie. The nurse had handed me my care package and reminded me that my doctor wanted to see me in his office the following week.

Her reminder had triggered a memory. I'd nearly startled Gordon to death by grabbing his arm as he'd started to shut the door. "Gordon! Call Detective Wallace! I forgot about Geraldine, Dr. Granger's nurse! Katherine and I both thought she had mental problems."

He'd nodded and pulled his cell phone from his pocket. He got Detective Wallace on the phone and handed the phone to me. Quickly, I'd told the detective about Geraldine's surliness, and how she wasn't able to have children because of her husband's violent attack.

"Okay, I'll put her first on my list," he told me.

"Will you let me know what you find out?" I asked.

"Yes, ma'am, I will," he promised.

At Gordon's insistence, I'd tried to take a nap when I got home, but my mind kept running in circles. Just thinking about the terror my sister must have gone through the last hours of her life had made my stomach heave, and made me break out into a cold sweat. I'd wondered if Mom was having the same terrible thoughts, thinking about her daughter's last hours. She had a grandchild close at hand—was she thinking about the other grandchild she had yet to see, and might never see?

James was a rock. Since he had retired, he had time on his hands. He either cooked for us or brought in expensive takeout food. Mom tended to Katie most of the time. I was feeling so anxious and sick that I was afraid the baby would pick up on my nervousness, so I'd let Mom take over without protest. It had seemed that my stress was affecting my milk flow, as well, so I'd given up my dream of doing everything just right and put Katie on formula.

The day after my release from the hospital, Detective Wallace had come to see us.

"I've got some news," he stated without preamble. "Geraldine Sweeney didn't show up for work last week. She didn't give anyone any notice or anything, and when I went to her apartment, the landlord said she'd moved out. She didn't leave a forwarding address."

Alarm and elation had warred within me. I'd tried to get up from the couch, but Gordon had pushed me gently back down. "Honey, you've got to heal. Stay put."

Frustrated, I'd fallen back against the cushions. "Can you find her? Do you think she did it? Do you think she has my sister's baby?"

Detective Wallace grimaced. "We're working on it, and yes, I think it's a definite possibility that she might have the baby. I did an FBI check on her and came up with some interesting results. It seems that she was charged with aggravated assault with a deadly weapon about ten years ago, but she didn't have to do any time, due to special circumstances."

"Aggravated assault?" I frowned. "She told us that her husband stabbed her in the stomach."

The detective nodded. "He did, and then, she shot him in the chest with a hunting rifle. He didn't die, but he almost did. She claimed that it was self-defense." He shrugged. "Since she had the stomach wound to prove it, the judge ruled in her favor."

I'd squashed a ridiculous surge of sympathy for the woman. If she had killed my sister and stolen her baby, I had no room for sympathy. The woman was insane, and she needed to be locked away. "How will you find out where she is?"

"We're checking into a few possibilities. If she rented a moving company, or a van, then she had to give them an address." He'd shifted from foot to foot. "We've interviewed nearly everyone on your list, and so far, everyone checks out. They've all got alibis."

"Someone could be lying for them." I watched crime shows on television. I knew that it happened.

"You're right, but I've got a gut feeling about this Sweeney woman," Detective Wallace confessed. "It's too big of a coincidence that she left around the time your sister disappeared."

I'd closed my eyes and moaned, remembering the sullen-eyed nurse and her curt manner. Was my niece in the hands of that madwoman? I hated to think that it could be true, but, at least, it was a lead. "Thanks, Detective Wallace. You'll keep us posted?"

"Yes, ma'am," he said.

"And you'll call us if you find the baby? Immediately?" I'd shot my husband a determined glare. "I want to go to her the moment that you find her."

After he'd gone, I couldn't stop the tears. Would the nightmare never end? The sound of the doorbell had made me jump. No, it couldn't be the detective again. He'd just left.

Mom had gone to answer the door. I'd waited, barely breathing, on the couch. When Mom returned, she wasn't alone. Patricia, Stephanie, Amanda, and several of the other women from the group my sister and I had belonged to were with her. They'd filed into the living room, solemn-faced, and obviously nervous. A few looked red-eyed from crying.

Patricia spoke first. "We heard about Katherine from that detective," she said, coming forward and taking my hand. There were tears in her eyes. "We all feel terrible."

I'd swallowed the bitter, ugly words that I'd wanted to say. "Thank-you," I mumbled woodenly, "and thanks for coming over." Although the detective felt certain that Geraldine was behind the murder and kidnapping, I couldn't help but view the group with suspicion. What if he was wrong? What if Katherine's murderer stood in that very room, mouthing platitudes and pretending to be upset? I'd given myself a mental shake, suspecting that my exhaustion was making me irrational. "Would you like to see the baby?"

I'd had to admit that their sudden eagerness had fooled me. Mom disappeared down the hall and returned with Katie. The women gathered around her, oohing and ahhing, fighting over who would hold her first. With obvious reluctance, Mom had handed her over. By the time that Katie had been passed to the last woman in the group, she was wide awake and hungry. She began to cry, and I felt a sharp pang of sympathy for the women when they reacted to her cries as if it were laughter.

I hadn't forgotten how deeply I had yearned to hear a baby's laughter, or even her cries. The group of women stayed for an hour or so, offering words of comfort and encouragement. I'd hesitantly told them about Geraldine and her suspicious disappearance. I'd wanted desperately to spread my hope that soon, we'd find my sister's child, and bring her home where she belonged.

Two days later, we buried my sister in the family plot. Instead of placing a rose on her coffin, I laid the ultrasound picture of her baby on the wreath of roses. The women from the group attended. Michele hadn't been able to make it back for the funeral, but she had thoughtfully sent a tree sapling and a card, telling me to plant the tree in my sister's memory.

After the funeral, I'd slipped into the bedroom and used the phone to call Michele. I'd wanted to thank her for the tree. I already had decided that I would plant the tree when my sister's baby returned home, and that, together, with Katie, we would nurture it and remember Katherine.

When I got Michele's answering machine, I'd left a brief message, asking her to call me back. On impulse, I'd found my address book, called the clinic where she worked, and asked for her.

"Michele isn't here. Can I take a message?" a woman asked.

I'd hesitated, thinking that I should just try her home phone again later, or wait for her to return my call. But it was such a wonderful, thoughtful gesture that I just couldn't wait. "Do you know when she'll be back?" I asked.

From the way the woman had spoken, I'd thought that Michele had gone on a dinner break or something. What she'd said next had totally floored me.

"She should be back from vacation next week, if you want to try then," she suggested.

Vacation? I shook my head, thinking that the woman had gotten Michele confused with someone else. "I'm sorry, I think I've confused you. I'm referring to Michele Richardson."

"Yes, Michele Richardson. It's the only Michele that we have working here." Concern edged her voice. "Is something wrong? I have her home number, if you can provide some sort of identification over the phone."

Hastily, I'd told her that I had the number and would call her there. I'd said that I must have forgotten that she was on vacation. I was still sitting on the edge of the bed when Mom came in and found me there. She'd sat beside me and put an arm around my shoulders.

"How are you holding up?" she asked, hugging me.

I'd hugged her back, taking a hard look at her tear-ravaged face. I'd lost a sister, but Mom had lost a child. I couldn't imagine the depths of her grief. I could barely handle my own. "I'm hanging in there. How about you?"

She'd tried to smile and failed miserably. "The house is full of people, some of them laughing and talking as if nothing has happened. I just want to scream at them to leave, and to take their darned food with them. We'll never be able to fit all that into the refrigerator, anyway."

Silently, I'd agreed. "I was just trying to call Michele and thank her for the tree sapling." I'd blinked to clear the tears from my eyes. I'd cried enough for a dozen people. "I know how badly she wanted to be here."

Mom blew her nose and wiped her eyes. Like my own, her tears were constantly streaming. "I know. She's such a sweetheart, but with that horrible flu bug going around, she just couldn't get away."

I'd frowned at that, still half convinced that the woman on the other end of the line hadn't known what she was talking about. "I just had the weirdest conversation with someone from the clinic where she works," I said. "They told me that she was on vacation until next week."

"That's silly. She couldn't take off from work, even if it was her vacation time, not with so many employees out sick. I just talked to her last night, and so did James. I heard him reassuring her that we would understand."

"Maybe I should try calling her at home again," I ventured.

But Mom had vetoed the idea. "I think we both need a nap, don't you? There are plenty of people out there who would love to take care of the baby for us, James included."

"Mom, I don't—" I began.

"Humor me, will you?" Mom squeezed my shoulders. "You're my only child now."

Well, when she'd put it that way, how could I have refused? My mom had lain down next to me, putting her arms around me. Just when I'd thought I'd never sleep in a million years, I'd felt myself drifting off.

It was getting dark in the room when I'd jerked awake. Mom was gone, and Gordon was sitting on the side of the bed. He was staring at me as if he had bad news. My stomach clenched painfully as I'd quickly sat up and swiped at my face.

"What is it? Is it the baby?" I couldn't help the panic in my voice.

"No, nothing's wrong with the baby. Detective Wallace called. They found Geraldine Sweeney."

My heart had lurched and my throat had gone dry. "And? Please, Gordon! Don't make me suffer!"

He'd reached out and clamped both hands on my shoulders, as if to anchor me to the bed. I didn't blame him. I was getting the reputation of reacting hysterically to any news concerning my sister or her baby.

"Honey, Geraldine didn't have the baby, and she claims that she doesn't have any idea of where she could be."

"She could be lying! Did they search her house? Did they give her a lie detector test? Where's Detective Wallace?" I asked.

"He left. You were asleep, and I wouldn't let him wake you." He'd ignored my furious glare. "Hearing the news thirty minutes later wouldn't have made a bit of difference, and you know it."

I ground my teeth, reminding myself that my husband was not the enemy. "Maybe not, Gordon, but I would have asked him questions."

"I anticipated most of them, honey. Geraldine Sweeney was living with a woman, if you get my meaning, and the woman testified that Geraldine had been with her for the past five days. They were painting the apartment. Detective Wallace said that he believed her."

"Who the heck does he think he is—God? Is he a mind reader? Heck, no, he isn't! Maybe this woman helped Geraldine abduct Katherine, and maybe she—"

"Shelby," Gordon interrupted patiently. "Geraldine didn't have anything to do with Katherine's death, or the disappearance of the baby."

The truth of his words had finally sunk in. I'd pulled from his grasp and sunk back onto the bed, curling into a fetal position. So, we were back to square one. "Will you get me some pain reliever?" I mumbled, just loud enough for Gordon to hear me.

I'd hastily sat up as I'd recalled the phone call I'd made to Michele. I supposed I was desperate, but the conversation I'd had with the woman on the phone kept bugging me.

I'd reached for my address book and looked up the number to the clinic again. Slowly, I'd dialed it. I didn't want to make any mistakes. The same woman answered the phone. I'd recognized her voice.

Still, I'd pretended that I hadn't already called. "Could I speak to Michele Richardson, please? This is her stepsister." Well, it was sort of true, I told my conscience.

There was a brief silence on the other end. It was as if the woman had recognized my voice, but wasn't quite certain. Finally, she'd spoken. "If this is her stepsister, then you should know that she's been on vacation since last week, and that she isn't due back until next week. Have you tried calling her at home?" she asked.

"Yes, I did. I couldn't get an answer," I hedged.

"Would you like for me to try?" she asked.

And just what makes her think that Michele would answer the phone to her, and not to me? I thought. I was more confused than ever. But what did I have to lose? "Yes, would you? I'll hold."

Less than a moment later, the woman had clicked back to me. "I got the answering machine, so she must be out."

"Did she happen to mention to you where she'd be going for her vacation?" I persisted.

"No, she didn't," she said coldly.

Realizing that I wasn't going to get any further information out of her, I went in search of Mom. I'd found her trying to fit a huge spiral ham onto the second shelf of the fridge. James was waiting behind her with a gigantic bowl of baked beans.

Mom had glanced at me as I'd entered the room. "Did you sleep at all, honey?"

"Yeah," I said absently, surveying the enormous amounts of food that were covering every inch of cabinet space. Unlike my mother, I couldn't summon the energy to care if it got put away or not. "Mom, when you talked to Michele this morning, where was she calling from?"

Mom paused with her hand on a jar of jam, frowning. "Her cell phone, I think." She'd looked at James. "Hon? Did you notice?"

He nodded. "Yeah, I checked the caller ID before I answered the phone. She was definitely calling from her cell phone."

An odd chill had skittered down my spine. If Michele had been calling from home, why wouldn't she have used her home phone? The reception was almost always better than on her cellular phone. Trying to sound casual, I'd continued. "Can you give me that number? I can't reach her at home, so maybe she'll answer her cell phone. I wanted to thank her for the tree, and update her on the latest. She said she wanted to know the instant we found out something."

James had shrugged and dug out his wallet. "Sure, I'll give it to you, but she's probably at work."

I opened my mouth to tell him what I'd found out, but quickly closed it again. Until I cleared up things, I didn't see the point in confusing or alarming Mom or James. For all I knew, Michele had a secret lover she wasn't ready to share with the rest of us.

He handed me a card with several numbers scrawled in the corners. He tapped the top right-hand corner. "That's it."

"Thanks. I'll just use the phone in the bedroom."

"Give her my love," James called as I headed to the bedroom.

"Me, too!" Mom added.

I'd told them that I would, but deep down, I didn't really believe that I'd be talking to Michele. Gordon met me in the hall with the pain reliever and told me that he had to go out for a while. I'd absently waved him off and gone into the bedroom.

I was pretty startled when Michele answered on the third ring, sounding breathless. "Dad?"

"No, it's Shelby. I wanted to call and thank you for the sapling you sent to the funeral home."

"You didn't have to thank me." She'd said it with just the right amount of sympathy and understanding. "I just thought it would be nice, you know—to honor Katherine's memory."

"And you were right." I'd hesitated, feeling sneaky and foolish, but unable to help myself. "I tried your home phone, but got your machine." That would have been the perfect opportunity for Michele to tell me that she wasn't at home—that she was in her car, or at the market, or at the hair salon. A simple explanation; that's all I'd wanted. Well, not exactly all I'd wanted. I'd also wanted to know why her coworkers would have told me that she was on vacation. Maybe there was a simple explanation for that, as well.

But Michele hadn't cleared up anything. She'd made it even more confusing.

"I was probably on my way home from work," she told me. "And, just now, I was taking out the trash. I try to remember to take my cell phone, especially in light of what's happened."

She'd sounded sincere, and it certainly answered two of my questions—which left a pretty big one still glaring. "Oh, so you worked today?"

"Of course. I told you that half the staff was out with the flu." I could almost hear the puzzled frown in her voice. "Otherwise, I would have been there. You know that, don't you?"

Did I? Right then, I wasn't sure about anything. "You still work at the same clinic, right?"

"Yes. I've been there for six years. Why?"

Before I'd been able to give it a second thought, I'd blurted it out. "Because I called there, and they said that you were on vacation."

There was a long silence. "Oh, that. It's kind of embarrassing, but I've had a credit card company calling for me at work, and they'll say anything to get me to the phone. I told Alice to screen all my calls. She knows Dad's voice, of course, but not yours."

Her explanation had sounded perfectly logical, but why had it taken her so long to reply? In my experience, that only happened when people were forced to think up a believable lie in a short amount of time. I'd never been really good at lying, so I knew that it would have taken me a lot longer.

Again, it had occurred to me that Michele might have someone in her life that she didn't want us to know about. But she was a grown woman and recently divorced. Why would she want to hide it from us?

I'd thanked her for the tree again, and she'd asked me about the funeral. As I was telling her about the service, a loud, male voice in the background had interrupted me.

"Hey! Can't you do something about that racket? I can't even hear my television!"

Michele's reply to the angry-sounding voice had been muffled—as if she'd put her hand over the phone. When she came back on the line, she'd sounded urgent. "I've got to go, Shelby. Give Dad and your mom my love."

Then, the line had gone dead. Dazed, I'd kept the phone to my ear until it began that raucous noise that told me the phone was off the hook. I'd dropped it into the cradle and sat back, my eyes glued to the wall.

My heart was pounding slowly, heavily. Michele was lying. I knew it. I didn't know how I knew it, but I knew it as well as I knew my own husband. There was a way I could check out her story, but that would have involved telling James about my suspicions. It would also mean convincing him to call the clinic and ask for his daughter.

Although I didn't want to believe that he would be a part of such a heinous murder-kidnapping scheme, I couldn't risk him alerting Michele before I could get to Miami.

In order to set my plan in motion, I would have to lie to James and, worse, to my own mother.

But it had only taken me two seconds to dispel any guilt I might have felt for lying. For Katherine and my niece, I would have lied to the devil himself.

When I came back into the kitchen, I didn't have to try hard to look shaken and pale. "I just talked to Detective Wallace. He wants me to come down to the station. He says there's been a new development on the case," I said.

Mom dropped a platter of cold cuts onto the counter. "I'm coming with you."

"No, you need to stay with the baby. I don't know when Gordon will be back. Somebody vandalized one of his construction sites."

"Then I'll go with you," James volunteered, always the gentleman.

He was a little harder to put off, because I didn't have a good excuse to make him stay. Praying my explanation would work, I'd gestured to all the food still left out. "Mom needs you here," I told him. "I'll be fine—really. I'll call you from the station the moment I find out anything."

Before they could argue further, I'd snatched up my purse and car keys and raced out the door. The drive to the police station took fifteen minutes. It took another twenty minutes for someone to track down Detective Wallace. I was glad when he led me into a small office and closed the door. If I'd had to resort to begging to convince him to help me, then I would have, but I wasn't too thrilled with the idea of there being witnesses to my groveling.

Quickly, I'd told him about calling Michele and the clinic where she worked, and about how she'd lied to me. With his arms folded, Detective Wallace had heard me out before he'd responded.

"And just because your stepsister claims she's working and the clinic claims she's on vacation, you want me to fly to Miami to see if she's hiding a baby, or a lover," Detective Wallace concluded. Somehow, he'd managed to make my speech sound ludicrous, and more than a little crazy.

I'd thrust out my chin stubbornly. If I had to, I would make the trip without him, but I desperately wanted him to come with me. "I'll pay your expenses," I offered. "Either way, I'm going." I wasn't above pulling punches. "And if my instincts turn out to be right, and I get shot or something, then you'll have to live with that. Look, it makes sense. There was no sign of a struggle. It was as if Katherine knew and trusted the person who took her to that hotel room. She would have trusted Michele."

Detective Wallace slowly closed his eyes. I couldn't be certain, but it looked as if his lips were moving. I'd figured he was counting to ten. Finally, he opened them again and sighed. "Call the airlines and get us the first flight out." He shot me a severe look. "And you'll do exactly as I say, understand? I could get suspended for taking a civilian along on a police matter."

I'd crossed my fingers over my heart and forced myself not to jump for joy. "I won't tell a soul. I won't even speak to you, or act like I know you, on the flight."

He wasn't able to suppress a smile. "You don't have to go that far, Mrs. Wiest."

"Please, call me Shelby." I reached for his phone to call the airlines and make reservations. I didn't know what I was going to tell Mom, Gordon, and James, but I knew that I couldn't tell them the truth, and risk the chance of one of them tipping off Michele that we were coming.

By the time I'd made the reservations, I had thought of a plan. I quickly dialed Patricia's number, explained the situation, and got her promise that she would cover for me. Then, I called home and told Mom that Detective Wallace had left on an emergency before I got to the station. I told her that I was going to Patricia's to help the group console one of the members who had suffered another miscarriage. I also said that I didn't know how long I would be.

I didn't like to lie, but I didn't have a choice. I knew that if Mom called Patricia's, Patricia was prepared to give her one excuse after another about why I couldn't come to the phone, and why I needed to stay longer. I hope that Patricia could stall them long enough for Detective Wallace and me to get to Miami.

The flight was six hours long, and it felt like it lasted eighty. My mind wouldn't be still. My foremost fear was that I might have been totally wrong. What if I surprised Michele in bed with her lover? Detective Wallace would probably find a reason to arrest me. He'd be furious with me for leading him on a wild goose chase.

True to my word, I'd barely spoken to him during the flight, although I'd sat in the seat directly behind him. The moment we'd gotten off the plane, we'd hailed a cab and given the driver Michele's address. Just before we arrived, Detective Wallace had used his cell phone to call the local police and ask them to send a car to meet us. He was out of his jurisdiction, so he had no choice but to involve the local authorities. I'd secretly admired the fact that he'd waited until we were nearly there. If he'd called the local authorities too soon, they might have alarmed Michele and caused her to run—or to harm the baby in some unthinkable way.

The driver stopped in front of a modest apartment building. I'd paid the fare as Detective Wallace was giving me stern instructions. I was to remain so far behind him that he wouldn't be able to see me if he turned around, he insisted—and there were to be no exceptions.

Despite the fact that I was trembling over the possibility of catching my sister's killer and finding my infant godchild, I'd nodded meekly. We took the elevator to the fourth floor. I'd waited in the hall, behind a huge potted fern, as the detective had surveyed the apartment numbers. Finally, I'd watched him pause in front of a door and push the buzzer.

I'd held my breath as the door had opened, but, to my frustration, I couldn't see the person's face, and they were talking too low for me to hear what they were saying. Disappointment coursed through me when the door closed and Detective Wallace strode in my direction. When he reached me, his mouth was set in grim lines. But one look at the gleam in his eyes had made me gasp.

"Was it Michele? Did you see the baby?"

"No." He'd waited long enough for disappointment to set in before he'd continued. "I just talked to the neighbor—probably the disgruntled man you heard on the phone when you were talking to Michele. He confirmed that the racket he was complaining about was a baby crying."

My knees buckled. Detective Wallace caught me.

"Easy, Shelby. I can't have you passing out on me now," he said.

"What do we do now? Can we just go in and arrest her?" I asked. "Can I take the baby?"

He shook his head. "We have to wait for the Miami police to get here. I don't think we'll have a problem getting them to cooperate with us. Once we get her into custody, I can start the extradition."

The wait had seemed interminable. Finally, the elevator doors had slid open and two uniformed cops had stepped into the hall. Detective Wallace called them over. He showed them his identification, and quickly explained the situation.

Once again, I'd had to stay behind as the three men had stood outside Michele's apartment and rung the bell. Waiting in that spot was one of the hardest things I'd ever done. I'd wanted so badly to confront Michele. And, of course, I was yearning to find my precious niece.

I couldn't hear what they were saying, but it was obvious when they asked her to step into the hall and began cuffing her that Detective Wallace and I hadn't flown to Miami in vain.

Risking his anger, I'd rushed down the hall and barreled past the police officers. I'd found Detective Wallace in the living room of Michele's apartment. He'd given me a chiding look and shoved me behind him.

"We haven't checked the apartment," he growled. "Stay behind me. For all we know, she had an accomplice."

He'd saved the bedroom for the last. Once he'd checked the closets, he'd gestured for me to come inside. I'd headed straight to the crib.

There, dressed in a pretty pink sleeper and fast asleep, was my sister's baby. My niece. My godchild—soon to be my daughter. With trembling hands, I lifted the baby and brought her to my chest. She stirred and stretched her little limbs, then settled against my breast and went right back to sleep.

She appeared to have been cared for well. But that fact didn't soften me toward my sister's killer. I was grateful to God for keeping her safe, and so very thankful that we'd found her. Finally, I'd felt as though my sister could rest in peace, knowing that her daughter was in good hands.

My tears had fallen fast and hot as I'd rocked my niece back and forth. The baby was safe. My beloved sister was dead, but her daughter had survived the ordeal, and, someday, when she was old enough to understand, I would tell her all about her brave, wonderful mother. She would not be forgotten.

THE END

Made in the USA
Monee, IL
19 May 2020